Praise for t...

SWEETWATER BURNING
(Originally published as *Blackbelly*)

"Sharfeddin has captured the family-like entanglements in a small community—by showing us what happens when those relationships begin to come apart."
—*The Philadelphia Inquirer*

"A good old-fashioned cowboy tale that's as gritty as they come...a nice piece of emotional storytelling."
—*Chicago Tribune*

"[An] accomplished western...Authentic descriptions of the stark, isolated landscape, rustic conditions, and the bitter winter form a backdrop to the characters' turmoil, suggesting a timelessness that is only occasionally broken with touches of modernity....Impressive."
—*Publishers Weekly*

"Superbly crafted...Characters are wonderfully drawn.... Explores a wide range of themes related to sin and guilt, personal integrity, and the destructive power of prejudice. Essentially, however, this is a story about the miracle of love blossoming in unlikely places. Highly recommended."   —*Library Journal* (starred review)

"Comparisons will be made to Kent Haruf....Sharfeddin's...eye for detail...and her unsentimental compassion for her characters...will entrance readers. The stark terrain is beautifully rendered."
—*Kirkus Reviews* (starred review)

"Striking... A deceptively simple contemporary western about two loners who have learned from their mistakes and flaws, but not overcome them."
— *The Portsmouth Herald* (New Hampshire), in selecting *Blackbelly* as one of the top novels of 2005

"Juicy reading [with] some powerful themes: faith versus religion, sin and forgiveness."
— *The San Diego Union-Tribune*

WINDLESS SUMMER

"In the stark beauty and eerie weather of the new West, people get what they have coming. Or do they? Tom Jemmet's motel in the Columbia River Gorge might be haunted. Might be blessed. Might be both. A whirlwind of misunderstandings can blur the difference between karma and curse, between miracle and coincidence, and even between love and hate. Heather Sharfeddin's characters are so complex and well-meaning and so frequently wrong you'll want to step in and hug the one you just slapped around. The woman can write. Imagine Annie Proulx taking on the Salem witch trials."
— ROBIN CODY, author of *Ricochet River* and *Voyage of a Summer Sun*

"Sharfeddin's best work yet." — *Publishers Weekly*

"An intense, disturbing story." — *The Boston Globe*

MINERAL SPIRITS

"A thoughtful blend of crime (high-country style) and social commentary."　　　　　*—The Seattle Times*

"Sharfeddin's writing is sharp, the characters real and the setting grittily recognizable to anyone who has driven a stretch of I-90 between Spokane and Missoula. There is no mistaking this place for any other, from the particular sound of the semis on the highway to the lonely geography and the decided chill in the air."　　*—The Oregonian*

"Sharfeddin's empathy for her characters and sense of place keep the reader engrossed.... A spellbinding, high-country thriller."　　*—Kirkus Reviews* (starred review)

"A first-rate page-turner from start to finish."
　　　　　　　　　　　　　　—The Denver Post

"A sharp, perceptive blend of crime and contemporary life issues ... Tight and emotionally satisfying, this impressive novel should gain the author new readers."
　　　　　　　　　　　　　—Publishers Weekly

"Exquisite use of language and detail...Neither a typical mystery nor a standard western, [*Mineral Spirits*] examines themes of love, hope, and aloneness-versus-loneliness....With its strong characters...as well as its good story line, the book will appeal to a wide variety of readers." —*ForeWord*

"Masterly...Transcend[s] the conventions of a simple whodunit and plunge[s] the reader into a fully realized world populated by believable, complex and fascinating characters...*Mineral Spirits* explores important issues: poverty, longing, loss, sorrow and the consolations and discontents of life in a small town."
—South Florida *Sun-Sentinel*

"[Sharfeddin's] intimate understanding of the land and characters of the West comes across smoothly in her writing....Sharfeddin's writing is clear, precise and full of true-to-life details that bring the story to life. Her dialogue captures the wary tone heard throughout the remote West, imparting a sense of tension that keeps the reader hooked." —*The Lewiston Tribune* (Idaho)

"A hybrid modern-western-murder-mystery: taut, gritty and layered with enough subplots to keep the arc steady...

One hopes for more explorations from Sharfeddin of the psyche of a modern West which still retains some vibrancy while struggling to maintain identity." —*Booklist*

"A book fill[ed] with strong characters . . . Sharfeddin is a master at writing conflict in almost every chapter. . . . Her memories of the beauty of rural Montana and Idaho are reflected in the authentic settings and in her ability to draw such realistic characters, all believable."
—*The News-Review* (Roseburg, Oregon)

"[*Mineral Spirits*] blends western and mystery genres into a fine, heady concoction. Recommended."
—*Library Journal*

SWEETWATER BURNING

SWEETWATER BURNING

A NOVEL
(Originally published as *Blackbelly*)

HEATHER SHARFEDDIN

Bantam Trade Paperbacks
New York

2010 Bantam Books Trade Paperback Edition

Copyright © 2005 by Heather Sharfeddin

Published in the United States by Bantam Books, an imprint of The Random House Publishing Group, a division of Random House, Inc., New York.

BANTAM BOOKS and the rooster colophon are registered trademarks of Random House, Inc.

Originally published in hardcover as *Blackbelly* in the United States by Bridge Works Publishing Company, Bridgehampton, New York, in 2005.

Published in trade paperback by Bantam Books, an imprint of The Random House Publishing Group, a division of Random House, Inc., in 2010.

Library of Congress Cataloging-in-Publication Data
Sharfeddin, Heather.
Sweetwater burning : a novel / by Heather Sharfeddin.
p.   cm.
ISBN 978-0-385-34128-8
1. Sheep ranchers—Fiction. 2. Muslims—Crimes against—Fiction.
3. Conflict of generations—Fiction. 4. Arson—Investigation—Fiction.
5. Fathers and sons—Fiction. 6. Hate crimes—Fiction.
7. Clergy—Fiction. 8. Idaho—Fiction. I. Title.
PS3619.H35635B58 2005
813'.6—dc22   2005001642

Printed in the United States of America

www.bantamdell.com

2   4   6   8   9   7   5   3   1

For Samuel, my inspiration

SWEETWATER
BURNING

1

"Easy now, I ain't gonna hurt ya." Chas McPherson, forty-one and looking it, heaved a nearly grown ewe onto her hind end. The thrashing animal immediately went limp, her legs splayed out like a collapsed marionette. The phrase, *Ever had a Blackbelly? They're mild . . . tender—not like woolies* rolled around Chas's head as he dabbed a cream on the ewe's eye from a tiny tube his fingers could barely manipulate. Mild and tender; not like woolies. He gripped the ewe hard between his knees and screwed the cap back on. He examined the animal's hooves, then slid his hand into the pocket of his muddied canvas jacket and exchanged the ointment for a pair of heavy, medieval-looking trimmers. He used the scissor-like instrument with quick precision to snip the hooves into sharp triangles. The phrase playing in his mind was one his father used to sell his butcher lambs, ever the salesman. When Chas released the animal, she remained motionless in a heap at his feet as if paralyzed.

"Git on now!" he yipped, giving the ewe a mild kick in the flank and sending her bounding back to the safety of the flock.

He slipped the trimmers back in his pocket and strode to the gate. The flock darted to the other side of the catch pen to avoid him. He unlatched the gate and swung it wide to let them out. They bunched together in a mass of wiry hair and black ears, pressing against the cold metal bars on the far

side of the pen from the gate. Shrugging, he left them to figure it out and started for the barn. When he was some distance away, a single brave ewe bolted toward the pasture,
leaping high in the air to clear a barrier at the gate only she
could see. The others quickly followed, mimicking her precisely, springing over the unseen obstacle on blind faith.

Chas snapped the twine on an alfalfa bale and tossed it
through the barn window to the feeder below. His sheep
streamed toward it in a long single-file line, as if they'd forgotten that only moments ago they were terrified of him.

He paused and looked out on the Sweetwater River that
ran along the southern boundary of his three-hundred acres
and into the tiny hamlet that shared its name six miles to the
west. A grove of black walnut trees stood leafless and bleak
along its banks. The river ran dull and sluggish, like liquid
lead under the gray December sky. The water was low, leaving a wide, black crescent where his animals waded up to
their knees in mud to drink.

He poured a bucket of oats over the hay, then lumbered
across the muddy yard toward the house. His eyes skimmed
the decaying eaves of the building, looking at the hooks his
father had spaced every six inches–for Christmas lights. He
thought briefly of putting them up before the old man came
home, as a welcoming gesture. But the idea dissolved with
the realization his father wouldn't see the lights, only the
grass sprouting from the gutters, or the thick slabs of moss
on the shingles–keeping the roof in one piece, really. Assuming his father would even recognize the place, and that was
a large assumption.

Chas stomped up the wide porch steps, loosening
clumps of mud and sheep shit from his boots, which he
kicked off next to the door. He dropped his jacket on a table
already piled high with broken tools, tractor parts and
chipped dishes never brought in from last summer's suppers.

He pulled two fir logs from a disorderly pile in the

entryway and added them to the woodstove in the living room. He stoked the fire up. In no time it burned so fiercely he opened the front door to let out some heat. He sat in the kitchen at a pine table gouged deep with time, his dirty breakfast dishes pushed to the side with last night's, and jotted notes in a small book where he recorded which animals he'd treated for which ailments and the date.

As he finished up, the phone rang. "Hello," he said.

"May I speak to Charles McPherson, please?" a woman asked.

"It's Chas. And you've got him."

"Um, my name is Mattie Holden, and I'm calling about your ad. I'm a nurse."

Chas listened.

"Are you still looking for a home-care nurse, Mr. McPherson?"

"Yeah. Where ya from?"

"Spokane. But I can be there with two day's notice."

"You ever been to Sweetwater?"

"No, but I see here on the map, it's not too far from Salmon City."

Chas took a deep breath. That wasn't what he was getting at. "I can't pay you much."

The woman hesitated.

"This ain't a rest-home; it's a sheep ranch. You're gonna be a long way from any shopping malls and movie theatres."

"I understand," she said.

"You better."

"I'm sorry, sir, I–I thought you were looking for a nurse."

He scowled. Why the hell else would I put an ad in the paper, he wondered. "I am. Just making sure you've got the whole picture before you waste your time driving down here."

"Do you want to ask me any questions? I mean, about my experience?"

"You're a nurse ain't ya?" He looked around his house at the piles of clutter and filthy dishes. Before she could answer, he said, "You know how to cook?"

"Well . . . yeah. But, that's not what you're hiring for."

"I know what I'm hiring for. And if you're gonna live here, you're gonna do your share of the cooking."

The woman went silent, and Chas sighed. She was the fourth to call, and he'd scared every one of them away. "Look, why don't you come down and we can talk in person. Then you can decide if you want the job."

She agreed, and he gave her directions. When he hung up, he looked at the mess again, seeing it in a different light, now that someone was actually coming. He'd need to do something about it before she arrived or she'd never agree to live here, but he didn't feel like getting started now. He pulled the rubber band from his hair, letting the greasy blond curls at the nape of his neck loose around his shoulders. Then he stripped off his clothes, leaving them where they fell as he made his way to the bathroom and started the shower.

Chas worked for three days, clearing decades of newspapers, magazines, ball bearings, twine, and grease-smeared auto parts that filled his house, moving his things to one of the two bedrooms on the second floor, and fixing the other for the nurse, deciding which room to give her based purely on which mattress smelled less moldy. In the room he'd been using on the main floor, he changed the sheets and swept the floor. His father would sleep here. He dragged piles of old furniture, books, and all manner of unwanted items, some as old as the house itself, into a large heap in front of his barn, where he set fire to everything. As the bonfire rose ominously, he went back for more. He found a box of women's clothing in the back of one of the upstairs closets; he guessed they once belonged to his mother. He hesitated a moment, looking at the dress poking out–small white flowers against a navy background–trying to remember her, then tossed the box into the fire whole. He stood and watched until the cardboard turned black and sparks took the darkening sky, then he went back to the house.

He poured himself a glass of whiskey and stood at the front window, watching the fire. His sheep came to the fence and watched, too.

It poured rain the day Mattie came, coating the landscape in a dismal gray, punctuated by simple black tree limbs against the dull-white sky. Chas stood at the window and stared out at the bleakness, waiting. She'd said to expect her at noon; it was one-thirty. Was she lost? Had she changed her mind? He looked at his flock, hunkered under a cedar tree and thought to let them into the barn, but it wasn't that cold, just wet. He almost poured himself a whiskey, but decided not to risk it. He needed a nurse. Without her he couldn't bring his father home from the institution where he languished. And he owed the old man this–to let him die in his own home. It was all he could do at this point.

When Chas glimpsed the blue sedan, lights on in the middle of the day, bouncing down his pocked drive, he thought his resolution would fail. He glanced around. The house wasn't cluttered now; it was sparse. He'd purged it of trash and memories alike, as if there were no distinction. But he hadn't scrubbed anything. And now, as she approached, he saw the dust, the grit, the coating of neglect on everything. There was no time to clean. She'd decline the job; there was no question in his mind. He looked forward to the whiskey when she was gone.

"Miss Holden?" he asked, stepping off the porch, which had also been scraped clean of rusted parts, sheep shit, and a three-legged, sagging chair.

"Yes, but you can call me Mattie," the woman said,

extending her hand. They shook, and she paused to look up at the century-old homestead. She was expressionless. She turned to survey the other buildings, the large sway-backed barn and its vast meadow cropped low by sheep. She turned back to Chas, but her eyes went past him, up the hill behind the house to the rock ridges that scraped the bleak sky.

Chas said, "Would you like to come in out of the rain?"

Inside, she pulled off her coat. When he didn't offer her a place to put it, she draped it over her arm. Rain seeped into her dress sleeve. "Your father is home?" she asked, looking around for evidence.

"No," he said. "No, I can't bring him home until I have a nurse. He's in Lewiston."

"Parkinson's, right?"

"Uh-huh. Late stages. He doesn't talk. Doesn't walk. Barely eats."

She nodded.

"I'd just rather he didn't die in that place. If ya know what I mean." He ran his hand over his stubbly chin and wished he'd shaved.

"Yeah," she said. "I know what you mean."

"Well, this is it. Your room would be upstairs. My father will take that one." He pointed at the doorway off the living room. "Taking care of him and sharing in some of the household chores—that's all I really expect."

"May I look around?"

He nodded and showed her the kitchen—surveyed her face as she looked in the sink, assessed the mildewed bathroom, and tested the bed in the musty upstairs bedroom. She hated it, he could tell.

"I'll have Sunday afternoons free?" She sat on the bed as if trying to imagine herself sleeping there.

"Uh-huh."

"No farm chores," she clarified.

Chas looked at her more closely. She didn't strike him as particularly attractive, but she wasn't ugly–his father would hate an ugly nurse. About thirty-five, he guessed. Her hair was pulled up in a tight bun at the nape of her neck; fine dark wisps escaped it, though. Her skin was clear and smooth, and she had the beginnings of deep crow's feet at the corners of her eyes. Which were pale gray–icy. He wondered if an occasional request to feed a bummer lamb in the cellar constituted farm chores. Of course it did. He shook his head.

"And if things don't work out?" She tilted her chin up, studying Chas.

Surprised, he answered slowly, "You saw all those sheep when you drove up?"

She nodded, looking at the wall that blocked her view of the meadow.

"Well, this job is sorta like them. I can't just change my mind about 'em. I'm committed–for the winter anyway. I've got ewes that'll be lambing in a few weeks. Then a whole lot of work to keep the little buggers alive. It's like that. You want the job, I expect ya to commit to seeing him through–at least for the winter."

She frowned. "When are you bringing him home?"

"Soon as you can start."

"I can start now."

He stared at her. She was taking the job. He couldn't believe it.

Chas arranged for Mattie to start in a week. As the days passed between hiring her and expecting her, he wished he'd made it a month. He put off chores that beckoned urgency, like repairing the fence where the ram got tangled up and tore out several yards, leaving a gaping hole for the flock to meander through at will–if they were smart enough to find it.

He watched the contents of a half-gallon bottle of Jack Daniels recede steadily while he tried not to anticipate his father's presence—or the nurse's.

Mattie put two suitcases and a cardboard box in the trunk of her car—all she owned in the world. The landlady who lived on the main floor already had a new tenant for Mattie's second-floor room and couldn't wait to get the cleaners in. Mattie wondered why the woman wasn't just a little sad to see her go. She'd hauled out the old lady's trash every week for the past eight months, despite the fact it wasn't part of the contract.

Mattie checked the phone; it hadn't been turned off yet. She dialed her sister in Orlando, Florida. "Kathy, it's Mattie."

"Oh, Mattie, this isn't a good time right now. I'm on my way out to Jacob's basketball game."

"This'll be quick. My phone's about to be turned off, anyway."

"What? I didn't hear you. Mattie—I need to go. Can I call you later?"

"No, I'll call you."

"Okay. Talk to you soon." She hung up.

Mattie held the phone in her hand a moment, her lips pulled tight. "Yeah, just try and call me back," she said. She looked around to make sure she hadn't forgotten anything, then pulled the house keys from her keychain and set them on the ugly, green-formica table. Which she was glad she would never see again.

As Mattie drove south toward Lewiston, a book about Parkinson's Disease on the seat next to her, she went over in her head the proper care of a patient like Mr. McPherson. Chas had said his father was in the final stages of Parkinson's Disease, which meant he would be incapable of even the

8

most basic tasks. He'd need feeding, diapering, bathing, massage. She promised herself to do her best in making this man's last days comfortable.

The eastern plains of Washington slipped away and she found herself winding through the mountains of northern Idaho. A beautiful range of steep, rocky peaks flanked by icy, boulder-strewn rivers. Idaho, she thought, was double—maybe triple-blessed with beauty. So why didn't she know anyone who wanted to live there?

In Lewiston, she waited outside a low building with peeling paint and thirsty shrubs. An attendant lifted Mr. McPherson into the passenger seat of her car. When she glimpsed the old man's face, she saw Chas—not simply a father-son resemblance, but an aged prototype. He seemed unaware of what was happening to him, showed not the least alarm at being taken away by a complete stranger. But she imagined that somewhere in his age-spotted head with its thin, curly hair, he saw, he knew.

The attendant gave Mattie a wary glance as he shut the door. "Is he a relative?"

"No, I'm his nurse. This is the first time I've met him."

He eyed the old man and stood back from the car, as if anxious to get away. "Well, good luck with him."

Mattie turned to her new charge. "I'm Mattie," she said as she fastened his seatbelt. "Chas has hired me to take care of you at home. That's where I'm taking you, Mr. McPherson. I'm taking you home."

She drove quietly for several miles, but something about the man's presence compelled her to talk. He seemed somehow bigger than he was, even though shrunken and frail. He was positively imposing next to her.

"I've been to your house, Mr. McPherson. Don't worry, I'll clean it. It's a mess right now, but I have to live there too, so I'll clean it. Not because Chas hired me to be a housekeeper."

Mattie shot the old man a meaningful glance. "I'm no one's maid. But it's bad. So I'll do it." She slipped a rogue strand of hair behind her ear. "I always seem to find myself in these situations. Where I have to do more than what's my job." She looked over at Mr. McPherson again. His blank face and frail limbs reassured her she didn't need to prattle.

"Chas calls that herd of goats, sheep. I wonder if he knows what he's doing? Even I can tell they're goats. He's got some problems—your son. That's pretty obvious."

The daylight was sifting away when Mattie turned onto the last road, a county road, long forgotten by the government. She wove her way around cavernous potholes big enough to swallow the wheels of her car.

"You grow up on that ranch, Mr. McPherson? I bet it was a beautiful place once upon a time. It's not much to look at now, though. Your barn's about to collapse right in on itself." She sighed and ran her tongue over her parched lips. "Guess you don't care to hear a lot of doom and gloom about the place you love. Someone could fix it up. It's not that far gone, but it will be if they don't hurry." She gripped the steering wheel a little tighter.

"I think it's real nice that Chas is bringing you home, Mr. McPherson. I'd do the same. If my dad was still alive, I mean." Mattie watched for the driveway, not taking her eyes from the road for fear she'd miss it and get lost. The longer she stayed focused on the road without looking at the old man, the larger he grew in the space beside her. She twisted the loose strand of hair around her finger, let it go, then twisted it again while she tried to take him in through her peripheral vision. "You seem a lot bigger to me than you are," she said. She didn't look his way this time, yet had the sense he was staring at her, though she knew it not to be true.

"My parents died when I was fourteen." She tapped the steering wheel in alternating intervals with her index fingers. "Where's the driveway? I hope I didn't miss it." She craned to see down the dark road behind her. Blackness. All the way up to the jagged tips of the trees on the ridge above. The canyon was deep—deeper than she remembered. And the ranches were farther apart. Miles, it seemed, between the faint yellow of kitchen windows, or the florescent blue flicker of televisions in darkened living rooms.

"Car accident. Lost 'em both, just like that." She snapped her fingers. "That's the thing about life, no guarantees." McPherson's hair was greasy and matted at the back of his head. She wondered if she should comb it before they reached the house, before Chas saw his father. "Guess you know that, though." She imagined the old man commanded a fair amount of respect from Chas, even in his current condition. He had an authoritarian air about him.

At last, Mattie spotted a battered mailbox missing its flag—Chas's mailbox. She could hear the river now as she turned down the lane. The sound soothed her, and the sight of the house, with all its lights ablaze, made her feel calmer. The figure pacing in the front window dampened her relief considerably though, when he caught sight of the car and stood motionless, watching. "We're almost home," she whispered. "Looks like your son is waiting for you."

Mattie waited next to the car for Chas to come out and carry his father inside. When he didn't, she started up the steps. As she reached for the knob the door burst open, and there, steeped in grimness, stood Chas. His eyes lingered on her face a moment in the pale porch light, then out to her car. And remained there.

"I'll need your help bringing him inside," she said.

She followed him into the yard. He opened the car door, then stepped back as if stunned by the sight of his father, who wore his same vacant expression.

"Hello, Dad," Chas said in a voice so tight Mattie's shoulder blades contracted into her spine. Mr. McPherson showed no recognition. Chas hesitated, then bent and lifted his father out of the car, turning so abruptly he nearly knocked Mattie aside with his father's feet.

As he brushed past her, she smelled the whiskey. Great, she thought, a drunk. Then wondered if he'd share.

Chas cranked the come-along used to stretch fence wire so tight the mesh in its teeth threatened to snap. It would leave a nasty wound if he was in its path, and he knew it. But he worked his way down the fence-line, hammering large metal staples into the rickety wooden posts, three to each one, anyway. Occasionally, he glanced at the house, tried to see the nurse as she scrubbed every inch of it. It pissed him off, her cleaning. And it pissed him off more that he hadn't done it himself.

He'd hardly slept the night before, despite his whiskey stupor. His father had visited him over and over again as the night dragged by—not the father who lay mute in his bed now, but the father of his childhood. The stern instructor of his youth. Reprimanding him for his failure, for his neglect: the house, the barn, the yard. In the stark light of day, Chas looked around and had to agree. He'd done a pathetic job. If his father could speak, he'd have no good thing to say to him. Chas pulled the brim of his hat down low against his brow to keep the rain from pelting his eyes as he worked. His fingers ached with cold, and there was a measure of justice in the pain that satisfied him. He worked all morning outside, barely making a dent in the years of work he'd put off—or never intended to do at all. But his hunger eventually forced him inside.

She sat at the table, his father next to her in the high-backed wheelchair Chas had purchased at the last minute from an estate sale. A vestige of someone else's unfortunate journey, too anxiously gotten rid of for a fraction of what they'd paid. Chas didn't consider it a find, bargain though it was. When the day came to pass it on, he'd be inclined to burn it, himself.

"I made you a sandwich," she said. "It's in the fridge."

"You don't have to make me lunch." He stalked past her to the still hot coffee pot and poured the last of it into a cup. The heat stung his frostbitten fingers.

"Well, I didn't do anything special. Just thought you'd be hungry and I was making one for myself. Don't take it like I'm always gonna make you lunch." She shook her head and went back to feeding his father.

Chas leaned against the counter and sipped his coffee. It wasn't his kitchen anymore. She'd taken over. She'd cleaned it, sanitized it, feminized it. Now he'd have to be careful not to make a mess or she'd be nagging after him. He watched her with his father a moment, then took the sandwich into the living room where he ate in privacy and watched his flock. Most were still huddled under the cedar, trying to stay dry.

After lunch he took his calendar from the wall and opened it to the back page, where all the known holidays in the modern world were listed. He ran his finger over the names until he came to Eid–December twentieth, next week. He pulled out his address book and flipped through it, listening to the nurse rattle on to his father about her ungrateful landlady. He paused and listened more carefully, for clues to her mental stability. Why would she take this job if she were sane? He found the number and made the call.

"Mr. Teleghani? Chas McPherson." He paused, listening to pleasantries from the man on the other end. "Happy Ramadan. I hope your family is well." Another long pause. "I'm good. Listen, I noticed next week is Eid and you haven't called about a lamb yet." He listened as the man detailed his financial difficulties this year. "Yeah, hasn't it been that way

13

for us all," Chas said. "I understand. I wanted to call and check, though. I always save the best one for you, you know that. Well, maybe next year."

He set the receiver back in its cradle and stood looking out the kitchen window at the mountains behind the house. Too little money this year for Teleghani to buy a lamb for Eid, he thought. What would he do with it now? He didn't need two butcher lambs, even with the extra mouths to feed. And one lamb through the sale ring would hardly be worth the trip. He picked up his coat and started for the door.

"I'm going to town to buy some groceries," the nurse called after him. "You haven't got anything here. Do you want something in particular?"

He glanced over his shoulder, but when he caught sight of his father, he turned back. "No." He pulled the door open, then said, "I have an account at the grocery store. You can charge it. But don't buy anything extravagant unless you plan to pay for it yourself."

"I didn't know you could get anything extravagant in Sweetwater."

2

THE NURSE COOKED SUPPER after returning from town with several sacks of groceries. From the loft of his barn Chas watched her unload the car. When he came in to wash up, he scanned the kitchen for his father.

She noticed. "He's sleeping," she said.

He pulled the lid off to inspect the aromatic spaghetti sauce with hamburger added.

"Don't get any ideas I'm gonna cook supper for you every night."

"You were gone a long time." He replaced the lid and sat down at the table. "Don't forget I hired ya to take care of my father."

Mattie stood over the sink, draining noodles. She glanced over her shoulder and scowled. "Keep your kitchen stocked and I won't have to go running after groceries."

His eyes came to rest on the back of her head–her tightly twisted bun. Maybe it was too tight, he thought. Just what he needed . . . a mean nurse. She wore jeans today, and he could see her figure, her narrow waist and round hips–a little too round. She could lose a few pounds. He leaned his head back against the wall and let his eyes go out of focus and took her shape in again. Maybe they weren't too round

15

after all, maybe just a little plump. Some men liked that. He could be convinced with a drink or two.

"Shouldn't you put those goats in the barn before they melt away out there?"

Chas's eyes refocused. "They're sheep."

She gave him a sideways glance, eyebrows raised.

"Sheep tails down, goat tails up."

"What?" Mattie brought the noodles to the table and went back for the sauce. "You could make yourself useful and get some plates and forks."

He narrowed his eyes at her and remained in his seat. He might have been inclined to help had she kept her mouth shut. "You can tell the difference between sheep and goats by whether their tails point down or up. Sheep tails point down."

Mattie waited for Chas to get the plates, prompting him with a blatant stare. When he didn't move, she went for them herself. "Sheep coats woolly, goat coats smooth."

His lips curled at the corners briefly. "You ever see a bighorn sheep?"

"Yeah. Well, on TV."

"How woolly was that?"

"Different kind of sheep. That doesn't count."

Chas twisted his face, trying to understand her logic. "Bighorn *sheeeeeep*."

"Whatever," she said, sitting down across from him.

"Those out there," he nodded toward his pasture, "are Barbados Blackbelly sheep. They're hair sheep. And that's the beauty of 'em; I don't have to shear."

"What's the point then?"

"What d'ya mean, what's the point?"

"If you don't get any wool. What's the point?"

He sighed. "For meat, of course."

Mattie set her fork down. "Eew."

"What do you think happens on a sheep ranch? Where

do you think meat comes from? Even that beef you just added to the spaghetti?"

"From the store."

"Uh-huh, from the store." He rolled his eyes. "Next time you're down there, maybe you should pick up some lamb chops. I'd like to taste those store-bought ones that you don't have to kill a sheep to git. Maybe I'll start raising that kind."

"I'm starting to see why you live alone."

Chas snorted.

Mattie pulled the old man into a sitting position, then eased him from the bed to the wheelchair. "No offense, Mr. McPherson, but your son is kind of a jerk." When she had him situated she carefully folded his hands into his lap. She took a comb from the nightstand and raked it over his scalp, smoothing the curly, white wisps that usually flew out in all directions. "He seems like the kind of guy who doesn't handle conflict well, if you know what I mean. Like he'd just as soon rip your kidneys out than listen to a different perspective." She wheeled Mr. McPherson into the living room and positioned the chair at the window, where he could look out on the meadow. The rain had given way to snow—silent and peaceful—transforming the gloomy ranch into something resembling a Christmas card photo. A light burned in the barn, and Mattie wondered what Chas did out there all day while all his sheep, if indeed they were sheep, made snow trails in the pasture. As she pondered his perpetual absence, a dark red sedan coasted down the driveway toward the house.

A woman in her mid-thirties got out and picked her way across the muddy yard in a pair of suede pumps. Mattie watched the woman's feet. Suicide, she thought, to wear such delicate shoes in this weather. She opened the door before the visitor knocked.

"Hi, my name is Pam," the woman said, extending her hand. In her other, she gripped a clipboard with tattered pages. "I'm an aide at the Sweetwater School." The woman looked past Mattie into the house, as if hoping for an invitation in.

Mattie kept an open gaze on the stranger, not guarded, but not inviting.

"I'm collecting signatures to petition the school to eliminate the ritual Christmas celebrations."

Mattie frowned.

"We'd still have a holiday celebration, of course," the woman added quickly. "But we have children of other religions attending the school, and it isn't fair to them . . . focusing solely on Christmas."

Mattie shrugged and reached for the clipboard. "Okay, I'll sign it." She paused. "Does it matter that I don't live here? I'm the home-care nurse."

"No, anyone can sign."

"You might try Chas, too. He's the one who lives here." A noticeable tremor ran through Mattie's hand as she handed the clipboard back. She nodded toward the rickety-looking structure across the yard, diverting the woman's attention. "He's in the barn."

The aide looked in its direction, then back at Mattie with doubt.

"Probably ought to come back in boots," Mattie said.

"I'll be out in the area tomorrow. Will you tell him I'll be by?"

"Sure." Mattie watched her leave, then turned to Mr. McPherson. "Well, how 'bout that? We just saved some kids from being left out of the holiday celebration."

Despite her declaration to Chas, Mattie had fallen into a routine of preparing all the meals. What else would she do with all her extra time? And she needed to eat, too.

It was nearly dark before he came in. Mattie wondered if he waited until she took the old man to his bedroom before returning. His absences coincided precisely with the time his father spent in the common area, except for lunch, which Chas ate alone in the living room like some freakish recluse.

He washed up at the kitchen sink, splattering black, soapy water across the clean porcelain. Mattie clenched her teeth as she watched him. Couldn't he see it was clean? How hard is it to rinse it down when you're finished? The constant cleaning required to keep the house livable astounded her. Chas tracked mud from the door to the sink with every trip, except for the rare occasions he left his boots on the porch. The firewood he dropped in the entryway was infested with bugs and the dry bark found its way into every corner of the place, even upstairs stuck to the bottom of his socks. His jacket stank of animals, and the odor lingered even when he was gone. She watched him scrub his blackened fingernails to no avail. His hands were rough and cracked, and she doubted even soaking them in bleach could sufficiently clean them.

"Who was that this afternoon?"

Mattie had forgotten the visit.

"The woman in the red car," he said with irritation. "Who was that?"

"Oh. Just someone from the school with a petition. They want to change the winter holiday so it's not about Christmas. She's coming back tomorrow so she can talk to you."

He leaned against the counter and dried his hands. "What the hell else would it be, but Christmas?"

"Just a holiday celebration . . . without the religious stuff. To include the families that aren't Christian." Mattie finished setting the table and opened the oven to check the potatoes.

"Sounds like a witch hunt to me."

"There're a lot of people who practice other religions. It makes 'em uncomfortable to have all this Christmas stuff going on."

"Well they shoulda thought of that before they moved to Sweetwater, where people celebrate Christmas." He threw the towel on the counter and sat down. "I suppose you signed it?"

"Just because you're Christian doesn't mean you have to force it down someone else's throat." She put the potatoes on the table next to a dish of steamed green beans and two cod filets and sat down.

Chas squinted at Mattie a moment, then dug into the food without waiting for her to offer it. "Who said I was Christian?"

They ate a while without speaking, Mattie wondering why he cared if he wasn't Christian. "You gonna get a Christmas tree?"

He held his gaze on her as he swallowed. "You're a bit contradictory ain't ya? Fist you wanna wipe the holiday from schools, then you turn right around and ask for a Christmas tree."

"It would be nice for your father. Give him something to look at."

Chas kept his eyes on his plate as he wolfed down the rest of his dinner.

"What kind of books does he like?"

He got up and dropped his dishes into the sink.

"How 'bout a clue? Give me something to work with here."

"Here's a clue: he was a Pentecostal minister for forty-five years." Chas pulled his coat on and headed for the door.

"I guess that explains the Bible next to his bed," Mattie said. But he was gone, pulling the door shut behind him with a thud. "The only thing in the room."

It was the eve of Eid, and Chas still hadn't decided what to do with the extra lamb. He inspected the two he'd selected back in May—the ones he culled from the flock and grain fed since Halloween. He didn't really save out the best for the

Teleghani family; it was the second best. He kept the best one for himself, and this year there was a clear difference. One had grown rapidly and put on good muscle, making Chas regret having castrated him–he would've made a nice breeding ram. But his stunted horns, which should've been a half turn in the first spiral by now, were simply two short spikes. Devil horns.

He wished he'd advertised the extra lamb in the paper. Now it was late in the season for that. The only people he knew who slaughtered an animal and ate its meat the very same day was the Muslim family. Everyone else would have a butcher hang the meat, let it cure for a week or two, then cut and wrap and freeze it. Too late for Christmas.

He backed his pickup into the barn, craning behind him to see through the darkness. He loaded the better of the two lambs into the bed. The metal gate on the stock rack slammed shut with a clang that made his head ache. He didn't tell the nurse he was leaving, but saw her standing in the window, so he knew she knew.

He parked on the road outside the Teleghanis' driveway. It was early yet; everyone would still be awake. But he hoped the darkness would allow him to slip in and out without being seen. The Teleghani clan lived on the outskirts of town on a small, one-acre lot. Just big enough to raise a few chickens and tend a garden that was the envy of every family in Sweetwater, with six-foot bean poles and straight, weedless rows of okra, cayenne peppers, eggplant–some of which the locals had never seen before. They were poor, with seven children. Middle-eastern, but he didn't know from what country. Had only wondered how they ended up in Idaho. He imagined sweltering sun, arid sand, and oppressive dictators might have brought them to this very different place.

He tied a rope around the lamb's neck and pulled it off the end of the lowered tailgate. The lamb struggled, pulling away from him until the noose was so tight Chas slid his hand under the creature to keep it from strangling. He finally carried it to the front steps where he tied the loose end to the Teleghani's porch post, working quietly, hoping not to be heard. The house was as old as his own, and in no better condition. He hoped the animal wouldn't rip the support out and collapse the porch roof during the night, but there was no place else to tie the lamb.

Chas ran the back of his fingers down the lamb's nose trying to recall the words he'd heard Nuri Teleghani use before he slit the throat. A prayer. A statement of thanksgiving. Or was it a declaration of God's oneness? He couldn't recall—wasn't sure he ever really knew. He turned his collar up against the chill wind and crunched back to his pickup in the hardened snow. As he pulled away, he looked back at the lamb again. And thought of his father, helpless and waiting for death.

When Chas got home he felt tired deep in his bones. He drove slowly past the front window and peered in to see if his father sat in the living room, or at the table, being fed like an infant. She was there, but his father wasn't. It was late and he imagined she'd put him to bed by now. But the all too familiar thoughts of his father's condition stayed with him.

He found a glass and went to the cupboard above the refrigerator where he kept the booze.

"Hello," she said in a pointed manner, clearly accusing him of not being civil.

He looked in her direction and nodded. Then he poured himself a glass of whiskey and stood at the sink staring at his reflection in the window as he sucked the top quarter inch off.

"You must be the busiest man on the planet, the time you spend out there working."

He turned and rested his hips against the counter. She sat at the table, writing a letter. He lifted his glass to her. "Would you care for one?"

She sat back and put the pen down. "Yeah, I'd love one."

Chas wondered if he'd made a mistake in offering it, but poured her a glass anyway. She accepted it a little too quickly–didn't appear to think about it. Like she'd already been thinking about it. I hope she's not a boozer, he thought. He set the glass down on the table and pulled the chair on the end out, spinning it around and straddling it. He slumped forward and it creaked under him.

"Thanks," she said.

"Who ya writing to?"

"My sister. She lives in Florida."

Chas watched Mattie's mouth as she spoke. It was small and red, like a bing cherry. She wore no makeup; her lips were naturally red like that–blood red. "How'd you get so far apart?"

"Her husband got a job down there."

He nodded, then looked over his shoulder into the living room.

"You got any brothers or sisters?"

"No." He was quiet a while. "How's my father doin'?"

"He's okay. There isn't much you can do for him now but make him comfortable. I'm sure he wouldn't mind you sitting and visiting with him. Or reading to him."

Chas looked away again.

"What happened to your mother?"

He kept his eyes on the front window, as if he could see more than the pale reflection of his kitchen light out there in the blackness.

"Sorry, it was none of my business," she said after a long silence.

"She left when I was ten. I don't know what happened to her."

"I'm sorry."

"Don't be. I'm not." He sucked down the last of the warm whiskey in his glass and stood to refill it. He brought the bottle to the table, poured himself another, then topped off Mattie's too. He set the bottle down hard—too hard, as if punctuating a point.

"Thanks," she said, looking up from behind softened gray eyes.

He picked up his glass and took it to the living room, where he didn't bother to turn on a light. He eased his tired body into the overstuffed chair in the corner, out of sight from her. The very moment he sat down he wished he'd brought the bottle with him.

Chas watched for the woman in the red sedan as he worked in the open doorway of the barn, soldering the broken clutch pin on his tractor. He had specific, carefully thought-out questions ready for her.

He'd taken to eating lunch late. The nurse always fed his father at noon. So he waited until one o'clock to come in. He couldn't bear the dribbling, the gurgling.

The petitioner arrived while he paced the living room with a half-eaten ham sandwich with too much mayonnaise. He'd peeled the bread back and removed the pickles, putting them on his plate as hint to the nurse. The house was cold; he hadn't shown her how to use the woodstove, and she seemed afraid of it. Her lack of resourcefulness irritated him. He'd decided not to stoke the fire at midday until she asked him to.

He opened the door before the woman reached the porch. "Are you the one from the school?"

"Yes," she said. She looked at him as if she could sense his opinion before he asserted it. "Chas?"

He held the door open for her. She wore jeans and snow boots. Mattie turned from the kitchen sink and gave the woman a warm smile, but didn't join them.

"I'm Pam," she said, extending her hand.

Chas gripped her fingers hard. "What is it you're trying to accomplish with this petition?"

"Well," she said, lifting the clipboard, as if the answer were written across the dog-eared pages of scribbled signatures. "We'd like to refocus the holiday celebration so it isn't about religion."

"Why?"

"Not all the children who attend the school are Christian, Mr. McPherson."

"Well, no kiddin'. You guys just figuring that out?"

"Excuse me?"

"Those kids ain't celebrating Christianity. They're celebrating Santa Claus. You gonna take Santa away?"

The woman stared at him. "Well, it's based on Christianity. And still has strong Christian overtones."

"Good point. So does the golden rule. Better get that on your petition too."

"I'm sorry I interrupted your lunch, Mr. McPherson." She started for the door.

"Wait, don't go. I have some questions."

"I can see you're not interested in signing the petition."

"You're right, I'm not. But can't I ask my questions anyway? I wanna understand this. Maybe you'll persuade me."

She paused at the door, her knuckles white stripes across the backs of her hands where she gripped the clipboard. She pursed her lips and waited.

"Who specifically are you doing this for?"

"What do you mean?"

"I mean, who's got a problem with Christmas?"

"There're a number of families who practice other religions."

"I know that . . . well, one family, anyway. But did they ask you to do this?"

"Of course not."

25

"Then why do you assume it's what they want?"

She turned and pulled the door open.

"Wait! Don't you think you're putting those people in a difficult position? You're assuming they don't want anyone else to enjoy Christmas."

"I'm sure they're thanking me in the privacy of their homes, Mr. McPherson," she said over her shoulder as she skipped down the porch steps.

"Why don't you ask them? This is America. It's allowed."

She paused with the car door open and said, "I think asking them *that* would put them in a difficult position, don't you?"

Chas watched her taillights until they were out of sight. When he turned, Mattie was leaning against the wall between the kitchen and living room. "What?" he barked.

"Nothing."

He stood at the window a moment longer, then he picked up his plate with the unfinished sandwich and dropped it on the counter. "What a buncha nosy do-gooders!"

She scraped the leftovers into the garbage and started washing the plate. "Why does it bother you so much?"

He went back to the living room, added two hickory logs to the woodstove, and stirred the fire up until it crackled. "Hey, nurse," he called.

She appeared in the doorway. "My name is Mattie. Not nurse."

He frowned.

"You wouldn't want me calling you *farmer. Hey, farmer!*"

"That'd be *hey, rancher*, Mattie."

"What is it, rancher?"

"Let me show you how to use the woodstove so my father doesn't freeze to death."

3

IN THE BLUE DAWN, Mattie sat on the edge of her bed with her feet flat against the cold, pine floor, pondering the marvelous invention of thermostats and wishing Chas had one. She'd never been so cold, so often, and for so long in all her life. She put on her robe and slippers and went quietly downstairs so she wouldn't wake Chas, whose cave–rattling snores had penetrated her brain like a buzz saw, driving her out of bed too early. It was just past five, and she opened the door of the woodstove and peered inside–just a heap of ash with a few orange coals glowing in the bottom. She opened the flue, just like he'd showed her, then added a couple of logs. Her hands shook, and she paused to rub the tremors away, sharply aware that she couldn't rub away the cravings that accompanied them. She focused on the fire, worked up a flame and wadded newspaper that she stuffed under the logs to keep it going. She stood in front of the stove waiting for the heat to spread, her eyes wandering the dim light of the house, looking for clues about this odd family.

She crept into the old man's room and stood over his bed. Everything was veiled in gray–the coming light muted by white muslin curtains. She could feel the old man's spirit floating in the air above the bed, suspended there. His soul ready for the afterworld, but tethered to this one by the last ounce of strength in a slowly dying body.

"I'm only here to see you through, Mr. McPherson," she whispered.

His eyes snapped open.

Her scalp prickled, and she reminded herself of his frailty. "Good morning, Mr. McPherson." Her voice quavered. "You're awake early today."

When Chas came in for lunch, he dragged behind him a six-foot Noble fir tree, which he propped next to the woodstove to dry. He said nothing about it to Mattie, found the ham sandwich she'd made for him, without pickles, and took it to the living room.

She followed him. "Nice tree."

Chas chewed his sandwich. Didn't look in her direction.

"Your father will love it." She sat down on the tattered sofa opposite him.

"I'll get the stuff outta the attic so you can decorate it," he said. "After I eat."

"Will you stay and help? It'll be fun."

He ignored her.

Mattie fidgeted with her hands, twisting her fingers together in a knot, letting them out, then doing it again. "Tell me something about your father."

He turned and stared at her, as expressionless as the man she inquired about.

"I mean from when he was younger. Before Parkinson's."

"Why?"

"Because he's not like anyone I've ever taken care of before. There's something about him—something . . . "

"What?"

"I don't know."

Chas turned his face to the window again.

"He just seems bigger than he is. When I turn my head, I have this sense that he's enormous. It sounds crazy."

Chas put his sandwich down. "He *is* big," he finally said. "Illness can't diminish a man like that."

Mattie let out a long-held breath. "I thought it was just me."

Now he turned and locked eyes with her. Hard. Piercingly. They were the eyes of the old man, but in the employ of his son—a viable man, a man of tremendous girth and physical strength.

Mattie shivered.

"When he was still alive, he killed a bobcat with his bare hands."

She blinked, trying to imagine it.

"Climbed a tree, clubbed it on the head, then strangled it." He turned back to the window, as if searching for the details of this odd memory in the snow. "Dropped it at my feet so I could skin it. Thought I'd like to have the pelt." Chas swallowed the rest of his sandwich and abruptly stood. "Its eyes bugged out when he hit it on the head."

Chas set the tree up for Mattie, then carried several dust-coated boxes marked "Christmas" down from the attic and dropped them in the middle of the living room. The scene reminded him of his mother, untangling strands of lights and singing *Oh, Holy Night*. She could never get the lights on the tree right; she was too small. But she had the voice of a bird. Bright and clear. He looked at Mattie. She seemed a lot smaller than his mother had, at least if he remembered right. "Do you want me to do the lights?"

"Yes," she said quickly.

He began opening boxes and pawing through the musty contents in search of the lights.

"I was thinking about what you said yesterday . . . to that woman from the school." Mattie went behind Chas, pulling out glass ornaments, checking the hangers, and laying them on the sofa. "Do you really think it puts those families in an awkward position?"

Chas plugged in an ancient strand of lights, illuminating the room in green and red. He unplugged it again, set it aside, and looked for more. "Well, if you lived in . . . Egypt. Say you moved there to have a better life. Would you want 'em to change their religious habits just so you wouldn't be offended?"

"It's not exactly the same."

"Why not?"

"Because this is a free country, Egypt is questionable."

"Okay, make it France, then."

"Hmm." Mattie found an ornament with a fuzzy black and white photo of a small boy, about four years old, mitten-clad and grinning at the camera. She carefully separated it from the others and set it on the arm of the sofa. "Well, I wouldn't want them changing anything for me. I'm not particularly religious myself."

"That's my point."

"What?"

"No one should assume to know anything about you without asking."

"You don't think it's a nice gesture to those people? A way of welcoming them into the community?"

"For starters, they've lived here for decades. And I don't claim to know any of the families they're trying to welcome personally, but I don't think it's what they'd want. How would you like to walk around town wondering if everybody hated you for changing long-standing customs?"

"Yeah, I guess you're right."

Chas paused and looked at the tree. "I don't know if my father's gonna like this or not. We haven't had a Christmas tree in probably thirty years."

"Why not?"

Chas frowned and shook his head, muttering, but nothing comprehensible.

"That's the hardest part about caring for someone in his condition. I have no way to know what he'd want and what he wouldn't. I want to make his last days comfortable and happy. But I can only do so much by myself, without knowing some history."

"Who wouldn't enjoy a Christmas tree?" Chas mumbled as he put the last strand of lights on the tree. He wished he hadn't brought it in in the first place. Why'd he let that nurse talk him into this foolishness? He bent and plugged the lights in and the tree became a radiant display of red, green, and gold. "It's all yours."

"Won't you stay to help decorate? I'll bring your father out."

He pulled his coat on. "Sheep await."

Chas stood in the open window of his barn loft and looked out on the Sweetwater as it rolled past his meadow like a band of cold, gray metal cutting a swath through the snowy land. All shades of white and gray. It was as bleak a scene as he'd ever laid eyes on. Nothing like the blue-sky day his father killed that bobcat. He fished in his jeans pocket and pulled out a large, bone-handled pocketknife. He ran his fingers over the yellowed surface, now scratched and worn. His father gave it to him for his eighth birthday—a man's knife. The bobcat was just to let him try it out. He opened the long blade and tested it. He kept it sharpened; it was the same knife he'd used every day since then. He held it up and remembered his father's rough hands diagramming where to cut the soft underbelly so he didn't ruin the pelt. It was still warm when he cut into it. It steamed in the early morning air, and Chas had to swallow back the vomit in his throat. He was a man now; the knife was proof. He couldn't throw up.

He flipped the blade closed and slid it back in his

pocket. He took in a deep breath of cold winter sky and closed his eyes. He wondered how long it would take the nurse to finish decorating that tree. He wanted to go in for a whiskey.

"Chas," she called from the house. "You have a phone call."

He stepped to the front of the loft and waved, then climbed down and started for the house. Inside, the heat was suffocating. She'd certainly learned to keep the fire going, and now she never let the temperature drop below seventy-five degrees. He picked up the receiver. "Hello?"

"Mr. McPherson, you are so kind. I am calling to thank you for your generous gift."

"You must have me mistaken with someone else, Mr. Teleghani."

"No, no. I know your lambs. No one else raises those blackbelly lambs."

"I'm sorry, I don't know what you're referring to."

"Of course. But, thank you. You have made my family very happy. God be with you, sir. And Merry Christmas." And he hung up.

Chas held the receiver in his hand for a moment, then gently hung it up.

"Whoever that was, he was awfully thankful to you." Mattie said. She stood at the table folding laundry.

He turned to her. She had one of his white cotton under-shirts between her fingers. Where did she get that? "What?"

"He went on and on about the lamb you gave him. I could hardly get him to be quiet long enough to call you in."

"I didn't give him a lamb. He has me confused with someone else."

"It didn't sound very characteristic of you." She reached for another shirt.

"How do you know what's characteristic of me?"

"From what I've seen anyway."

32

"No one told you to wash my clothes."

"I didn't have a full load with just my stuff and your father's. I didn't think you'd mind. Most people hate laundry."

Chas walked out into the living room in his habitual manner, to gaze out the front window. But the tree now obstructed his view. He circled back to the kitchen.

"Doesn't it look nice?" she said. "I swear your father almost smiled when I showed him."

Chas doubted that very much, but if it made her feel better to believe it, he wasn't going to ruin it. Maybe she'd leave him alone with all her questions if she thought the tree made his father happy. "Yeah, it looks nice."

"Where's that man from?"

"Who?"

"The one on the phone? He had an accent."

"I don't know. Somewhere in the Middle East, I think." Chas got himself a cup of coffee and leaned against the counter. It irked him that she was folding his underwear. "He usually buys a lamb from me in December. But he didn't have enough money this year."

She peered at him suspiciously. "And you weren't the one who gave him a lamb?"

"Nope."

Mattie started to put the folded laundry back in the basket.

"Leave mine. I'll put it away," he said, realizing she'd be pawing through his dresser. "If you insist on doing my laundry, I'll put them in the hamper in the hallway. But don't go rummaging through my bedroom."

"You're welcome," she said. "Besides, don't expect me to do it again. I just needed enough to make a full load."

The old man sat in the living room, his gray skin blinking red and green with the Christmas lights. He stared ahead, expressionless, emotionless, perhaps even thoughtless. Mattie had carefully combed his hair over from a part she made on the left. And she had buttoned his shirt all the way to the collar. He looked like a little boy dressed for Easter Sunday. On his lap was a red plaid blanket of wool. Mattie sat opposite him on the sofa, drinking her fifth cup of coffee and imagining the day he strangled a bobcat.

"I believe you did that, Mr. McPherson. I believe you strangled a bobcat with your bare hands. There's something about you that's mighty fierce. Chas says you haven't had a tree in thirty years. I hope you're not mad that we put it up. I wish you could tell me why you quit having a Christmas tree. But I suspect if you could say something to me, you wouldn't say anything about that. Am I right?" She took a long slow sip and studied his face. The drink was bitter and she thought briefly of Chas's whiskey. "Let's see . . . if you could say something to me, what would it be?" She twisted her mouth, trying to guess. "Well, you were a preacher, so I guess you'd ask me if I know Jesus. Isn't that right?" She watched the old man's face for any sign of change. He remained as still as a stone. "I think that's what you'd ask. But I'm not very interested in religion, so that conversation would be a disappointment for you. What else would you ask?" Mattie pulled a loose lock of hair behind her ear. "You might ask me about my parents. I think you're about the same age as they would've been. But you already know they're dead. And I don't remember all that much about them anyway. My dad was a lumberman. My mom, she stayed home. Like most women did in those days." She looked at Mr. McPherson with new interest. "Does it bother you that so many women work now? I mean you being a preacher and all. I think you'd have an opinion on that."

Mattie got up and stoked the fire again. The house was finally warm, and she wasn't going to let it get cold. She started for the kitchen to check the ribs she was baking for supper. As she passed from one room to the next, she felt the old man behind her. It brought the short hairs on the back of her neck up. A small pulse rippled up her spine. She stopped and turned in the doorway, scanning the living room. Mr. McPherson was facing away from her, staring at the tree and the rapidly darkening sky outside. Her eyes roamed the corners of the room, the hallway, the stairs. Nothing. She shook it off and started into the kitchen again. But still he seemed to stalk her. She turned and looked again. All was as it had been. She crossed the large, open room to the oven, quietly, setting her feet so lightly on the cracked linoleum she could barely hear her own steps. Before she bent to open the oven, she turned and looked behind her once more. The room was empty, but she sensed someone was there. She waited a moment, then pulled the oven open, breathing lightly. "Chas? Is that you?" she called, trying to keep her voice even and light.

Silence.

She pushed the near-cooked ribs back into the oven and quickly shut the door. Her rapid footsteps tapped out her anxiety as she returned to the living room. She stood next to the old man and studied him. His ominous presence diminished as she surveyed his helplessness. *Small, frail, sick,* she chanted in her mind. *Small, frail, sick.*

"Okay, if that's what you want, we'll talk about religion," she said. "You see there's one thing I can't get past. Well, there's more than one thing, but I get hung up on this one and can't move on." She held her coffee in both hands to control her tremors. When she spoke aloud to him, he seemed normal. Just the old man she took care of in his last days. It was the silence that seemed to send him wandering. She knelt in front of him on the pine floor. The wood was soft, sanded dull from Chas's boot soles. She'd scrubbed it; even waxed it. But no shine could be coaxed out.

"If God talked to those people in the Bible in plain language like you and me, why doesn't he talk to us now? Would certainly clear up all this misunderstanding." She gulped her coffee and thought. "Imagine what the world would look like right now if He did."

Mattie stayed on the floor at the old man's feet where she could see his face. Perhaps it wasn't him who had followed her to the kitchen, but something else. And perhaps he, in all his mysterious bigness, could protect her from whatever it was. She'd never have agreed to take this job if she'd known Chas was a drunk and his father was . . . well, she didn't know for sure what he was. Except that he wasn't normal.

Chas came in and dropped several split logs onto the woodpile, destroying her neat rows. He stood near the stove, glowering at her as if she stayed uninvited. She got to her feet and went to the kitchen, cautious as she entered the room. But whatever was there moments before was gone now. She pulled the ribs out to cool and started setting the table. Chas followed her to the sink and washed black grime from his fingers, splattering it over the clean sink. She eyed him. He reminded her of a little boy, wandering about oblivious to her work, leaving disarray and mud trails in his wake.

"You just gonna leave him sittin' there?" he said of his father.

"He's okay."

Chas grimaced.

"I'll take him to his room."

"No, leave him." Chas slumped down at the table with his back to his father.

"You ever have anything weird happen in this house?"

He looked at her, puzzled. "What d'ya mean?"

"I mean . . . is it haunted?"

Chas laughed. "No. Where'd you get a crazy idea like that?"

Chas immediately wished he'd been nicer in answering Mattie's question. She was obviously disturbed by something, although her suggestion that his house was haunted was stupid. He dished up his plate before she sat down, then paused and waited for her. He'd forgotten proper table etiquette. Not that it mattered. When she joined him she was quiet–too quiet. Not chattering about senseless things as usual. It'll do her good to shut up, he told himself.

When Chas took his dishes to the sink, Mattie had only eaten a few bites. She stirred the food around on her plate. He got his half–drunk bottle of whiskey and two glasses, poured one for him and one for her. "You look like you could use one," he said.

She took a swallow nearly as quickly as he filled the glass, sloshing the whiskey over her shaky fingers.

Chas watched, then took the bottle to the living room, where he sat in the overstuffed chair, facing his father. The Christmas lights gave the old man an oddly animated expression. Chas tipped his head back and let his eyes go out of focus, pretending his father was taking a nap, the way he used to before supper. He lifted the drink to his lips and let it pass slowly over his tongue, warming his throat. It was smooth and soft, and as he swallowed, he kept the glass to his lips so it was an everlasting flow from lips to tongue to throat. Until his glass was empty.

"Got thirty–two pregnant ewes out there," he said. "Should be a good spring. Maybe see fifty lambs if near all of 'em have twins." He watched his father's expressionless face. "Probably can't hope for that many." Chas poured himself another drink. "Hope you don't mind." He raised the glass in a mock toast. "You always knew. May as well not pretend otherwise."

He listened to Mattie washing dishes. "What do you think of that nurse?" He reckoned she could hear him, too. "She treatin' you okay?" The old man's silence stifled Chas's conversation. He couldn't think of anything else to say and stared at the floor for a long time, trying not to think of anything at all. Mattie came into the living room and wheeled his father away. He watched her hips swing from side to side until she was out of sight, then tipped his head back and groaned.

The next morning Chas headed to town. He drove past Hinkler's Market without slowing—he had the nurse to buy groceries now. Despite the intrusion she posed on his solitude, it was nice not to have to grocery shop.

Sweetwater had been a thriving mining town in the late 1800s, then a lumber town during much of the twentieth century. But it was a diseased little hamlet now, holding onto the last and most tenuous of its industries—agriculture. Main Street was pocked with empty storefronts and crumbling brick facades, the rest of the buildings suffering a steady turnover of second-rate, but overpriced, antique shops in a vain attempt to cash in on the charm of an authentic old-west town. As if tourists would simply materialize from nowhere. Chas went first to Ruark's, the local farm store, to get milk replacer for the inevitable orphans. He didn't want to be caught without it when his ewes started lambing. But he hoped simply having the stuff on hand would ward off the need for it. Most of his ewes were second- and third-time mothers. Proven. Those with poor mothering instincts were promptly sent to the sale ring. But he had a handful of yearlings in the bunch.

"Guess it is about that time a year, ain't it?" Dean Ruark, a schoolmate who'd inherited the store from his father, said as Chas set the items on the counter.

"Hope I don't need this stuff. But you can bet your ass I will if I don't have it."

"That's a fact."

"Put it on my account, would ya, Dean?"

"Need a protein block? Got some for sheep 'n goats over there." He nodded toward a wall of carefully stacked salt and mineral licks.

"Damn, you could build a house outta those," Chas remarked, staring at the one-foot square blocks stacked to the ceiling. "I'm fine, though." Dean was the perfect man to inherit a failing farm store, Chas thought. Not only had he reinstated the rural custom of carrying tabs for farmers–making it easier for them to buy things they wouldn't normally–but he always tried to sell a little something extra with every visit. No matter what it was, he'd ask each customer if they needed it. Last month he pushed rubber mud boots. And Chas had bought a pair.

"Hear 'bout that petition?" Dean said.

"Shit."

"What's the world comin' to?"

"I don't think it's got a damn thing to do with *other* religions."

"Yeah, you bein' the preacher's son, that don't surprise me."

Chas shook his head. "The only thing I got from my old man was his looks and the practical aspects of sheep ranching. Never went in for other forms of shepherding, if ya know what I mean."

Chas stopped at the liquor store and bought two half-gallon bottles of Jack Daniels, a bottle of brandy, and some eggnog. He didn't care much for the sweet stuff, but thought the nurse might like it. And he didn't intend to buy her a Christmas gift, so it would have to suffice as good will.

He turned down Harper Street on his way home to see if the petitioner had succeeded in eradicating Christmas from the school. A large pair of red tinsel bells hung over the front doors. "Guess not," he said aloud with a measure of satisfaction. In the turn-around stood a large fir tree decorated with ornaments, lovingly made by the hands of Sweetwater children. Chas pulled to the side of the road and looked at the familiar old building. It was an immense brick structure with row upon row of tall windows cased in white. He could almost see Sarah walking through the front doors, wearing a pink angora sweater and tight jeans, her blonde hair spilling around her shoulders. He yanked back on the stick shift, threw it into second gear and pulled onto the road, spinning gravel along the soft shoulder. Two high school students loitering on the steps gave him the finger as he passed.

4

Mattie mixed a brandy eggnog and toasted Chas. "Thanks."

"Merry Christmas," he said flatly.

"I'll get your father."

"No." Chas turned his back and looked out the kitchen window into the darkness. "He needs his rest."

"But it's Christmas Eve."

"So?"

Her eyes rested on the back of his head and his blond ponytail of delicate ringlets, and she was reminded of how often physical attractiveness and personality clashed—often causing onlookers to come to see such people as ugly as trolls. That was it; Chas was a troll. As she contemplated this epiphany, the phone rang.

"Hello?" Chas held the receiver several inches from his head, and Mattie could hear a high-pitched, frantic, woman's voice. "What?" He nodded to Mattie. "Yeah, she's here. Hold on." He started to hand her the phone, but stopped and listened again. "Yeah, hang on and I'll get her," he said with clear irritation. But he waited a moment with the receiver cupped in both hands, then hammered it down hard on the counter and shouted, "Mattie, it's for you!" as if she were in another county. "Whoever that is, she's pissed at you," he said, smiling, then took his drink and sat down at the table. He watched Mattie scramble to pick it up.

She pressed the phone close to her ear, turning her back to Chas. "Hello?"

"Mattie, thank God you're alive. I've been worried to death about you! Where have you been?"

"Kathy—"

"I'm so angry with you."

"Kathy, I'm fine." Mattie glanced over her shoulder at Chas, hoping he'd get the hint and give her some privacy. But he looked on in amusement. "I'm fine. I wrote and told you where I was."

"Why didn't you call? I just got your letter today."

"I *did* call, Kathy. You didn't have time for me. Remember?"

"Mattie . . . "

"I did call you."

"Mattie, I'm sorry. I was just so worried. I didn't know if you were dead, or kidnapped, or what. You can't just keep disappearing like this. You scared me. Again!"

"I'm sorry. I took a home-care job to save some money."

"What happened to your job in Spokane?"

"Nothing. I–I got laid off. Things are tight. Too many nurses right now, I guess."

"Where are you?"

"I'm in Sweetwater, Idaho."

"Where?"

Mattie didn't respond. She was hyper aware of Chas's ears prying into her conversation.

"Why didn't you just ask for some money? You could've been on a plane the next day."

"On a plane to where?"

"Here, of course."

Mattie was silent.

"Where's the nearest airport? I'll book you on a flight out tomorrow, or the next day if you want."

"No. I can't, Kathy. I told you I have a job."

"So, they can find someone else. Give them a week's notice."

"No." Mattie glanced at Chas. A week wouldn't get him another nurse. A year might not get him another nurse.

"Mattie?"

"No. I have an obligation. Tell everyone Merry Christmas for me. Tell them I miss 'em."

"Wait, Mattie—"

"I'm fine. You don't have to worry about me."

Kathy sighed. "Okay. I love you."

"I love you too." Mattie kept her back to Chas, biting hard on her upper lip and blinking at the ceiling. When she returned to the table she avoided his gaze.

"Must be the sister in Florida."

Mattie sat in silent confirmation.

He studied her face as he peeled the dry skin from his lower lip with his teeth. "I take it she offered to pay your way to Florida?"

"Don't worry, I'm not leaving. I agreed to take care of your father." Mattie swirled the yellow liquid in her glass, watching the spiral pattern it made in the brandy.

"Thanks for not bailing on me."

She looked at him. His eyes were soft, and she noticed their color for the first time. They were deep brown, just like his father's. His pupils were dilated, and Mattie wondered if it was from all that whiskey. "It was tempting."

"I'm an asshole to live with."

She laughed. "Yeah, well, I've dealt with assholes before. But there's something about your father that gives me the creeps." She eyed Chas. "Either that or there's a ghost in this house." She rubbed her hands over her arms as if she were sitting in a draft.

"Well, you're the first to say that about my house, but not about my father. He's always scared people. His fury is beyond any normal man's. Drove away my mother."

"But he's so frail. No matter what kind of monster he was, how can he scare anybody now?"

"I never said he was a monster."

"Sorry. You sort of implied it."

"No I didn't. I just said his fury was great."

"What do you mean?"

"Everybody has fury. Well, most everybody."

Mattie gave Chas her full attention. It was the most information he'd offered about his father since announcing that he had killed a bobcat with his bare hands.

"You ever see the way bighorn sheep ram their heads together until one either dies or takes off?"

Oh, here we go with the bighorn sheep again, she thought. "Yeah, I guess."

"My blackbellies would do that too. If I had more than one ram." He grinned at the idea. "That's fury."

"I thought that was just testosterone."

He studied her, making her uncomfortable.

"So your dad walked around banging heads with people?"

"Pretty much. He used to walk up the road to old man Fenton's place with his Bible tucked under his arm. He'd go up there like he wanted to talk sheep—Fenton raised woollies. When the old man invited him in for coffee he'd start in on him about shacking up with a married woman. She was really just a whore that never divorced her husband. She moved in with Fenton when nobody would pay for it anymore." He paused, thinking about it, a deep frown etched on his face, as if the concept of an old whore that no one wanted disturbed him. "Anyway, on the fourth or fifth visit Fenton ran him off with a shotgun. Swore he'd blow his head off if he ever came back." Chas took a long, slow drink. "Dad has a way of knowing people's sins . . ."

44

"Huh?"

"I mean how he knew Fenton was shacking up with a whore . . . probably before Fenton knew it."

"Information like that travels on the wind–people can't get enough of that kind of gossip."

"No, he had some kind of special gift."

She laughed. It seemed absurd.

Chas's eyes were hot on Mattie. "You're the one said you were afraid of him. I'm just givin' you a little insight as to why. He knows your sins. Even sins you don't think are sins. He knows; that's why he scares you."

Mattie thought Chas was a complete loon. Or drunk.

"Don't worry, nobody can live up to his standards," he finally said. "You're probably no worse a sinner than the average bear." Chas smiled again. "The best day of my life was when I figured that out."

She waited for him to explain, leaving an expectant silence hanging between them.

"Say you were standing at the foot of a mountain that you knew there was no way of climbing," he said. "Would you even get your gear on?"

"No."

He nodded and lifted his drink to her.

"What about your mother?"

"What about her?"

"You said she left because of him."

Chas sat quiet again, leaving Mattie to believe he wasn't going to answer. When he did speak, his tone was resigned. "Well, I assume she left because of him. How'd you like to get a sermon on gluttony every night at the supper table?"

"That would suck. But it isn't a reason to leave."

"Little things have a way of pilin' up."

Mattie looked at the clock and swallowed the last of her eggnog. She was tempted to have another, but had already broken the promise she'd made to herself that morning, and

45

the previous one. "I better check on your father. Then I'm going to bed."

"G'night," he said.

Mattie lay in bed contemplating Chas's outlandish claims about his father. She tried to dismiss it as complete absurdity, but Chas's starkly realistic perspective on life made his observation nearly impossible to disbelieve. How could that old man know anything about her? *He could not*, she decided and rolled onto her side with her back to the window. The winter sky had cleared and was bright with a nearly full moon that burned into her room, illuminating her every thought. And even as she worked to clear her mind of all they had discussed, her sins shown bright in the moonlight, forcing her to take inventory. She lined up her small, simple sins next to deeds she wished she could undo, or even just forget. If that old man could know her worst sins, she thought, he'd do a whole lot more than haunt her.

Mattie found Chas sitting at the table sharpening a long, thin knife against a whetstone. It was just past seven and the sun was making a slow appearance over the mountain behind the house. Chas had made fresh coffee and she got herself a cup and leaned against the counter. "What's that for?"

"Cuttin'."

"No kidding?" She rolled her eyes.

He tested the blade against his thumb, underestimating its sharpness and drawing a fine line of blood. "I wouldn't recommend coming to the barn today."

"Since when do I go to the barn?"

"Well, in case you're inclined to. I wouldn't today."

"Okay. Care to tell me why?"

"I'm gonna butcher that lamb this morning."

"On Christmas?"

"It's a day same as any other day to me."

"Then I guess you wouldn't want me to bake a ham, or make mashed potatoes and gravy, or any of that nonsense."

He slid the knife into its leather sheath and set it on the table. "You could do that if you want. I'm not here to stop you from celebrating. Not like that petitioner from the school."

"No, I think you're right. It's just a day like any other. I'll skip the big dinner and just boil hotdogs." She looked out on the brilliant, eye-stinging snow.

"My father would want you to make a big dinner."

"Your father?" She'd have to purée it for him.

"Yup, he's a Christian man. That'd be a nice thing to do for him." Chas gulped down the last of his coffee.

Mattie watched him gather his knife and put on his coat, calmly going out to kill a living, breathing creature. *Barbarian*.

"Easy now. Easy." Chas spoke softly as he entered the pen, trying not to spook the lamb. A frightened animal would release lactic acid into its muscles, making the meat tough and gamey. "Easy now," he repeated as he caught the lamb up with one arm. He heaved it off its feet and shoved it down on its side, straddling it with his knees. He pulled its head back and swiftly cut its throat, slicing it nearly through to the bone. The animal had no time to struggle. The first cut went deep, through the windpipe with a whistle. He cut again, deeper, then again until the lamb's nose lay back against its withers. Blood pooled at his knees, and the animal kicked reflexively with its hind legs, as if trying to leap up–to leap into the next world. He held it firm, its nearly severed head bent back, until it lay limp and the bleeding slowed from a gush to a trickle.

He stood, wiped the bloodied blade against the leg of his coveralls and set it on a post. He looked at the twisted animal and tried again to remember the words Nuri Teleghani spoke before killing his lambs. Wanted to know them now more than ever.

"It wasn't any fun for me either," he said as he lifted the carcass and hung it on a chain suspended from the rafters. Then he carefully slit a line down the belly to pull the hide away.

Once skinned and gutted, the lamb was no longer an animal, but meat. Simply meat. Chas set to work cutting it into portions. He didn't imagine what the meat would taste like, or how he would prepare it. He could not cross that line from livestock to Sunday supper so simply. He'd have to freeze it; leave it for a time. Then in March or April, when the memory of this moment, no matter how many times repeated, was only a distant nib in the back of his brain, easily shoved down to the darkened depths of his soul, would he reach for the ribs or shanks and think of rosemary and apple chutney.

Mattie peered out at the barn, imagining what Chas was doing. She turned to Mr. McPherson. "Can't imagine the kind of man who could slaughter a lamb on Christmas day."

The old man stared at the tree.

"Chas says you know people's sins." She gave a quick laugh, then went serious. "That's ridiculous. I can't believe a grown man could walk around thinking something so silly."

She wheeled the old man into the kitchen. "Even if you did, I wouldn't have anything to hide." Mattie took the ham from the refrigerator and checked the oven. It was old and didn't maintain an even temperature, making it difficult to bake anything without constant monitoring. She'd spent the entirety of her third morning at the ranch on her knees, scrubbing away decades of baked-on food in the hope it would work better. She sliced a pineapple into thin rings and pinned them to the ham with cloves.

"Your son wanted me to prepare Christmas dinner for you. Wouldn't admit that he wanted it himself. He's a strange bird. But, sometimes he can be nice. Not very often, mind you. Just often enough to put me off guard. To make me think he's not so bad.

"So how would a body come across the ability to know another person's sins without being told?" She put the ham back in the oven and washed her hands. "I mean someone would have to tell you. Right?" She glanced at him as if he might confirm her suspicion. "Does God talk to you like he did to people in the Bible?" She ran a sponge over the sink with a quick back-and-forth motion. "No. He wouldn't tell you about other people's offenses. What's that thing Jesus always said? Get the mote out of your own eye before you go helping someone else get the speck out of theirs? Yeah, it was something like that."

As she was peeling potatoes, someone knocked. She dried her hands and went to the door. She stepped back and caught her breath.

"Is Chas McPherson home?"

Mattie stared at the police officer a moment, then smiled politely. "Yes, he's in the barn." She pointed the way. "You might want to come back tomorrow, though. He's out there slaughtering a lamb."

"This won't wait 'til tomorrow," the officer said. "I have some questions for you as well."

"Oh, what about?"

"I'd like to speak with Mr. McPherson first. Please wait here."

"I wouldn't set foot in that barn with him out there cutting up an animal."

The officer stepped off the porch and started through the snow without another word. Mattie pressed her shaking fingers to her temple and wiped away tiny beads of sweat. She closed the door, but watched the officer until he was out of sight, then stared at the open barn door until he emerged again, grim-faced, and heading for the house. She waited for him to knock before she opened the door.

"May I come in for a moment?"

She stepped aside.

He held a small spiral-bound notepad in his left hand

49

and a long, sharp pencil in his right. "What's your name?"

"Mattie Holden." She tipped her head back to answer his questions; he was uncommonly tall. Well over six feet, probably halfway to seven. She thought it a pity that he'd ruined his good looks with the uniform. His square jaw, his smooth skin. Sharp and clean.

"How are you acquainted with Mr. McPherson?"

Mattie glanced at the old man in the wheelchair staring at the kitchen sink. "You mean Chas, right?"

"Yes."

"I'm the home-care nurse. He hired me to take care of his father." She pointed at Mr. McPherson. "He's got Parkinson's Disease."

The officer looked at him and nodded. "Was Mr. McPherson here last evening?"

"Yes, he was here."

"Did he leave at any time during the evening?" He had a habit of piercing her with his stare after asking each question. She imagined he could invoke the truth from people with his compelling blue eyes alone.

"No."

"What time did he go to bed?"

"I don't know. I went to bed before him."

"What time was that?"

"Ten-thirty. Why?"

"Did you ever hear Mr. McPherson talk about a family by the name of Teleghani?"

Mattie fidgeted with her fingers, twisting them, and letting them go. "It sounds familiar . . . yeah, Mr. Teleghani called the other day . . . to thank Chas for giving him a lamb. I'm pretty sure it was him. He had a very heavy accent. I had a hard time understanding him. But he went on and on about the gift–the lamb."

"What lamb?"

"He said Chas gave him a lamb. But Chas says he didn't."

The officer jotted notes in his book.

"What's this all about, anyway?"

"Someone burned the Teleghanis' house down last night. The family got out okay, but the building and everything in it was a total loss."

Mattie's mouth gaped. "Who would do such a thing?"

"There's at least one person who says Chas's pickup was parked on the road in front of the house recently."

"Last night?"

"A few nights ago." He closed his notebook and slipped it into his pocket. "Said he appeared to be casing the place. Do you know if he signed the petition about the holiday celebration at the school?"

"Whether he signed a petition or not doesn't make him guilty of arson."

The officer waited for her answer.

"No, he didn't sign it. He thought it would put the families in an awkward position."

"What families?"

"The ones the petitioner claimed she was trying to include in the celebration."

"Thank you, ma'am." The officer started for the door.

"Wait." Mattie hurried after him. "He cares about those families."

"How do you know that?"

"He didn't sign the petition because no one asked them if it was what they wanted. He thought it would make them worry that everyone hated them for taking away the holiday." Mattie could see she was making it look worse for Chas. "No one asked them. How would you feel if you were in a strange country and someone banned the local holiday on your account?"

"Wasn't Franklin McPherson a minister?" The sheriff nodded at the back of the old man's head.

"Yes. But Chas isn't religious. He doesn't care about Christmas."

51

The officer looked at the tree blinking in the window and pulled the door open. "Thank you, ma'am."

Mattie stood on the porch until the cold forced her back inside. She stoked the fire and went back to the kitchen, but couldn't keep her mind on her work–starting to peel a potato, then turning and looking at the old man, then picking up another potato and starting again. Finally, she pulled on her coat and boots, and started for the barn. She stood outside and called to Chas. He didn't answer.

"Chas?" she repeated, stepping into the cavernous building and waiting for her eyes to adjust to the dim light. "Chas?"

"What're you doing out here? I told you not to come to the barn." He was on the other end of a long hallway that ran the length of the barn. His tone was harsh, and she immediately regretted coming.

She could see the naked carcass hanging from a chain and turned her face away. "I came to see if you're okay."

He faced her, a knife in his hand, his arms and coveralls greasy red with blood. "Go on back to the house. I don't need nobody worrying over me! I didn't burn nobody's house down."

She nodded and started back, but paused in the doorway. "It's what you were worried about. You were right."

"It didn't take a fucking genius to figure out that something like this would happen. All anyone had to do was stop and think about it for one goddamn second."

She nodded, covering her nose and mouth with the collar of her sweater to shield herself from the smell of the blood. Which she only imagined.

5

CHAS TOOK THE MEAT TO THE CELLAR, where he kept a large chest freezer. He moved the remainder of last year's lamb and put the new one at the bottom so the meat would be eaten in the order he'd killed it. He stripped off his coveralls and hung them on a peg near the door. He'd come back when the blood was dry and the nurse was gone and put them in the washer. He wouldn't ruin her Christmas by dragging them into the house now. He used the large sink to scrub his knife and himself, up to the elbows, and wash his face. He thought about Mattie coming to the barn to see if he was okay. He'd so specifically told her to stay away from the barn today. Now she'd probably refuse to eat the meat, forcing him to buy meat from the grocery store with money he didn't have. Why couldn't she take him at his word? Instead she had to come out and see for herself, all because some sheriff came to question him about something he didn't do. He shook his head and thought about the whiskey waiting for him. It was early, but it was Christmas. Everyone would be drinking early on this day.

Chas dried his hands on a crusty yellow towel and threw it on the floor beneath his coveralls to remind himself to wash it. He put his hands on his waist and pressed his shoulders back to stretch the muscles across his chest, then slowly twisted to one side, then to the other to stretch his upper back. A brilliant pain seared across his lower back and he held his breath through the spasm. When the pain diminished, he bent and pressed his palms against the cool, cement floor, stretching his lower back, opening the vertebrae and easing the pressure on his pinched nerve. He felt old.

Upstairs Mattie beat potatoes with an old electric mixer. She didn't hear him come in. He went directly to the cupboard for his whiskey, but instead of pouring a glass, nudged her arm, startling her. She jumped, pulling up on the mixer and spraying gooey bits of potatoes around the kitchen and all over him.

"God! You scared the hell out of me," she yelled over the screeching whir of the mixer, her eyes flashing.

Chas looked at his shirt, dotted with potatoes and scratched his eyebrow. "Sorry. Just seein' if you wanted a brandy."

Mattie turned the mixer off and dropped it back into bowl. She pushed a lock of hair out of her face and steadied her gaze on Chas. "What? I couldn't hear you."

He shook his head, wishing he'd simply gotten his whiskey and sat down. "Brandy?"

"Over there." She pointed at the bottle next to the refrigerator.

"You–do *you* want a brandy?"

"Oh." She paused, her mouth still open. "Sure. Yes. That would be nice. Thanks." She turned back to the potatoes with a perplexed expression.

"That was entirely too much trouble," he mumbled as he poured each of them a drink. He set hers on the counter, then sat down at the table.

"Warm enough for you yet?" he questioned.

"What?" She turned back, confused.

"Is it warm enough for you? It must be a hundred degrees in here."

"Yeah. It's warm enough."

"Good, I'm opening the door." He propped the front door open with a stick of firewood. Returning, he asked, "You fed him already?"

Mattie turned again and looked at Chas blankly.

"Jesus, am I speaking another language, or what?"

"Yes! Yes, you are." She took a breath and closed her eyes. "First you come in here and scare the crap out of me, then you start speaking in quarter sentences. What are you asking me?"

He scowled at her. "Never mind." He took a swill of his whiskey, rolling it over his tongue.

"Yes, I fed your father already, if that's what you're asking." She picked up the glass, and Chas saw her hand tremble before she steadied it. "I have to make his special, and I didn't want it to get cold. He's resting, but I'll get him . . . if you want to share Christmas dinner with him."

He shook his head.

She nodded and turned back. "You like garlic and rosemary in your mashed potatoes, or do you prefer them with just butter?"

"Never had 'em that way. However you want is fine."

Mattie was quiet, and Chas leaned his head against the wall and closed his eyes, imagining the burnt ruins of the Teleghani house. He wished he'd asked the sheriff where they were staying, then wondered how they'd make ends meet. Nuri made violins in his basement—violins that would be ruined now.

"Did you tell that police officer you gave the Teleghanis a lamb?"

Chas opened his eyes, but kept his head back, staring at the water-stained ceiling. "Sheriff. He was the sheriff."

"Whatever."

He tipped his head down and looked at the back of Mattie's head. "What lamb?"

"Come on, I know you gave them a lamb."

"What're you, psychic?"

She flashed him an annoyed glare. "I thought back on when I saw you leave in your truck the other night. You had a metal rack on it, like people use when they haul animals. It wasn't on your truck that morning, and it wasn't on your truck the next morning. And that police ... I mean *sheriff,* said someone saw you at their house a few nights ago."

"So you think you've got it all figured out, huh?"

"Look," she said, turning to him with a long wooden spoon in her hand. "If you tell the police you gave them a lamb, how could they suspect you of arson?"

"I didn't burn nobody's house down. They can figure that out whether I gave anybody a lamb or not."

"Why don't you change your shirt; dinner's almost ready."

Chas frowned. The last thing he needed was a woman telling him what to do. And they needed to get that straight right now. "I'll change it when I'm goddamn ready to change it."

She blinked at him, then stared tensely at the floor. Finally, she turned and spooned the potatoes into a serving bowl, which she carried to the table without looking in his direction. She pulled the ham out to cool, then set two places, carefully pushing Chas's drink out of the way to make room for his plate, and leaning over from the other side of the table so she didn't crowd him.

The aroma of baked ham with sweet glaze wafted over him. He looked down at his shirt, splattered with mashed potatoes. *Damn it!*

Mattie heard the chair legs scrape against the linoleum and glanced up to see Chas disappear into the other room. Then she heard his heavy footsteps on the stairs and saw he hadn't taken his drink; he'd be coming back.

The creaking of the floorboards overhead comforted her, no matter how surly his mood. All strange noises could be attributed to him when he was at home. But when he was gone, she had only to speculate at what lurked in the forgotten corners of this house. Or was this the effects of trying to get clean on her own? Had she taken her drug use to such a level that she was left imagining things, hallucinating? Had it been a mistake to sequester herself out here alone, believing she could kick her habit without help? Whatever the cause of her unease, it intensified her craving for painkillers and cocaine, anything narcotic. She drank down the brandy—her third that day, but to Chas's knowledge only her first, and quickly fixed herself another.

When Chas returned, he wore a blue western–style shirt with mother of pearl snaps, tucked into a pair of nearly new jeans. "Happy?"

She gave him a weak smile. "You didn't have to go to all that trouble. Just didn't think you'd want to eat dinner with potatoes all over your shirt."

He grunted and sat down. She brought him the whiskey, knowing he'd want it. Then they ate silently, without a prayer of thanksgiving. Chas didn't comment on the dinner she'd worked so hard to prepare, but filled his plate three times, satisfying her that she hadn't done it all in vain. Then he abruptly stood and took the whiskey to the living room, leaving her with the greasy pots and pans, and a table cluttered with dirty dishes. She sat a long time, thinking about the situation she'd gotten herself into, feeling remarkably like Chas's unattractive housewife and wondering if she should accept her sister's offer of an airline ticket. But the idea evaporated as she played it out to its natural conclusion. She pushed away from the table, reminding herself she chose this isolation for a reason, and began gathering dishes, clanking them together unnecessarily and running the water for no reason, all to disturb Chas's whiskey retreat.

By the time Mattie finished up, Chas was snoring in his chair, his feet propped on an old wooden ammunition box. Mattie went to his father's room and began the evening ritual. As it was early yet, she sat down, picked up his Bible, and began to read from the gospel of Matthew–the nativity story–a little Christmas gift, she reasoned. She tried to picture Mr. McPherson at the pulpit, pounding out revelations for his flock. It all seemed so open to interpretation to her, such a wide margin for error. What's the punishment in heaven for a preacher who leads his flock astray?

Mattie tiptoed past Chas and unplugged the Christmas lights, then climbed the stairs to her room. She undressed in the dark and slid between the cold sheets, shivering and wishing she'd thought to stoke the fire one more time. It'd been a long day–a hard day. And the most unpleasant Christmas she could ever recall–not that she'd ever known one that was special.

She awoke in the dark to a cool, eerie howl. The sort of howl that cuts through the night in every werewolf flick– guttural and throaty, sending the heart galloping and visions of yellow fangs glinting in the moonlight skittering through the mind. It was followed by another, then a symphony of yipping. Mattie gasped and scrambled out of bed, pulling her robe from the bedpost and running into the hallway between her room and Chas's. She looked out on the meadow and the river, her skin prickling as she scanned the snow. It sounded like there were dozens of them–whatever they were. She looked at Chas's closed door and wondered if she should wake him. But the howls went silent then, and she waited, her breath shallow and her fingers trembling. Had she dreamed them? Seconds ticked by and she began to believe she'd imagined sounds from Hell, but she couldn't calm herself. She sat on the top step to wait, listening to the slow ticking of an old clock in the living room below. It was loud beyond proportion, and she wondered how she'd never noticed it before. How could she have missed the way it articulated each second? Then the howling started again; one lone, long howl followed by the same chorus of yipping. She squeezed her fingers together and put her head between her knees.

A loud thump came from Chas's room, as if he'd fallen out of bed, then a series of clatters. She imagined him hopping across the floor on one foot. His door flew open, banging hard against the wall and shuddering back. He didn't see her, but went straight to the window, his jeans on but his fly unbuttoned and one sock still in his hand. His broad back rippled with tension as he peered down at the meadow. He pulled his other sock on and turned to go downstairs, nearly tripping over Mattie.

"What're you doing sitting here in the dark?" he snapped.

"What is that?"

"Coyotes. They must've found the rest of that lamb carcass." He slipped past her and thumped heavily down the stairs. She scurried after him. He turned and looked up, stopping her cold. "Go back to bed!"

Mattie froze until he was out of sight, then sat down again on the stairs, too afraid to go back to her room. She listened as Chas slammed the front door. She followed him down and watched his shadowy figure move across the yard toward the meadow, the moonlight shining on the barrel of his rifle. He paused at the fence, raised the gun in the air, and discharged a shot. Mattie looked up at the night sky, as if expecting to see where the bullet had torn it open. Her eyes went back to Chas. He stood motionless for several seconds, then he climbed the fence and went further into the meadow. She wanted to yell at him to come out of there. Coyotes, in Mattie's mind, were synonymous with wolves. And wolves traveled in packs, drawing victims in to attack.

She waited, but didn't hear another shot. The longer he was gone, the more she worried he'd been attacked and dragged into the woods. She wondered if she should call the police, but reckoned if Chas were still alive, he'd kill *her* for doing that.

A half hour passed and Mattie was on the sofa, her feet curled up under her, when she heard Chas's footsteps on the porch. He came in like a storm, swinging the door open wide and upsetting the silence. He leaned the rifle against the wall and kicked the door shut with his boot. He looked at Mattie, then pulled off his coat, exposing his still-bare chest.

"Did you kill them?"

He shook his head, but an amused smile broke across his face. "They can't git ya in here. Besides, they're more afraid of you than you are of them." He paused, studying Mattie more closely. "Well, maybe not in your case. It was the sheep I was worried about. Go on back to bed."

Mattie didn't move. She wasn't getting off that couch and returning to a freezing bed to stare at the ceiling, alone and scared.

Chas put a log in the woodstove and stoked up the fire. Then he went to the kitchen, pawed through the leftovers, and made himself a plate of ham and mashed potatoes, which he warmed in an old microwave oven so crusted with grime Mattie refused to clean it.

She marveled at how he could eat with vicious animals loose in his meadow. She pulled her robe down over her feet and lay her head on the armrest. The musty smell of the sofa prickled her nose, but she didn't move. Chas brought his plate and sat across from her. She closed her eyes and listened to his fork scraping across the stoneware. Whatever he was, he was strong. She felt safer to be near him, even if she didn't especially like him.

Mattie was drifting back to sleep when Chas dropped his dishes into the sink with a clatter, startling her awake again. She looked at the clock: just past one–the whole night ahead of her still.

He turned the light off and stood over the couch peering down at her. "I'm going back to bed. You best do the same, or those coyotes might come in here and gitcha." He sported a wide grin.

She got to her feet and started for the stairs.

"They'll come right through that window," he said, pointing at a small double–hung window at one end of the living room. "They can open it, you know."

"Shut up."

"I swear it. But they only come after people that're scared of 'em. So Dad and I don't have to worry. Just you."

"Leave me alone or I'll poison your food."

"Ooh, you're mean when you're riled, ain't ya?"

Mattie hurried up the stairs and into her room, shutting the door with a swift kick.

Chas stood in the meadow at blue dawn and surveyed the remains of the carcass. The coyotes had strewn it across the landscape, dragging most of it away before he'd scared them off. When he'd tried to bury it the day before the ground was frozen, so he covered it with snow instead. He'd have to hook up the backhoe on his tractor to dig a hole. Which, he conceded, is what he should've done in the first place.

He thought of Mattie, sitting on the stairs in the dark, then curling up near him on the couch. At least she wasn't a screamer. He gave her credit for that. She reminded him of Sarah. She had been afraid of coyotes too, and spiders and snakes. He had teased Sarah, too. But not too much, just enough to make her grab him and beg for protection. She'd press herself against him so tightly it felt like she was trying to climb inside him. He liked that. He'd put his arms around her and kiss her. He could still remember the soft rose scent of her hair.

The memory blew away with his breath in the frigid air as he looked back at the house and thought of his father, lying still in his bed. A vile bitterness crept into his mouth, threatening to choke him.

Chas walked the meadow after he buried the carcass, looking for a ewe due to lamb soon. The coyotes would be back, scouting around for a while, and he didn't want to risk losing a newborn, or possibly two. He carried a green laundry detergent bucket with grain in the bottom, shaking it lightly as he went, attracting the flock. A long single-file line formed behind him, lead by an old ewe that if Chas were inclined to keep a favorite, which he was not, would be it.

"Come on, old girl," he coaxed. He brought them into the catch pen and poured the grain out into the feeder, then circled back and pushed the gate closed. Simple. As the latch clanged, their heads popped up, eyes wide. "Tricked ya again," he sang softly.

He inspected the flock and selected three ewes likely to deliver within the week and let the others out again, watching for signs of ill health as they darted past. Then he herded the ewes into pens in the barn.

"Welcome to the maternity ward, girls." He put hay in the mangers and filled buckets of water from the outside spigot. Then he did what he almost never did; he paused to admire his animals. He studied each brown face, their perky black ears. The bars over their eyes, and the stripes down their necks. They were beautiful little creatures–like deer. There was a danger in stopping to truly look at them. It reminded him that his life would only be this–day-in and day-out, lambing, feeding, butchering, and lambing again. To be dreaming of other places and other lives at forty-one. When he knew in his soul it was too late. One morning in the not-so-distant future he'd come out to find a pair of twin lambs, then another, and another in the weeks ahead. And he knew he'd turn his back as they frolicked in the grass, springing on slender legs, like a circus of tiny acrobats. He wouldn't take pause to peer back at the curious faces when they found a new vantage point from which to contemplate their master, such as the low branches of a maple tree.

He trudged out of the barn, disappointed in himself for indulging in this moment of self-pity and wondering how he'd make it until dark before cracking open the other bottle of whiskey.

6

SHERIFF EDELSON SURVEYED THE BURNT RUINS of the Teleghanis' house. He'd found scraps of cloth soaked in gasoline
abandoned near the chicken shed. He guessed the house had
gone up so quickly the arsonist had made a hasty retreat.
The walls had been stuffed with newspapers in a vain
attempt to insulate the place.

He walked circles around the house, combing the
ground, finding nothing but a few forgotten toys. Red chickens scratched in the muddy snow, looking for food. He jotted a reminder to call animal control. Didn't want oppor-
tunists to steal the fowl. The Teleghanis would need the food.

He thought about Chas McPherson, bloodied to the
elbows, wielding a knife, begrudgingly answering questions.
Hostile. Why? The sheriff's gut reaction was heightened suspicion. And the nurse–her story about Chas's refusal to sign
the petition–it seemed only to point to his guilt. And already
half a dozen reports incriminating the man had been called
in, and it wasn't ten o'clock in the morning. As if the news
blew through town on the night air.

During his two years in Sweetwater, Edelson had not gotten to know McPherson. Though the sheriff had seen him in
town a few times, it had been simply in passing. It took him

some time to recall exactly who Chas McPherson was when the tips came flooding in. His secretary finally described McPherson's blue truck in exasperated tones–as if Edelson were an idiot. McPherson wasn't one to frequent the local tavern, or any of the various community functions like the Independence Day Parade or the lighting of the Christmas tree down at the corner of Main and Railroad Streets. To the sheriff, Chas McPherson seemed almost reclusive.

Edelson slid into his cruiser and backed out of the Teleghanis' driveway and onto the highway. He idled in the road a moment as his eyes roamed the scorched hulk of their house. He could taste the smoke at the back of his throat, though he knew it was only imagined. That this happened was not at all surprising to him; there were a lot of folks around who resented foreigners. What surprised Edelson was the unanimity of Sweetwater's residents in pointing out who was responsible. He hoped they were right for two reasons: it made his job easier, and he had a particularly venomous hatred for arsonists. Ever since he was a boy Edelson had suffered an irrational fear of fire. At different times in his life he'd tried to overcome it, shrug it off, and even confront it head on. This thing that plagued him sprang from nowhere. He'd never been the victim of a fire, nor had he personally known anyone who was. But still, it stalked him. At the mere mention of a fire, he couldn't prevent his mind wandering into the terror of his own blistered flesh or his lungs choked with smoke.

Edelson took a hard breath of the clean December air, and headed back into town. Anyone who would see human beings burned alive deserved swift and severe punishment. And Edelson intended to see that they got it.

Mattie chattered on about the coyotes as she took ornaments off the Christmas tree and packed them into boxes that might never be dragged from the dusty attic again. She doubted the old man would live to see another Christmas. He was having bouts of bleeding from his nose and genitals. Alarmed, she'd promptly made a doctor's appointment. She wondered about telling Chas. But he was so put off by his father's illness, she doubted he could cope with information of such an intimate nature.

She rambled about anything she could think of to keep the old man from lurking in the air around her. "You hate me, don't you?" She waited, knowing it was pointless to expect a response. "Why do you hate me? I'm only here to help you." She studied him, believing he understood. Parkinson's patients rarely suffered a loss of mental ability. "Don't hate me, Mr. McPherson."

She turned back to the tree and pulled down the ornament with the picture of Chas. She held it up for the old man to see. "I love this ornament; he was so cute. Too bad he turned out so mean." She turned it over and examined the back. In cursive it said *Chas '63*. A woman's handwriting. She placed the ornament on the sofa arm and wondered what could make a woman leave her child. Mattie compared the all-too-familiar sense of abandonment she'd felt after her parents died to what Chas surely felt; knowing his mother *chose* to leave. It was like being caught with something that didn't belong to her. Like she was indulging in a grief she wasn't entitled to. She began pulling the strings of lights from the boughs, walking in circles around the tree and draping them over her arm. "I hope you don't mind me taking this tree down so soon."

Chas came in as Mattie pulled the last strand of lights from the tree. "Taking it down already?"

"Yeah. You don't mind, do you?"

Chas gave her a wary look.

"What's the significance of the tree at Christmas?"

He shrugged. "How should I know?"

"Doesn't it strike you as odd we don't even know why we

have Christmas trees? I read the story of Jesus to your father last night and I didn't find anything about a tree in it."

"You what?"

"I read him the story about Mary and Joseph and Jesus."

Chas sat down with his sandwich. Between bites, he said, "The sheep'll eat it."

"What?"

"The tree."

She looked at the tree in amazement. "Really?"

"Vitamin C."

"How do you know that?"

He shrugged and wolfed down the second half of his sandwich. "I'm going to town. You need anything?"

She was surprised he would even ask. "No, but I'll need your help tomorrow morning. Your father has a doctor's appointment in Lewiston at eleven. I need help getting him in the car."

"An appointment? What for?"

"Just . . . thought it was a good idea. That's all."

"Can you make me two sandwiches tomorrow? I git hungry with just one."

Mattie saw a fleeting presence of the boy in the photo just then, even as she remembered she wasn't obligated to make him *any* sandwiches. "Okay."

Chas cruised down Main Street slower than usual in his battered blue Dodge four-by-four. He paid attention to the twenty-five mile-per-hour speed limit, as well as to the faces that turned and stared. Severe faces. Suspicious faces. He didn't have specific business in town that day, but came to prove he had nothing to hide—to drive down to the farm store, or the grocery store, or wherever he felt like going, just like any other day.

He pulled up at Ruark's, drawing the attention of two men discussing weather reports on the sidewalk. He nodded curtly with the brim of his hat as he passed. They stood silent, following him inside with their eyes. He strode to the counter with a deliberate measure of confidence, setting his boot soles hard on the dirty, tile floor. "Dean," he greeted. "Changed my mind about those protein blocks. I'll take two."

Dean nodded. "Can I get ya anything else? Got a delivery of whole oats this morning."

"No, that'll do it for me." Chas leaned against the counter while Dean rang up his order. "Terrible thing about the Teleghanis' house, ain't it?"

Dean lifted a shoulder slightly, but didn't look up.

"You wouldn't know where they're staying, would you?"

Dean took his time answering. "Don't think I should be having this conversation with ya, Chas. You know . . . with all that's going round town. Lotta folks think it was you."

"I didn't burn nobody's house down. You know that."

Dean blinked several times. "I believe you, Chas." A tense silence passed between them, Dean refusing to look up. "I guess, it's because of your old man," he finally wheezed.

"Christ! He can't even wipe his nose. How's he got anything to do with this?"

"It's why they suspect you, Chas. You're the preacher's son."

"So I'm to assume then that you'll never make this place turn a dime's profit because your daddy was a lousy businessman?"

Dean's face flushed crimson.

Chas pulled down a twenty-pound protein block. "Put it on my tab, would ya?"

Dean nodded to his clerk, who scrambled to get the other one, and followed Chas out the door.

Chas worked a small key to open the metal box in the bed of his pickup. He dropped the block in and held the lid up for the clerk to deposit the other. "Keeps honest people honest," he said.

The clerk smiled nervously. "Nice day, Mr. McPherson."

Chas watched the boy, pimply faced and probably no older than sixteen, run back to the store. He wondered what the rumor would be at the high school when classes resumed. Kids were more imaginative when it came to placing blame. He could be called the Jesse James of Sweetwater, or the Grinch that stole Ramadan, assuming the kids–or anyone in Sweetwater–knew what Ramadan was. Or better, maybe he'd inherited his father's gift. Maybe he would stalk them at night, tormenting them for their sins, lurking in the dark like a vampire. He smiled to himself.

Before going home Chas stopped at the County Sheriff's office, which was housed in the old Idaho State Bank building. It was the first thing people saw when entering Sweetwater, and the last they saw when leaving. It had been built of brick and cinderblock in 1882, with large iron bars on the windows and doors, and a vault that could hold its contents through a sizeable dynamite blast. Just the sort of bank a silver mining town needed in those days. But now it only served the sheriff for restraining an occasional rowdy cowboy, or a sneaky arsonist.

He hadn't given much forethought to the visit, but had been seized with a sudden urge to show the sheriff his congenial side after realizing he might've made a bad impression the previous day, dripping with blood and all. He pressed the silver bell on the counter. A pleasant "ding" resonated through the high–ceilinged room. Moments later a vaguely familiar woman in her mid-fifties stepped out from the back and assessed Chas harshly with her eyes. He assessed her back; she looked as though she'd moussed her hair with pine pitch.

"Yes, can I help you?"

"Chas McPherson. Number one arson suspect. Here to speak to the sheriff."

"Is the sheriff expecting you?"

"No. I thought I'd surprise him."

"Sheriff don't like surprises, Mr. McPherson." She gave him another severe look. "I'll see if he's available."

Chas sat in the waiting area and read a week-old edition of the Spokesman Review. He sifted through it for nothing in particular, and nothing in particular caught his attention. He didn't care much for world affairs, thought governments would do what they wanted, whether anyone reported on it or not. And people everywhere would form opinions based on their own narrow view of the cosmos. He accepted his part in the grand scheme of things as minute beyond measure; the world would hardly notice if he simply disappeared—the sheriff notwithstanding. In a hundred years no one would remember the name Chas McPherson, perhaps even fifty. But that was the beauty of life, the anonymity of it. He was down to the community pages when the woman appeared again.

"He'll see you in a minute, Mr. McPherson. Says you shoulda called ahead, though."

Chas nodded. "Next time." He scanned the police reports: stolen cars, homes burglarized, DUI arrests. A summation of all bad things he believed about the city. At the bottom of the page was a brief article about the problem of drug addiction among nurses, recently on the rise.

"Sheriff Edelson'll see you now," the pitch lady said.

Chas tossed the paper on the coffee table and followed her around the counter, down a long corridor into the bowels of the building. It occurred to him she might be leading him straight to jail. But she halted at an office door and nodded for him to enter.

Sheriff Edelson sat behind a large antique desk of solid oak, adorned with a dentil cornice. It was likely part of the original bank furniture. Chas looked the sheriff straight in the eye and nodded his greeting.

"Have a seat, Mr. McPherson," the sheriff said, motioning

to a hard-backed chair opposite his desk. "What can I do for you?"

The sheriff was a formidable man. Not in girth like Chas, but in height. Over six feet tall, with broad shoulders and large hands. A badge adorned the front of his cowboy hat. And he wore boots. No self-respecting western sheriff would chase an outlaw down on foot. He'd ride after him on his horse. Or just shoot him dead—so Chas imagined. He wondered if the sheriff even had a horse.

"I came to ask about the Teleghanis. I'd like to help 'em out, but I don't know where they're staying. And with all the jawin' that's going on in this town, nobody's inclined to tell me either."

"You'd like to help them out?"

"I have some extra meat from that lamb I butchered yesterday. I thought they could probably use it."

The sheriff squinted suspiciously.

"Ain't a crime to help a family in need, is it?"

"No . . . no, it ain't a crime. But, it is a bit suspicious. You wanting to help now that people think you're the one who could've done it."

"You've got no evidence on me."

"How do you know that?"

"Because I didn't do anything wrong."

"Got an eye witness says your truck was parked on the road in front of the house a few nights before it happened."

"How's that make me guilty of anything?"

"Got two more who say you were hanging around the school on Christmas Eve."

"Didn't know reminiscing 'bout the old days was against the law either." Chas scratched his chin. "I guess I'm learning all kinds of things today."

The sheriff looked Chas straight in the eye. "Did you give the Teleghani family a lamb on the night of Eid?"

"What difference does it make?"

"Intent."

"And if I said yes, would you believe me now, anyway?"

The sheriff twisted a new, sharp pencil between his fingers. "Pam Cook says you were aggressive with your opinions when she came by with the petition."

"Yeah, I s'pose I was. Just trying to git her to think the whole thing through."

"You have something against Moslems, Mr. McPherson?"

"I didn't have to ask you what Eid was, did I?"

"It was a yes or no question."

"No."

"Sorry, I can't tell you where they're staying. It's not here in town, though."

Chas felt heat rising in his cheeks, then stood to go. "Tell you what, I'll send it over here. You'll see they get it, won't you?"

The sheriff neither agreed nor disagreed, and Chas tipped his hat as he walked to the door.

"Don't be leaving town without letting me know."

Chas paused in the doorway. "Who the hell would feed my sheep if I left town?"

Sheriff Edelson sat a little further back in his chair. "It's just a formality. I tell all my suspects that."

Chas pulled the brim of his hat down low over his eyes and left the building with sharply punctuated steps.

Edelson sat back in his chair and went through the interchange, word by word. What was it about Chas McPherson that left him so uncertain about the man's motives? Was it that McPherson believed he could waltz in here and offer some token of generosity and his name would be wiped from the list of suspects? As if Edelson were so green that he'd believe anyone capable of burning a house down wasn't also capable of plotting an elaborate display of innocence by following it up with a good deed. But . . . was that really it? He went through the conversation again. If McPherson had only come to save his neck, wouldn't he have gladly taken credit for giving the Teleghanis the lamb they claim he did? Why stonewall?

He went through the conversation again, recalled Chas's body language, his facial expressions, his direct and uncompromising style. Could it be that McPherson offered to help the Teleghanis because he honestly cared about them? There might have been other ways to help them than to show up at the Sheriff's office. Either way, he had to respect the man for his guts, guilty or not.

The scattered remains of iceberg lettuce and carrot shavings littered the snow in the meadow. Chas squatted down to get a closer look, then glanced over his shoulder at the house.

Inside, Mattie folded laundry on the kitchen table. Jeans and dark colors today. His jeans.

"Did you throw all those vegetables out there?"

She smiled, as if proud of herself. "Yup. For the sheep."

"I've got grain for the sheep. You don't need to feed 'em."

"It was going in the trash anyway."

He pulled a pair of jeans from the basket. "These weren't in the hamper."

"Figured you forgot. I found them on the floor."

He didn't know what to say. What didn't she get about staying out of his bedroom? "Don't be making pets outta those sheep. They're livestock. They ain't pets."

"What's the difference between feeding them a Christmas tree and feeding them rotten lettuce?" She snapped the wrinkles out of a shirt and laid it over her chest, folding the arms in. She folded clothes like department stores, causing him to carefully lift them out of the drawer looking for the right one, then carefully setting them back inside so he didn't mess them up. She turned to him with a look of wonder. "Did you see that tree?"

He hadn't noticed it.

"They stripped off all the needles and bark. Left the trunk and branches perfectly intact. It's cleaned bare, like a big, spiny toothpick. Amazing."

Chas looked to see if she'd been drinking, but saw no evidence of it.

Mattie worked her hands over Mr. McPherson's rigid calves, pressing gently with her thumbs, warming his muscles, limbering them. She talked as she went, keeping her tone adult and conversational. She'd worked with nurses who spoke to their elderly patients as if they were infants, cooing in high-pitched voices, and she would not do that to her patients. Could not do that to this patient.

She surveyed his face. It was as it had been every night in her dreams. Cold. Accusing. She'd awaken with a powerful sense of foreboding deep in her center, his presence so real she could feel him brush her skin. And she'd lie awake recounting her most damning sins.

"What's the worst sin you ever knew of, Mr. McPherson?" She ran her fingers down his scaly legs, then squeezed another yellow glob of lotion into her palm and started again. "Robbery? Rape?" She paused and listened for the answer, which did not come. "Did you ever know anyone who'd murdered someone?" She sat down on the bed and lifted his hand and began working his wrist and arm. He was frozen in place like a department store mannequin. But her twice-daily massages were helping; she could see the difference already.

"Chas says you know sins that the people who commit them don't even *know* are sins. Is that true?" She bit her left cheek into a deep wedge. Her eyes slipped from his face, down to the chapped, shriveled hand in hers. "Can you absolve people of their sins too?" Her eyes bounced back to his. "I mean . . . if God gave you this gift to know people's sins, he must've given you the gift to absolve them. Otherwise, what's the point? Certainly he didn't mean for you to simply torment people."

With her finger, she followed the blue veins like thirsty roots in depleted soil under his translucent skin. After a moment, she placed his hand on his stomach and pulled the blankets over him. She moved to the chair, where the light of the stingy lamp shone brightest, and picked up his Bible. "What would you like to hear tonight?" She wished she knew something–anything–about the Bible. She knew there were verses to conjure heavenly images, or assure the weak and weary. Or maybe to persuade him to stop haunting her dreams, to leave her alone and let her sleep. But she knew not where those little gems lay hidden in the sea of impossible to pronounce names and cryptic, seemingly pointless stories.

"How 'bout we pick up where we left off?"

Chas poured his fourth glass of whiskey and listened to Mattie singing out the verses of the gospel of Matthew. He couldn't quite hear the words, just her tone. She was good at reading aloud, a skill he'd never been bold enough to hone. But he guessed it was an asset in her line of work, if not a requirement.

A light floral scent seeped from the bedroom on the wings of her pretty voice, bringing to mind a soft, naked woman. His penis stiffened in his jeans. But his whiskey-soaked mind caught up with his nose, and he saw the image of her caring for his father, the helpless baby. He brought the glass close. The masculine aroma of his drink overpowered the stench of a diminished man, and he threw the whole glassful back in his throat and choked it down in a single swallow, shuddering.

CHAS AWOKE BEFORE THE FIRST DAWN LIGHT to what he imagined was a woodpecker hammering at his head. His tongue was parched and gritty. He swung his legs off the bed in pursuit of water, but was seized by an angry knot in the arch of his right foot. He groaned and scrambled to a stand, pressing his weight onto his foot, onto the floor. The cramp persisted, pulling the tendons across the top of his foot taut like mean little violin strings. He clenched his teeth to keep from howling in pain. Gradually it let up, and he bent to massage the muscles, wider awake than he could ever remember being. He was filled with an acrid self-loathing. He'd crossed the line somewhere the previous night and drunk too much, which even he knew was a tough accomplishment.

He eased his foot into yesterday's jeans, trying hard not to incite it to cramp again. He opened the door to go downstairs, but stood a moment in the hallway. Her door was open. She never slept with the door open. Then he glimpsed the pale glow of her nightgown in the hazy darkness, hunched in a ball at the top of the stairs. Was she sick?

She let out the unmistakable wet sniffle that comes with crying. He turned, thinking to go back in his room, pretend he hadn't seen her. What else would he do? But he knew his father had done this to her. Even silent and crippled his father could torment people. Chas shuffled to the stairs and slid down alongside her.

"Up kinda early, ain't ya?" His voice was thick like honey.

She glanced up with red-rimmed eyes, then buried her face again. "I'm sorry if I woke you."

He waited, a loss for anything intelligent to say. "Whatever it is, can't be all that bad."

"That's just it," she said, getting to her feet and wiping her face with the sleeve of her nightgown. "I don't know what it is. I'm going out of my mind."

He told himself to let her go back to her room, leave it be, but then patted the step where she'd been. "Sit down."

She sat down again and resumed her head-buried pose, making it impossible for Chas to read her face. Not that he'd ever been any good at reading a woman, even when she spoke in plain English.

"I'm scared," she said, slumping against his arm, her knee digging into his thigh.

He sat rigid, jaw clenched. "Scared of what?"

"I don't know. I wake up at night and I can hardly breathe. There's something in my room. There's something in there." Her shudders sent tiny shockwaves through Chas's frayed, hung-over nerves.

He frowned and began peeling the dead skin from his lower lip with his teeth.

"I know I made you a promise. But . . . " She paused to sniff at her wildly running nose and wipe her hands over her cheeks. "I don't know if I can do it. It just keeps getting worse. Every night I get less sleep. I'm so scared."

Chas slowly straightened his leg out, still hyper aware of his angry muscles, and slid his hand into his pocket for his handkerchief. It wasn't clean, but it still had a lot of miles on it before it was ready for the laundry. "Here."

77

She wiped her face with it. "I'm sorry, Chas. I don't think I can do this."

"Whoa, now. Let's not jump to any rash decisions. You had a bad dream."

"No I didn't! It wasn't a dream. There's something in there." She straightened up and pulled to the other side of the step again. "How can a person have a bad dream over and over again, all night for a week?"

"Whatever it is, it can't hurt ya," he said, trying to figure out what he'd said to make her so mad all of sudden.

"You don't believe me," she said, scowling at the hand-kerchief.

"I never said that."

"I can tell."

"Make you a deal; I won't assume to know what you're thinking, and you don't assume to know what I'm thinking. All right?" He looked her in the face, trying to make eye contact, hoping to get her thinking rationally.

She ignored him.

"Let's go on downstairs and make some coffee. Maybe eat something. Things'll look a lot different in the light a day."

"How come you brought your father home?"

Chas sat up a little straighter. "What d'ya mean? I already told you."

"It doesn't add up. You won't have anything to do with him. You pretend he's not here. You won't even come in the house until he's in bed. You won't sit with him; you won't talk to him. If you want me to stay, you need to tell me the truth."

"There ain't nothing to tell."

"You're hiding something." She held her eyes firmly on his, waiting.

"I can't afford the nursing home. I don't have insurance. I can't afford it. It's that simple. And I don't want him to die there, anyway. Not in some strange place. Not like that."

Mattie slumped down again. "I'm sorry."

"I just wish he'd git on with this business of dying. I can't watch it. Makes me sick to my stomach." Chas's head pounded relentlessly. "Can we just go downstairs and make some coffee? My head is killing me."

She nodded and held his handkerchief out to him.

He looked at it, hesitated, wondering why she was giving it back, then took it and got to his feet. He didn't know whether to be pissed off or to feel sorry for her. Should've gone back to my room, he thought.

She made no move to get up.

"Don't leave just yet. If it happens again, come git me. Okay?"

She nodded, but he didn't believe she would.

Chas examined the ewe he'd been treating for pinkeye. Her eyes were clear, all the cloudiness passed on to another. He assessed each animal and counted three new ones with runny, white eyes.

"Damn it, ain't there any gettin' rid of this?" It was going on three months of treating animal after animal. Just getting one back to health and coming out to find another stricken with the disease the next day. He considered culling the three and sending them to the sale ring. But he'd lose money with such an obvious show of bad health. Besides, they were all pregnant, and his best ewe was in the bunch. He'd read about a rancher who had rounded up his entire flock and scrubbed their faces and ears with warm water and baby shampoo, then dried each one with a fresh, clean towel. *God, what a nightmare!* The very idea made his dehydrated brain ache in his skull.

He pulled his handkerchief out and ran it over his sweaty forehead. It smelled like Mattie. He thought again about her sitting alone in the dark. He believed her. Knew exactly what she meant. The old man haunted him too. But he'd long learned to see the truth about who he was and accept it, to quit believing he was either good or righteous. A truth everyone needed to accept, in his opinion. He wondered what offenses his old man was using against her. Couldn't imagine her capable of serious sins. Not that it mattered. Everyone had theirs. No one was immune.

She also reminded him of Sarah, and he didn't care to have those memories dredged up. The randomness with which they popped into his head now put him in a continuous state of mournfulness. After witnessing Mattie's fear that morning, he could only think of Sarah during their junior year of high school.

"He knows, Chas. He knows what we're doing," she had told him.

"No he doesn't, Baby."

"I can tell by the way he looks at me. He thinks I'm a slut."

He had kissed her forehead and pulled her against his chest, her nose nestled against his neck, soft and cool. "It ain't like that if we love each other."

"You promise you still love me, Chas?"

The question seemed so absurd. Of course he did. Even more so after they'd made love. How could she doubt it?

His chest tightened. It wasn't such an absurd question after all.

Mattie's silhouette moved across the window. He put the handkerchief lightly to his nose and breathed in her scent—talcum powder. How would he protect her from his father? He folded the square and put it in his breast pocket so the delicate smell would be with him.

Mattie had to force herself to touch Mr. McPherson as she went through the morning ritual. She recited to herself: *He needs my help. He can't hurt me.* Mr. McPherson sat in his high-backed wheelchair with his coat and shoes on. His skeleton-like hands emerged from the thick layers of fleece, giving him a grim reaper appearance. What could this old man do? How was it even possible for him to haunt anyone?

She wanted Chas to come with her to the appointment in Lewiston, felt near to the brink of begging him. When it was nearly time to leave, she stood on the porch and hollered across the yard. "It's time for me to take your father to Lewiston. Can you help me?"

He looked up, acknowledging her with a nod. "Give me a couple minutes."

Mattie stepped off the porch to warm her car. It was mid-morning, but the windshield was still opaque with a stubborn, white frost. She turned the ignition and the car chugged once then fell silent. She tried again. It groaned out three more belabored attempts, then nothing. She slammed her hand down on the steering wheel and burst into tears.

"That ain't gonna git it started." Chas was standing near the open car door. "Maybe you should go back inside."

"How am I going to get your father to his appointment if my damn car won't start?"

"C'mon." He pulled at her arm, and she relinquished the car. "Go on inside. I'll see if I can git it started."

Mattie watched from the front window as Chas worked on her car, lifting the hood, trying to start it again, fiddling in the engine, trying again. Her temples pulsed, and the muscles at the back of her neck were stretched so tight she thought they might snap. She glanced at the clock; they'd be late. Her tears returned.

Chas dropped the hood on the still-quiet car and came inside. "It ain't going anywhere. It needs a new alternator."

"Now what?"

He stood his distance, regarding her tear-streaked face. "How important is this appointment? Can't you reschedule it?"

She looked at his father. "He's bleeding from his penis."

"Jesus!" Chas turned his back and sucked in a hard breath.

She dropped her head in her hands and struggled with the onslaught of new tears.

"Call and tell 'em we'll be late. I'll git my truck. It's gonna be a tight squeeze."

Mattie wiped her hands over her cheeks again. "You don't have to go."

He stared at her. "I ain't handing my truck over to you in the condition you're in."

They rode silently, Mr. McPherson next to the door, Mattie sandwiched between the men with her feet on the transmission casing, her knees poking straight up like a cricket's. She tried to give Chas plenty of space, but that only pressed her into the old man, who remained wooden and unyielding. As they neared Sweetwater, she glimpsed the burnt ruins of a house. Its roof was collapsed, its windows crowned by angry black spires. Oddly, the porch stood untouched, adorned with its doormat and handmade welcome sign, as if the family might return at any moment. A handful of large chickens scratched the frost-frozen ground near a small shed.

"Is that it? Is that the house of the Moslem family?"

Chas fixed his eyes on it as they passed, giving a curt nod and turning back to the road. Mattie felt him tense beside her. And he drove the two-and-a-half hours to Lewiston in utter silence. Mattie fell asleep with her head tipped back at a painful angle, her mouth gaping.

At the clinic, Chas lifted his father into a wheelchair and looked at his watch. "I'll be back in two hours. I've got some errands to run." And he was gone.

She watched the dirt-caked tailgate disappear in a snarl of traffic. She'd hoped to be in and out in half an hour.

Mattie sat with her arms folded tightly across her chest,

legs crossed, her foot bouncing more vigorously with each passing minute. They'd been ready to go for over two hours. She gripped a new prescription for Mr. McPherson in her hand and watched for Chas's pickup, a wide assortment of magazines strewn across the table in front of her–nothing of interest left to read. Her head ached behind her eyes like a dried up reservoir baking in the sun, and she craved painkillers. She rattled the bottle of pills, staring at them, wishing they were anything she wanted. Then she turned her eyes on the old man. "Whatever it is–this thing you can do to people–it's not good or holy. It's pure evil. And you better stop it or I won't stay. Then you'll be stuck with Chas. And he'll send you back to the nursing home." She immediately felt guilty for her words, but couldn't bring herself to apologize to the old man. She believed that if she showed him any weakness, he'd only become more vengeful in his midnight intrusions.

When she saw the truck turning into the clinic parking lot, she jumped up and pushed the wheelchair out to the curb. She waited for Chas to pull into the pickup area, her eyes fixed on the pavement, her jaw tight.

"Sorry I'm late," Chas said, but offered no explanation.

She looked away.

"There's a burger and a coke in the truck for you." He pointed, but kept his eyes on her, as if afraid she might haul off and hit him.

Mattie ate while Chas drove. In the rearview mirror, she spied bags of animal feed piled in the truck bed. *Three hours for that?*

Chas waited until she finished her food before he spoke. "Is he okay?"

"The doctor thinks the Levadopa was damaging his bone marrow, causing him to bleed. He changed the prescription."

Chas nodded.

"Thanks for the burger," she said. "I was starving."

"Ordered extra pickles for ya."

She glanced at him. His beard stubble bristled red in the afternoon sun. "Sorry I was such a mess this morning."

He looked at her, but the closeness was awkward and she turned away.

The setting sun glinted off the windshield of a state police car parked next to the sheriff's patrol in Chas's front yard. He pulled in behind them and took a deep breath, as if preparing for a fight. The front door, which he never locked, stood open. A pair of upstairs windows reflected opaque in the evening sun, catching his house in a dumb gaze.

"Least they could do is close the damn door," he muttered.

Sheriff Edelson walked out onto the porch. "Afternoon, Chas."

"Let me get my dad inside, then you can tell me what this is all about." He brushed past, his father cradled in his arms. Mattie followed close on his heels, glancing furtively at the sheriff, who followed them back inside, a warrant in his hand.

"That for me?" Chas asked, emerging from the bedroom.

"No, just permission to search."

"Find what you're looking for?"

"Still searching your barn and out-buildings."

Chas gave him a cool stare, then began to rekindle the dead fire.

"You keep fuel on your place?"

"Do ranchers have tractors?"

The sheriff watched Chas blow on the fledgling flame. Finally, he said, "You know, it'll be a lot easier for you if you just tell us the truth."

"I already did."

"The problem is that your truth doesn't line up with everybody else's."

When the fire blazed again, Chas stood. "Mind if I move my truck? Rather ya'll didn't stay for supper. Nothing personal." He strode out into the yard so deeply angry his hands ached.

Sheriff Edelson remained in the dingy living room, waiting for the nurse to come out of the bedroom. He'd been surprised by the orderliness of the house, but suspected that was her doing, not McPherson's. The condition of the barn had been a different story—piled to the rafters with old junk and barely supporting its own weight. It was clear that McPherson didn't have much money, but that was a common affliction among residents along this remote stretch of the Sweetwater River. There weren't many barns in the area that weren't threatening to collapse from neglect. It wasn't a commentary on McPherson's character.

Edelson watched through the front window as McPherson pulled his pickup around and parked it in front of his barn, then disappeared into the dark cavern. Edelson tried to imagine Chas setting fire to the Teleghani house, wondering if the man was truly capable, but the idea was halted with his own imagined sense of suffocating from the heat and flames. He closed his eyes a moment to refocus on the task at hand.

The sheriff hadn't yet turned from the driveway, samples of fuel in the trunk of his car, when Chas got the whiskey, his hangover burned away by his fury.

Mattie watched him throw back a shot and pour another. "I'll make something to eat."

"I'm not hungry," he growled and took the bottle to the living room to be alone. But once there, his mind wandered back to her in the kitchen. He listened for the sound of her cooking. He strained for the sounds of weeping, but didn't hear that either. He tipped his head back against the chair and closed his eyes. Mattie disintegrating in tears after her car wouldn't start replayed in his mind. He tipped his face down again. "Mattie."

She appeared in the doorway.

"It's my father. He's the one who's bothering you at night."

She didn't deny it. Waited for him to go on.

"Whatever he's got on ya, you have to remember it doesn't make you a bad person."

"How can he know anything?"

Chas shrugged. "Somehow he does. But he can't make you a bad person because of what he knows."

She thought about it.

"Anyhow, what could you have possibly done that's so bad?"

She gave him a piercing glare, then went to his father's room. Moments later he heard her talking to the old man, and finally reading from his Bible. Chas felt like his insides had been scraped out with a sharp spoon. He got up and put the whiskey back in the cupboard and set his glass in the sink.

Mattie's breath came in short, sharp gasps. The old man was there with her, hovering above her bed in the darkness, unseen. He brought vivid a buried memory. A man . . . a stranger. A smoky bar. Thick cocaine lines across the tank lid of the women's toilet. Almost time to pay up. She adjusted her top, licked her finger and collected the loose powder around her nostrils, then rubbed it against her gums—nothing to waste. He took her to his car. It was parked in the alley. And in the blue–green glow of the tavern light she gave him head with her breasts popping out of her top like advancing torpedoes.

Chas awoke in the middle of the night, his eyes stinging and his mouth dry. He wished he'd remembered to bring a glass of water to bed. He rolled over to go back to sleep, but heard something in the hallway. It was Mattie, crying again. He got up and pulled on his jeans, buttoning the fly just far enough to keep them up, and opened the door. She sat on the stairs again, in the same place he'd found her the previous night. He sat down next to her. "Same thing?"

She buried her head.

"I told you to come git me."

"What can you do? How can it be him?"

Chas considered her questions, trying to decide which one to address. Not that he had a reasonable answer for either. "What d'ya think it is then?"

She didn't answer.

He went to her bedroom and looked up at the pitched ceiling, then scanned the entire room, turning a full circle. Nothing. "Mattie, there's nothing here. Come see."

"I know there's nothing there. That's what I'm telling you," she said, her tone laced with bitterness.

He slid down on the step again and looked at his watch: twelve-fifteen. He wanted to go back to sleep; his body was screaming with fatigue. But he couldn't abandon her here. If she were too afraid to sleep in his house, she'd leave. Then what would he do? It took six months to find her. "Do you wanna talk about it?"

Mattie leaned against his arm. Chas stiffened, biting his lip.

"It's awful. I keep dreaming he's floating in the air over my bed, staring at me. Then . . . "

"Then what?"

"How can it be him?" She drew in a long, wet sniff.

"I'm telling you, he's done this his whole life. You ain't the first person to feel his presence. But it don't mean anything."

She wiped her face.

"You can't stay all night on the step here. Would it help if I slept with my door open?"

She considered, then nodded.

He watched her as she went back to bed, then went to his room, leaving the door open as promised. It was awkward, he thought—sleeping so close to another person without the privacy of a closed door. He lay awake a long time, wondering about Mattie's sins, and wishing he'd remembered to get that glass of water.

Mattie pushed a shopping cart along the dim and gritty aisles of Hinkler's Market. The left front wheel stuck sideways every few feet, driving the cart into the shelves. She gave it a frustrated shove and gathered up the green beans and lettuce. At the back of the store she stood over the freezer case, staring at bags of frozen French fries and TV dinners, trying to remember what she needed. At last she gave up and took the vegetables to the checkout counter.

A fortyish woman with bleached hair leaned against the register, gossiping with an elderly customer. "Everybody knows he did it," she said.

"I hope they can prove it. That boy's been messed up since his mother left," the elderly woman said.

"That's the nurse," the cashier whispered when she saw Mattie.

Mattie's eyes bounced from the cashier to the customer. She set her things on the counter and said, "Charge it to Mr. McPherson's account, please."

"Sorry, but Mr. Hinkler says Chas needs to settle up before he can charge anything else."

"Are you sure?"

"Uh-huh." The cashier nodded. "He dropped Chas's credit limit since his trouble with the law. Doesn't want him hauled off to jail before paying his bill."

"He didn't burn that house down," Mattie muttered. She

got out her wallet to pay cash, tempted to give a more explicit response. Then she thought better of playing this game at all and shoved her money back in her purse and started for the door. "Never mind. I'll get this stuff some-where else."

"Suit yourself," the cashier called after her.

As she drove Chas's huge, hard-to-steer pickup home, Mat-tie imagined the foul mood he'd be in when he heard her news. He didn't need more reasons to be surly, and this was as good an excuse as any to retreat with his whiskey. He wasn't inclined to share when he was in a bad mood, and she needed a glass as much as he would.

She pulled up as Chas emerged from the barn with a syringe and a small, pink vial. He grinned, surprising her with a mouthful of perfect teeth she'd never noticed before. He waited for her to get out.

"Come see this," he said, and disappeared into the barn again.

She followed him inside, her nostrils tingling from an acrid mix of manure, alfalfa hay, and some other deep, earthy scent she couldn't quite identify. She hurried to keep up with Chas's long strides, taking careful steps on the mud-slick floor. He glanced over his shoulder to see if she followed, then led the way to a small pen at the back of the barn.

Mattie glanced around warily for evidence of the lamb he'd slaughtered, but the blood had been rinsed away.

"Look," he said, pointing into the pen.

She peered in to find the tiny, chocolate-colored lamb struggling to stand next to its mother. It wobbled on gangly legs—seemed to be all legs.

Chas smiled like a proud father. "First one this year."

"Can I hold it?"

He looked surprised. "No. It's gonna be butchered in the fall. It ain't a pet. Just thought you'd like to see it."

Butchered? Mattie was certain she wouldn't be here for that event. There was no way she'd make it that long, even if Mr. McPherson kept on breathing. "Then I guess it won't hurt to love it a little," she said.

Chas climbed into the pen, and the mother darted to the back corner. The baby sprang after her, but Chas scooped it up and held it out for Mattie.

She gathered the baby up in her arms and pressed it against her chest, dropping her face down between its ears. Chas watched with a mix of disturbance and curiosity.

"Is it a boy or a girl?"

"A ram . . . a boy. If it was a ewe . . . I mean a girl, with those markings, I'd keep her for breeding. See how nice the black is over his eyes and down his throat?" He ran his index finger over the animal, along the pattern of black. "Every once in a while I git an all-tan one, or one with a gray face. I don't know where those come from. Must be some mix back in the bloodline. I don't keep 'em unless they're marked right."

Mattie rubbed her nose back and forth over the back of the lamb's soft neck.

Chas reached for the animal. "Okay, that's enough. You're gonna ruin him, make him think people are nice. He'll be followin' me all over the place."

She ignored Chas.

"C'mon, give me the lamb."

She handed him over and followed Chas out of the barn. "I didn't get any groceries today. They won't let you charge anything more on your account until you settle up."

"What?" He stopped abruptly and faced her. "I just paid them. There can't be more than twenty bucks on that account." He narrowed his eyes at her. "Unless you're buying things I don't know about."

"No," she said. "No. The cashier said they lowered your limit because of this business with the sheriff."

"Son-of-a-bitch!" He spit in the mud.

She watched him cross the yard with wide and powerful steps, shaking his head as he went. Once inside, he turned back to collect the syringe and vaccine.

Mattie got the whiskey down and set it on the table. When Chas returned, she was standing at the refrigerator looking for something to fix for supper. He didn't pour himself a drink. Instead, he slid the vaccine into the door of the fridge, then pressed it closed, forcing her to step out of the way. "Let's eat out tonight? Seems all you been doin' is cooking."

"What about your father?"

"Feed him before we go. He'll be fine."

8

SHERIFF EDELSON RECORDED THE ITEMS he'd taken from Chas's ranch on a small sheet of paper with *McPherson Ranch* scribbled across the top.

"Find anything?" Loraine, his secretary, stood over his shoulder, scanning the list.

"Not really." He wondered if she were disappointed.

She clucked her tongue.

"Maybe the lab will come up with something. All I need is one little fiber; anything to tie it back to him." He realized he was a bit disappointed himself.

"There has to be something."

He nodded. "It seems fairly simple. He had motive and opportunity. We've got multiple eye-witnesses. Something'll turn up. Has to."

"Yup. Everybody knows he did it."

"Damn, that bread's making me hungry." The sheriff looked out at the bakery next door. The aroma of hot baking bread wafted over them, making his stomach growl. Too bad life isn't just about responding to the smell of food, he thought. Wouldn't life be great?

"Didn't you eat?"

"I skipped lunch to take the stuff to Lewiston. I need to

get this guy off the street." He thought back on Chas's visit. "I can't believe how brazen he was to just walk in here and ask where the Teleghanis are living? It's almost like he thought I would strike him from the list of suspects."

Loraine snorted. "I'll see if I can find you something to eat."

He sat back and wished he possessed the certainty of Chas's guilt that his secretary did. In light of this unexpected lack of evidence, Edelson was beginning to wonder if he really did have the right man, despite what the rest of Sweetwater believed.

Mattie adjusted the temperature in Chas's pickup for the third time. It was either too hot or too cold; she couldn't find a happy medium. She saw him scowling at her.

"I'm cold," she protested.

"You musta been born in the desert or something. Can't take anything less than a hundred degrees."

"Well, get a decent truck."

"Hey."

She smiled privately out the window.

"How many days before we need groceries?" Chas said, glancing across the cab at her.

"I don't know. If I'm creative . . . four maybe."

"We'll go to Salmon City. Wednesday. Hinkler can take his credit and shove it up his ass."

"His store is gross and his shopping carts don't roll straight, anyway."

Chas smirked.

"Why don't you name that lamb Cocoa?" Mattie said, still enchanted by him. The baby was an unexpected high point in her gloomy association with Chas's ranch.

His smile disappeared. "I already told you, he ain't a pet."

"Won't hurt him to have a name."

"No—no, it won't hurt him. It'll hurt *you*. I can see it

comin' a mile off. You'll beg me not to kill him, then we'll starve to death because you wouldn't listen to me."

Mattie thought it was awfully presumptuous of Chas to think she'd still be there when the time came to butcher that lamb.

"Shouldn't of showed it to ya."

She pondered the idea he'd do anything she wanted. Unlikely, she thought. More likely he'd kill the lamb on Christmas just because she gave the baby a name.

A bell over the door jangled out their arrival at the nearly full diner. Faces turned and stared. The room went silent. Mattie turned to Chas for direction, a nervous energy flitting through her. He pointed to a booth still cluttered with dishes along the back wall. He slid in across from her and surveyed the crowd. Some stared openly, others pretended not to notice, but no one spoke for several seconds.

Chas nodded to a man sitting at the bar, who immediately turned his face. "Forgot to tell ya, I'm the town pariah. I'm an arsonist, you know."

"Stop it," she said, giving him a sharp glare.

He shrugged. "Doesn't matter if it ain't true. People believe what they want to believe. They don't need proof."

A fact Mattie was familiar with. "Yes, they do."

"Small town life has its advantages. But when you're the bad guy, it just plain sucks."

A waitress handed each of them a menu without saying a word. Then she set a large tray on the edge of the table and gathered up the dirty dishes. "Anything to drink?"

"Beer," Mattie said.

Chas paused, looking at Mattie. "Coffee please, Annie."

The waitress gave him a chilly nod and carried the dishes away, leaving the table littered with crumbs and water rings.

"I always wanted to live in a small town," Mattie said.

"This ought to cure you then." He studied her a moment before opening the menu. "You grow up in Spokane?"

"Uh-huh."

"I recommend the bacon cheeseburger." He folded the menu and put it down, already decided. "Seems people from the city have a skewed idea of small-town life. It ain't like in the movies."

"Life in the city can suck too, you know."

"I'll buy that. Where would you live if you could just go anywhere?"

She didn't have to think about it. "Joseph, Oregon. Have you ever seen it?"

"Once, a while back. Sold some sheep to a guy over there."

"Wasn't it beautiful? I mean . . . it's got everything, a lake, the mountains. And . . ." She smiled to herself.

"And what?"

She was suddenly uncomfortably warm. "And a full-size shirtless cowboy in bronze right smack in the middle of town."

Chas laughed out loud, drawing the attention of the room.

"Laugh if you want. It's something to behold." She pressed her hands over her cheeks to hide her embarrassment.

"I guess I missed that," he said, still chuckling. "Yeah, I didn't see the cowboy; I guess the mountains got in my eyes. They were something to behold, too."

Chas was amused by Mattie's moment of discomfort and realized that the promised unpleasantness of this trip into town was diluted by her presence. Almost forgot his purpose of making Sweetwater residents uncomfortable. It both delighted and disturbed him. He'd forgotten the gentle laughter of a woman–had barely experienced it at all in his life. Couldn't remember it in his mother. Had pushed away all memory of it in Sarah. Never heard it once from the infrequent prostitutes who'd satisfied his interminable ache. Mattie's laughter now seemed to be what defined her as a woman. The presence of her laughter brought him an unexpected sense of joy, especially because it had pained him to witness her weeping in the night.

Chas didn't drink his whiskey that night, but sat alone in the corner of the living room in his well-worn mohair chair, a relic from the 20's that had belonged to his grandmother. The dim light of a tarnished-brass floor lamp illuminated his thoughts as he listened to Mattie slur through the gospel of Mark, after she'd drunk three pints of beer at the diner. He realized she was working her way through the New Testament, a chapter at time. He wondered if his father could possibly accept this gesture from her–a gesture of peace. A plea to be left alone.

He waited for her to climb the stairs to bed before he turned out the lights. He didn't latch his bedroom door, instead left it slightly ajar so she wouldn't be afraid, but knowing it was no protection from his father's psychological wrath. The old man would cast his shadow over her, making her cry out. He dropped his clothes in a heap on the wood floor. His bed was made, and he stood next to it a moment. Why had she made his bed? When he turned down the covers, the sheets were tucked tightly under the mattress, and the smell of bleach and fabric softener filled the darkness.

He slid between the cool cotton and drew in a deep breath. The freshness was out of place in his house, wrong, but also rich with an odd ambition. He didn't want to be happy about it, or to accept it. She was worming her way into every crevice of his life.

When he heard Mattie weeping again, he swung his legs off the bed and felt for his jeans with his foot. The clock glowed two-eighteen in big red numbers. He rubbed his hands over his face and pulled his pants on, then tiptoed to the door. She was in her place on the stairs, this place she'd come to seek out as a refuge, for what safety it offered he did not know.

"I'm sorry," she said. "I'm sorry I keep waking you."

He slid down beside her, and she leaned into him, setting his teeth grinding against each other. Her hand circled behind his elbow, grasping his arm, clutching it tightly. She pressed her wet face against his shoulder. He frowned and pulled his arm away, peeling her fingers from his skin with his free hand, which she had latched onto like a frightened cat. He slipped his arm behind her and pulled her in against his chest.

"He knows," she sobbed. "He knows."

"He knows what?" Chas's deeply honeyed voice surprised him.

"I killed them. It was *my* fault."

"Shhh."

"I killed them." She gulped for air. "They would've lived." Her tears spilled down his belly, soaking into his denim jeans.

"I don't think you killed anybody."

"They forbid me from seeing him."

"Who?"

"My parents."

Chas worked at the skin on his lip as he tried to assemble the fragments into something coherent. "How's that make you responsible for killin' anybody?"

"They were coming to get me. They would've been home that night if it weren't for me."

Chas shook his head, still not getting the picture. She pressed her face against his chest again, and he ran his hand over her forehead and down her hair. Having thoughts he knew he shouldn't be. She smelled like flowers. She was silky soft.

"Tell me what happened," he said, hoping to divert his attention from his swelling crotch.

97

She rubbed her hands over her face vigorously. "The other driver fell asleep at the wheel. I didn't know my folks were coming for me. I was out with my boyfriend, and they were driving around looking for me. This man hit them head on. They had to pry the steering wheel out of my father's chest. And my mother bled to death in the road. It was raining . . . it rained on her."

Chas winced. "I'm sorry," he said.

She pulled away from him, to the other side of the step.

Chas watched her, wanting to comfort her, to run his fingers through her hair.

She got to her feet and said, "I'm sorry." Then she went to her room.

He sat on the step, wondering if he should have a drink now. Finally, he stood and looked out the window on the moonlit meadow dotted with dark figures–sheep sleeping in the snow. Then he went to bed. But he couldn't keep from smearing the fresh sheets with the unstoppable force that had risen within him.

Chas was up early, before dawn, unable to sustain even a fitful sleep. He sat at the cleanly wiped table, a bowl of perfectly symmetrical pinecones in the center, and sipped his coffee. Pinecones, he mulled. Who'da thought to put pinecones in a bowl on the table? He lifted one and rolled it around in his fingers. He tried not to think about Mattie's confession–a horrible sort of confession that she'd certainly regret when she woke up. What would he say to her? Nothing. He tossed the pinecone back into the bowl, stood and tipped his cup back, drinking down the last of the coffee. "Feels like a goddamn museum in here," he muttered.

In the barn he found a pair of twin lambs curled up at the feet of a nervous ewe. He climbed into the pen, and she warned her young in a low, guttural tone, bringing them springing from a sound sleep onto their shaky legs. He scooped one up and looked under its tail. A ewe. He looked at the lamb's face, ran his index finger over her black markings, down to her jaw and nodded with satisfaction. He set the lamb down and picked up the other. Also a ewe. Also well marked. "Good girl," he said to the mother. "Those are fine lookin' babies."

He started back to the house for the clostridium vaccine, but stopped in front of the next pen and surveyed the wide, sagging-bellied ewe that occupied it. This was his lead ewe. The dramatic droop of her pregnant belly accentuated the sharp line of her backbone. Wide as a barge, he thought. She waddled toward him, grunting with the effort, looking for oats. He ran his hand over the top of her head, between her ears. "Gotta be any minute now, huh?" He crouched to look under her; a nearly full udder. Within a day, he guessed. He hoped for twins, or even triplets. She'd produced them before. She was a trooper.

In the house, he found Mattie sipping coffee and gazing blankly out from behind disheveled locks. When Chas saw her in the light of day, her hair spilling all around her like that, the burning urge she'd spawned in him the night before returned. "Mornin'," he said.

Her eyes came up to meet his. They were swollen, still red. She set her coffee down and said, "Chas, I have to go."

He stood silent, struggling between acquiescing and begging her to stay. He wasn't surprised, but he actually prayed she wouldn't go. He needed her. For his father. "Please reconsider."

"I can't do this. I'm too frightened."

"Please," he said, his chest so tight the word evaporated on his tongue.

"I can't believe I told you those things last night."

"It's okay. I don't hold you in any judgment. I've done worse myself."

"Chas . . . " Her face contorted, as if she might cry again.

He started to speak, to plead. But stopped. What words could he offer? "It's okay," he said, finally.

Her tears splashed onto the table.

"Don't cry. It's okay. I understand." He fidgeted with his hands, at last shoving them into his jeans pockets.

She put her head down and sobbed.

He watched, wondering how she never ran out of tears. "I got a girl pregnant once." He looked up at the ceiling, immediately regretting his words. "I loved her. I wanted to marry her."

Mattie looked up, tears pooling under her chin and trickling down her neck in salty rivulets.

"My father . . . " he glanced back at the bedroom door where his father lay silent. "My father called her a whore. He went to her house and called her a whore in front of her par-ents." Chas looked at Mattie. This wasn't about his father. Git to the point, he told himself. "I didn't fight for her. I let him take control, like some kind of fucking coward. I loved her. And I didn't do a damn thing to protect her."

Mattie's tears had ceased. He could feel her gaze heavy on him.

"He wanted her to put the child up for adoption. I was so stupid . . . so young. Seventeen. I wasn't ready for that kind of responsibility." He drew a breath. "It was so goddamn selfish of me."

"What happened?"

"I don't know . . . her family moved away."

Mattie scowled.

"I waited all these years for Sarah to come back." Chas's tone was pulled tight, like a tendril from his heart was tied to a heavy stone that could only keep falling. "You can see," he said, looking around the house, "she never did."

Mattie's tears started again, slowly, and Chas suspected they were different tears. Cried for a different reason.

"So you see . . . I would never judge you for what you did. I got plenty to be sorry for myself."

Mattie stood up and poured her coffee into the sink. Chas's heart quietly splattered his hollow chest with tender emotions he had so long pressed down. He walked to the refrigerator and opened the door for the vaccine. He'd inoculate the new lambs, then call the nursing home in Lewiston and see if they could work something out. Maybe some sort of payment plan that would go on long after his father had ceased to torment people in this world. What else could he do?

She poured a fresh cup for herself and went back to the table. "I'll try to stick it out," she whispered. But she wouldn't look his way.

Mattie spoon-fed Mr. McPherson a pureed mix of green beans and overcooked ham. He stared straight into her eyes the entire time, as if judging her soul. He was having increasing trouble with swallowing, forcing her to give him only tiny amounts at a time. It dragged the chore out an hour or longer, and she said nothing to the unblinking face that haunted her nights. In her mind she went over Chas's confession. She hadn't believed him capable of love—not the kind of love he spoke of. And it made her curious to know what he was like with this girl he'd gotten pregnant. How could this man who barely spoke a civil sentence once have been a boy in love?

She saw the old man differently now as well. She tried to compare him with her own father, but her memories were increasingly vague and out of focus. A used, pink motorboat, she and her sister in bright orange life jackets, and her mother wearing a bikini; that was the only one she could find clarity in. Mattie was five and they'd circled Coeur D'Alene Lake. She leaned over the side, pressing her hand into the wake–the water surprisingly hard against the pads of her small fingers. Then, without warning, she was sailing into the air, like a rubber ball bounced hard on the pavement. She came down in the cool, blue lake and watched the boat speeding away, her amazement eclipsing her fear. The water stretched out long before her, sparkling white and orange into the setting sun. This memory somehow represented everything about herself and her family. After her parents died, she wished it'd been her last memory. But she was scooped up by a nearby fisherman, the only one to witness her fall. Pulled into his aluminum boat, slippery with fish slime, and returned to her still–unaware family.

She thought off and on about her midnight confession to Chas and the freshly opened wound it left–a scab that had never begun the work of mending itself. Bloody. Festering. Painful. She didn't believe Chas had confessed to a worse deed. Certainly he could see that.

She found a large, plastic cup–blue–dark enough to hide its contents, and filled it half–way up with brandy, which she sipped on as she went through the morning.

Chas sat high in the barn loft on the stacked bales of alfalfa hay, his head nearly touching the dusty crossbeam of the gable. Doves roosted nearby, cooing softly. He found their mournful voices disconcerting. Wished they knew his mood. Through the open flap he looked down at Mattie's blue sedan, three inches of snow blanketing its roof. He needed to replace the alternator for her, had promised to do so. But now . . . it might give her greater opportunity to leave. As it was, she'd have to wait the time it took him to fix it. He considered again the nursing home. Surely they could work something out; he'd paid his bills on time. He could sell the ranch to pay for it. The mean truth about why he'd stayed all these years was laughing in his face now–now that he'd admitted it aloud. Not that he ever really believed Sarah would come back. But still, what a fool he was.

The sheriff's car pulled up beside Mattie's, and Chas took a deep breath. Or, they could arrest him for something he didn't do and his father's fate would fall into the hands of the state, he thought. He started for the loft ladder, wishing he could intercept Sheriff Edelson before he disturbed Mattie, witnessed her swollen, tearful eyes and drew further conclusions to convict Chas. By the time he reached the barn door, the sheriff had been redirected and was on his way across the yard.

"Afternoon, Mr. McPherson," he said from some distance.

Chas glanced at his watch and realized it *was* after noon. He'd spent three hours sitting like an idiot in the loft. "Sheriff."

"Got a couple more questions for you."

Chas jacked a boot against the barn door and leaned back with his hands in his pockets.

"I asked when you came by my office if you had anything against Moslems," Edelson started.

"And I answered it." Chas looked resigned. As if it hardly mattered whether the sheriff cuffed him and hauled him away right then.

"What I didn't ask is how you feel about people of other races. I mean . . . people who aren't white. People from other countries."

Chas gave the sheriff a long, thoughtful gaze. "You see, Sheriff, that's why this whole idea that I was the one who did this is so absurd. I don't have anything against anybody. Black, white, purple . . . hell . . . Moslem, Christian, whatever." The sheriff listened, but Chas could see his patience was thin by the way he squinted with one eye. "With my old man there ain't no escaping one's obligation to think on God and man."

The sheriff's lip turned up in a benign smile.

"See those trees over there?" Chas pointed out at the river where a handful of black walnuts stood along the bank. "Now see those up there?" He pointed at a grove of Douglas firs crowning the ridge above his house. Sheriff Edelson followed Chas's hand, craning his head back to see the trees from under his hat. "And look at that one right there." He pointed at a poorly pruned apple tree in the front yard. "You ever notice how some have smooth bark, and some have rough bark? Some have leaves; some have needles. Some are green all year. Some look like they died in the winter. That one," he pointed at the apple tree again, "gits white and pink flowers in the spring. It's really somethin' pretty to look at."

The sheriff eyed Chas hard. "What's your point, McPherson?"

"Point is . . . they're all different. Ain't two the same when you git down to it. God created those," he gestured down to the river, "and those," he pointed at the ridge, "and that one too. God has a wild imagination. And I'd say it's a safe bet that he favors variety. This we have here in my yard doesn't even begin to touch the variety of trees out there in the world." He spit in the mud near his feet. "So anybody says there's only one right way, or only one chosen bunch a people . . . well . . . they ain't observed much about the nature of God, now have they?"

Sheriff Edelson stared down at the walnut trees, pondering Chas's philosophy. He'd heard his share of opinions on God's favored people, especially here in what the locals called "God's country." But this perspective of Chas's was not at all consistent with a reclusive man with no allies. Indeed, it provoked him to think hard about Chas's analogy, and wonder to what depth a man must ponder life to come up with this.

"Anybody that believes I burned that house down ain't observed much about me either," Chas said. He stood away

104

from the barn and took a few steps toward the house, then paused and looked back at the sheriff. "You can choose to believe what people tell ya 'bout religion. Most do–rather than undertake the hard work of thinking it through for themselves. And you can choose to believe there ain't no difference between a man and his father. People do that, too."

The sheriff looked back at Chas, but he was already on his way to the house, not waiting for, or expecting, a reply. Edelson shook his head, wishing that Chas McPherson was less complicated. Or less clever.

9

CHAS ATE TWO BOLOGNA AND CHEESE SANDWICHES in the living room, alone, out of Mattie's view, and fought an intense craving for whiskey. She was scrubbing the bathroom, down on her knees in front of the tub, scouring away the top layer of yellow–stained porcelain. He wanted to tell her it was no use, but didn't. As long as she believed she could make a difference, maybe she'd stay.

He had a mind to tell his father to leave her alone, but did the old man even possess the capacity to know, or control, his actions? His father's tormenting presence was a way of being. And now, like an old dog burying imaginary bones, he was living the last days of his life repeating a habit. But even a dog stopped when given a sharp order–for a little while anyway. So he went to his father's room. The old man was sleeping, and Chas stood in the doorway a long time before he sat down in the chair. His father reeked of floral–scented body lotion. Mattie did a good job of keeping his muscles massaged and limber, despite her fear of him. Chas respected her for that.

"Dad," he whispered. "You gotta quit this. There ain't no good coming of it." The old man's bony chest rose and fell. Chas listened to the whistle of breath through his father's nose. "She's here to help you. Without her, I gotta send you back to the nursing home." Then he spoke in a clear, direct tone. "Please leave her alone. Please."

His father's eyes came open and a ripple raced down Chas's spine. "Please, Dad, leave her alone." Feeling like a very small boy, he pulled his coat on and went out into the newly falling snow. The sky was dark. It felt like dusk, but was just past two o'clock. He climbed into his pickup and started for town to order an alternator and get some clostridium for the non-stop flow of new lambs coming in the weeks ahead. He suddenly felt as exposed and bare as the newborns.

Chas pulled up at Guthry's Automotive and took a scrap of paper from his coat pocket with the make and model of Mattie's car. The bell over the door jangled his nerves.

Henry Guthry smiled at the visitor. "Afternoon."

"You got a glass door, Henry. What d'ya need a bell for?" Chas complained. "You can see people coming from across the street."

Henry looked up at the door, as if he'd been informed of something wholly new, and shrugged. Henry was in his sixties. He'd moved to Sweetwater some twenty years before to start the automotive business with his only son. But Guthry Junior didn't take to small town life and ran off to Los Angeles, where he married money. Henry had always been kind to Chas. Chas used to feel sorry for the shopkeeper after his son left, when he wasn't having jealous fantasies of doing the same thing.

"I need an alternator for a Mitsubishi." Chas slid the paper across the counter.

Henry took it in his grease-blackened fingers and studied it through bifocal lenses. "Don't carry that. Have to order it."

"I figured."

"Take 'bout two weeks."

"The longer, the better."

Henry peered up at Chas, curiously. "Never heard anybody say that before."

"I've got a habit of swimmin' against the current. If you hadn't noticed."

"Yeah . . . yeah, I have." He glanced around the empty shop, as if someone might've sneaked in without him noticing. "And I'd say we're better off for it, if you know what I mean."

Chas didn't. He squinted at Henry.

"We don't need their kind here in God's country. You done all right by me."

Chas pulled back and stared at the floor. The blood pulsed in his fingertips. He slid his hands into his pockets. "Haven't got any idea what you're talking about."

Henry gave him a sly wink.

Chas took the paper and slid it into his breast pocket. "Never mind 'bout that part." He turned and pulled the door open. The bell jangled in his ear. He grabbed it and yanked it down, ripping the metal clamp from the doorframe.

"Hey! What are you doing?" Henry shouted, coming around the counter.

Chas tossed the bell at his feet. "I didn't burn nobody's house down, you son–of–a–bitch!"

Chas didn't stop for the clostridium because he was worried he'd end up assaulting someone. He sped along the highway, doing seventy in a forty–five zone, and figuring if he got a ticket it would be satisfaction for the sheriff to finally pin him with something he could prove.

At home, he went for his whiskey. The house was quiet. Mattie was in his father's room, but she wasn't talking in her usual manner. It annoyed him—her silence. He threw back a shot before pouring another, and quickly finished the next while staring out the kitchen window at the trees he'd so moronically contemplated aloud to the sheriff. He imagined Sheriff Edelson at his office right now, laughing with the pitch-lady about Chas's ridiculous theory of God. He was pouring his third glass when Mattie appeared.

She looked at the bottle, then at him.

"Want one?"

"Okay."

He got her a glass. "They don't carry alternators for Mitsubishis in Sweetwater. We'll have to order it in Salmon City, or . . . Lewiston maybe."

"They don't carry them, or they don't sell them to you?"

"What difference does it make?"

"I'll make you something to eat."

Chas sat down and watched her. Her hair was still down. She hadn't pulled it back today. Watching it somehow smoothed out the hard edges of the day and he slumped back in the chair. "You know, Mattie, you should always wear your hair down like that. It's pretty." The moment he said it, he wished he hadn't. Why couldn't he just shut up? All day he'd done nothing but blabber on like some kind of jackass.

She smiled over her shoulder, surprising him. "Thanks."

"The old guy that runs the automotive place practically thanked me for burning down the Teleghanis' house. That asshole!"

Mattie turned and listened.

"Guess not everybody hates me. I'm a hero to some."

"You know, when I first got here, I figured you for a brutal kind of man. I could've believed those things too. You have a way about you that's hard—kind of like a jagged rock." She paused, seemed embarrassed for her words. "Anyway, last night when I was so afraid . . . you proved you're not hard. Not on the inside, anyway."

"Am too rock-hard. And don't go thinking otherwise."

"Yeah, right." She turned and began slicing a cucumber. "I meant to say thanks."

He watched her, wanting to thank *her* for staying another day, for not bailing out on him yet. But he couldn't find the words or the courage. He lifted a pinecone and spun it in his fingers. "Nice pinecones. Where'd you git 'em?"

She pointed out the window with the blade of her knife. "Down by the river. I found a bunch of pretty green and blue river stones I was going to bring up, but they were too heavy. I guess the pinecones are nice enough, though."

He wrinkled his forehead and tried to imagine a bowl full of stones on the table. He didn't get it. But he wouldn't have gotten the idea of pinecones either, if he hadn't seen them sitting there. "You have any hobbies? Besides decorating my house with the great outdoors."

She laughed. "You don't really like the pinecones, do you?"

"Now I didn't say that. I think it's a rare talent to be able to decorate from nature. Least you didn't buy those flowers down at the store, spend my money on things that just die."

"Everything dies sooner or later. May as well get some enjoyment out of them."

"Not stones and pinecones." He laughed, drunkenly. "You hear that, Mattie, I'm a poet. *Stones* and *pinecones*."

"No, you're just drunk."

"Then you should git drunk too." He got up and topped off her glass. "Go on, slam it back."

"No way."

"C'mon, you can do it."

She giggled, then lifted the glass and sucked down the whiskey, making a sour face as it went. She set her empty glass down and shivered visibly.

He poured her another and waited, trying to focus her face. "You've had some experience with this. I can tell by the way you drink."

"You don't know the half of it." She drank half the glass and set it down. "I can't drink it all at once, I'll puke."

"Oh, no, don't do that." He filled her glass again and went back to the table.

Mattie didn't manage supper, just a salad, which they ate with slices of cheese and bologna.

"We need some groceries," she stammered.

"Tomorrow. We'll drive up to Salmon City. Maybe order an alternator for your car." He gazed at her from behind hazy eyes. "Or not. If I don't fix it, I guess you can't leave."

"Are you holding me hostage now?"

"Maybe. They're gonna haul me off to jail anyway. You can leave then. Take my truck."

"Did you always want to be a sheep rancher?"

"God, no," he snorted. "No, I was gonna git my pilot's license and fly mail and stuff into remote areas, like down the middle fork of the Salmon, or up in the Denali Wilderness in Alaska."

"Sounds exciting . . . and dangerous."

"Better to die young and happy than . . . " his eyes wandered to his father's bedroom.

"I guess there's something to be said for doing what you love, no matter what the risk."

Chas poured the last of the whiskey into Mattie's glass.

"No, you can have it," she said, sloshing it across the table at him.

"No, I'll git the brandy."

"Ugh." She made a nasty face. "You'll be sick."

"Buck up, girl. We've still got a half a bottle to go. Don't quit on me now."

She pulled her glass back and took a sip. "I've always wanted to see Alaska. That sounds like a cool way to live, flying in and out of remote places."

Chas listened, believing her too drunk to really mean what she said, but wondering for the first time in decades if it wasn't too late for him. But with his luck, his father would linger for twelve or fifteen more years, just to spite him. He'd be ready for a nursing home himself before he'd be free of his obligations. Didn't matter so much that the sheriff might take him to jail, as he thought about it now. Couldn't be any more confining than the prison he already lived in. "What about you? Was this the glamorous career you always imagined?"

She stayed quiet at first. Then said, "There are worse careers to have."

"True. It's fine. I didn't mean it wasn't important."

She shook her head.

"It's about the most important career I can think of right now, given my situation. You know it took me six months to find you."

"For what you're paying, I'm surprised it didn't take six years."

Chas closed one eye. "You're kinda mean sometimes."

She smiled and ran her finger around the rim of the glass, collecting tiny drops, then sucked the liquid off with her tongue. "I always wanted to have a bookstore."

"That's not very exciting."

"Speak for yourself. Beats slaughtering sheep."

His eyebrows went up.

"But then again, those babies are really cute."

"There you go again, trying to turn 'em into pets."

"They ain't pets," she said in unison with Chas, mimicking his stern expression.

They both laughed. "Least you heard me."

"You're kidding, right?"

"You know, I never really looked at 'em. Not that close anyway. I mean . . . I check to see if they're marked right and all. But I never really looked. They're like deer. No, they're like . . . women."

Mattie sat back, her face scrunched in a scowl.

"They are. They're like women. Slender and sleek."

She tossed her head in disagreement. "You know you'll

never get a date if you compare sheep to women." She started laughing again. "Oh, now I finally get all those sheep jokes."

He tried to remember what made him make the comparison in the first place.

Mattie awoke face down on her blankets and fully dressed. Her pillow was smeared with drool, and her head ached. She rolled over and stared up at the ceiling. The room rolled with her. "Oh, God," she groaned. She tried to recall the evening, but all she could remember was a lot of silly laughter. Her stomach pitched, and she became acutely aware of her sour mouth. She lurched out of bed and skidded down the stairs, sucking back her breath. She sailed past Chas, snoring on the sofa, his arms wrapped tightly around his head.

She was kneeling over the toilet, staring at the muddy contents of her stomach, holding her hair in one hand, when Chas appeared in the doorway.

"You okay?"

She nodded gingerly without looking up.

"You need anything?"

She shook her head, wishing he'd just go away.

"Want me to make you some coffee?"

She shook her head again. "Please, just let me be."

"Okay."

She heard him in the kitchen making coffee anyway. She sat back on her heels and pressed her cheek against the cool wall, waiting to see if the vomiting was really over. This is why drinking was never my first choice, she thought. Finally, she stood on shaky legs and rinsed her mouth. Her fingers trembled horribly, and she felt poisoned. It was early still, so she climbed the stairs back to her room. She had another hour before she needed to tend to Mr. McPherson. Who, thank God, had not bothered her the previous night—could not have penetrated her drunkenness, anyway.

Sheriff Edelson waited for Mr. Teleghani at the burned ruins of his house. He hated asking the man to come, but was perplexed by Nuri's insistence that Chas McPherson could not have burned his house down. "He gave us a lamb for Eid," Nuri claimed repeatedly. "How can a man give from his heart one night, then burn my house down the next?"

The sheriff turned his collar up against the chill wind as he walked the property again, looking for new clues. He'd already been over it inch-by-inch three times. And he found nothing new today. The place was eerily deserted. Someone from the county had finally rounded up the last of the chickens. Wind whistled through the gaping windows of the house.

Nuri pulled up in a battered gray minivan.

The sheriff greeted him with a handshake. "Thanks for coming."

Nuri nodded. "It's in here," he said, giving the sheriff a stern look and leading him to a dilapidated shed behind the house. "You are wrong about Chas McPherson. I told you that already." He lifted his stocking cap and scratched his shiny head, then pulled it down snugly over his ears. "But you will agree with me when I show you the hide. It is one of his lambs. He is the only one around here who raises those blackbelly lambs."

The sheriff followed him into the dark shed that smelled of linseed oil. Edelson heard that Nuri used the oil when he cured his violins.

Nuri bent and dragged a frozen hide from the corner, out into the light. He pressed a boot down on one corner and pulled it into a wedge resembling a giant potato chip. "See the black underbelly," Nuri said, pointing at the edges of the hide. "Touch it. It is not wool. It is hair."

"Are you sure this isn't a goat hide?" The sheriff said, bending to inspect it.

Nuri straightened up and stared at the sheriff. "My family ate it. We know the difference between a goat and a lamb."

"Of course, I'm sorry."

"I have bought lambs from McPherson for the last six years. When he called this year, I had to tell him we could not afford it. Business is dead." Nuri Teleghani looked back at his house mournfully. "He just did not want anybody making a big deal about the gift. That is all. Chas McPherson is a proud man, and so am I. I do not believe for one minute he burned my home."

"An awful lot of people think he did," the sheriff said, still examining the hide. "Mind if I take this as evidence?"

Nuri shrugged and dropped the hide on the ground at the sheriff's feet.

Edelson mentally chalked up one positive vote for Chas McPherson.

Chas volunteered to go for groceries, leaving Mattie alone with her throbbing head and trembling hands. She slept off and on in the morning, then got up to make the old man lunch. She found the kitchen sink filled with blue and green river stones–the stones she'd collected, then abandoned under the tree for the pinecones. They were soaking in tepid water, which must have been hot when he filled the sink. She stared down at the wintry colors, more vibrant when wet. She laid a towel on the counter and spread the stones out to dry, then scrubbed away the grimy ring left behind on the white porcelain. Then she made a systematic, but ultimately disappointing, search of Chas's bathroom medicine cabinet for anything that would take the edge off her hangover.

When Chas returned, the stones were piled in a wooden bowl, which he usually used for popcorn, perched on the end table next to his chair.

The two of them unpacked groceries in silence. When

they finished, Chas handed her a small bag with two pieces of fried chicken. "Here, if you're up for eating."

She smiled. "Maybe a little. Thanks for bringing my stones in."

"Man, they weighed a ton!" He unpacked the last bag, pulling out two half-gallon bottles of whiskey.

10

CHAS FOUND HIMSELF ONCE AGAIN IN THE CHAIR next to his father's bed. Once again, he took a long, hard look at the man lying before him. He had never imagined this man at the mercy of others, and even now, with the old man dying, he felt that his father still had the upper hand. Always, he had the upper hand. "Mattie's not feeling well. I told her to go on to bed."

The old man stared ahead at nothing in particular.

"I drove up to Salmon City this afternoon. Had to git groceries." He watched for a change in his father's expression. Nothing. "Yup, they're treating me pretty bad in town these days." Chas sipped his whiskey and stayed quiet a while. "They think I burnt down the Moslem family's house." He raised his glass in a toast. "Thanks, Dad."

Through the window, the clouds had turned slate blue in the coming night and Chas switched on the lamp. "You had no right to do what you did to Sarah. She didn't get pregnant all by herself. You had no right."

Chas threw back the last of his whiskey and set the glass down. He pulled his ankle up and rested it across his knee and leaned back a little further in the chair. He thumbed the pages of his father's Bible. The old man had closed his eyes.

Chas willed his father to understand his words. "Leave Mattie alone, Dad, I'm asking you nicely."

Chas came awake shortly after one o'clock in the morning. Something was gnawing at him. He got up and wandered into the hallway and scanned the meadow, looking for things amiss, but all was quiet. His sheep lay scattered beneath the cedar tree, sleeping. He imagined little puffs of steam rising from their noses in the dark air. He listened to the silence and wished for the peace they had. He thought he'd seen Nuri Teleghani in Salmon City. Wasn't positive, and couldn't get through the check-out line quickly enough to follow the gray van he thought looked so familiar. What did it matter, anyway? The only two people who needed to know the truth were himself and the sheriff. There was no point in chasing Nuri down to convince him of anything.

As he grappled with his insecurity, Chas caught the pale outline of his face reflected in the window glass. He looked like his father in his younger years. He brought his image into focus and looked at himself—at his father. If he cut his hair, he would be his father. Is this who people see when they see me, he wondered. My old man, the man they hate?

Chas's mind wandered back to the summer of his freshman year, when his father had sponsored a revival. The old fashioned kind, with a big circus tent in the city park, with traveling evangelists and musicians. It was the last of three nights, and Mrs. Campbell, Chas's English teacher, had come, along with most of Sweetwater. She sat in the front row where Chas was required to sit. She patted his hand and told him how much he reminded her of his father. His gut had twisted in response. He knew by then he didn't want people to look at him and see Franklin McPherson. He was the only preacher in town, and he carried out his appointment like a plantation overseer, snapping the whip of righteousness across the backs of his sinning flock. Singing out affirmations of their depravity, then luring them in with the promise of redemption. And to Chas's surprise, they followed him in and scattered again just like the sheep in his meadow—driven by hunger and fear. His father called them each by name that night.

"Mary Haskins!" he shouted from the podium, eyes closed, face drawn in what appeared to be anguish. "Your adulterous affair has not gone unnoticed by your father in heaven." And the middle-aged housewife stumbled into the aisle and collapsed, weeping and begging for forgiveness.

"Albert Morris! Your God did not witness the gifts you say you have given in his name." And on he went until the citizens of Sweetwater had been admonished for their sins with horrifying accuracy, while groveling in the cool grass for some small intercession on their behalf.

But the frenzy of repentance and forgiveness under a billowy tent on a warm summer night turned to scalding humiliation in the stark morning light. Neighbor turned against neighbor with revelations of betrayal. Mary Haskins' husband left her. And children everywhere were soundly punished for crimes that had otherwise gone unnoticed.

An aura of divinity had floated about Franklin McPherson for months to follow, but as time marched on, as the glow of forgiveness faded in the hearts of those most vulnerable, the preacher's divine position came under increasing speculation. Perhaps it wasn't the Lord who spoke to him in the dark, when good citizens were home with their families. But none were so bold as to publicly question him, for fear their own closely guarded wrongs be brought out for all to see.

Meanwhile a veil of suspicion shrouded his son. Did Chas possess this frightening gift? Like all children of the clergy, Chas had learned to defend himself from schoolyard bullies. He didn't suffer the hazing that would have been the lot of a weaker boy. Instead, the children simply withdrew what friendship had once been extended. He was as alone as anyone could be after that summer night of the revival. Except for Sarah.

Chas's eyes refocused on the meadow. He questioned himself for standing in the dark in the middle of the night, dredging up memories he could do nothing about. Losing my mind, he speculated. He tiptoed to Mattie's door and stood looking in, seeing if she was still there.

"What are you doing?" she asked, startling him.

"Just checking . . . to see if you're okay. Thought I heard something."

"I'm okay. But thanks."

"'Night, then." He went to his room, but couldn't fall asleep. He lay awake most of the night, wondering if was too late to get his pilot's license.

Mattie rolled over and closed her eyes, trying to sleep. She listened for Chas's snoring, but he stayed quiet as the hours ticked by, making her wonder if he lay awake too. She wished she hadn't lied—wished she had begged him to hold her the way he had when he had last found her on the stairs.

She finally found slumber sometime before dawn, but awoke again to a persistent, urgent crying. It sounded like a baby. But it came from outside. She went to the window, where Chas was already peering out.

"What is it?"

"A lamb," he said, craning to see it in the misty morning light.

"Sounds like a person."

"It's looking for its mother." He went to his room and emerged a moment later with his shirt on and a pair of socks in his hand.

"I'll make some coffee."

He nodded, but disappeared down the stairs. Before she had her slippers on, the front door slammed.

The crying continued for a half-hour. Finally, she bundled up against the cold and went outside to see for herself. Chas was trying to lure a ewe into the barn by holding a tiny lamb out in front of her as he walked backward. When the lamb cried, the mother called to it, but would not follow.

"C'mon, girl," he coaxed.

As Mattie watched this odd event, she realized it wasn't the lamb in his hand that cried, but another one, loping around in the snowy field, instinctively following the nervous flock, tripping on its unstable legs. It was soaked. "Chas, do you need help?"

He tucked the first lamb under his arm, his face tense. "Bring me a couple dry towels from the house. Old ones."

When Mattie returned, he was chasing the second lamb around the cedar tree, one arm outstretched, fingers splayed. His magnificent strength was of little use now. Agility and finesse were what he most needed, and what he most lacked. His ungraceful stumbling would've made Mattie laugh had she dared. She opened the gate and started toward the cedar. As the lamb came round she scooped it up, and immediately realized with horror that it was wet with birthing fluid and manure. Its umbilical cord, long and sticky, wrapped around her hand.

"Oh, gross," she said, holding it away from her.

"That's what the towels are for."

She handed a towel to Chas and watched as he started to dry his lamb, methodically, from its head down its back and legs, ending at the underside of its tail.

"Start with its head, not its butt."

She glared at him. "I'm not stupid. What's wrong with them, anyway?"

"Nothin' I can see." He held his lamb out and looked it over. Then he scanned the flock for the mother. "Didn't think she was that close. It's her first time . . . and her last! A ewe that won't nurse her lambs ain't worth a damn."

"What are you going to do?"

"Eat her. Soon as these two are weaned."

Mattie wrapped her lamb in its towel like a baby, tipping it onto its back and looking into its eyes.

Chas gave her a sharp look of disapproval. "Let's take these inside and put 'em in a jug."

"Put them in a what?"

"A pen. It's called a jug," he said.

Chas carried his green bucket of oats into the field, attracting the attention of the flock. The temperature had risen above freezing, turning snow to rain. Tiny streams crisscrossed the meadow in a headlong gallop to the river. Mattie looked at her muddy, bloody coat and hands, now numb with cold, and wished she'd stayed inside.

"I'm gonna bring 'em all into that catch pen, then we'll let out the ones we don't want." He pointed at the round pen next to the barn. "I gotta catch this ewe and get some milk into these babies before it's too late."

"What do you want me to do?"

"I can do it by myself, if you wanna go in."

She looked again at her coat. It was already ruined; she may as well satisfy her curiosity about the outcome now. "I'll stay and help."

"Then stand over there until I git 'em all in."

Chas made a slow meander through the meadow shaking his bucket and calling, "Shee–eep, shee–eep," in a smooth drawl until the flock trailed after him in a long line. He poured the grain into a feeder at the back of the catch pen, then circled around and shut the gate. It looked so simple, Mattie wanted to clap.

"Okay, Mattie," he said. "You stand at the gate. When I shoo one over, open it just far enough to let it out, but not wide, or the whole bunch'll go. Got it?"

She nodded. And Chas stepped to the edge of the flock and separated the first one, pushing it toward her. She opened the gate.

"Too far," he shouted. "Just a little."

The flock was nervous now and began darting back and forth. Chas separated another ewe and pushed her toward the gate. Mattie opened it, and the animal sprang out into the meadow and kept running for a good distance, then turned and watched the fate of her mates. Mattie smiled triumphantly. But when she turned back, a large ram with corkscrew horns flew out of the center of the flock and butted the gate hard, knocking her backward.

"Let him out," Chas shouted.

She pulled the gate open too far and three ewes escaped with him.

"Close it!" Chas yelled.

"I'm sorry—I'm sorry."

Chas came to the gate frowning.

"I'm sorry," she said again.

"It's okay, he was the hard one. Just hold tight a sec and I'll see if I can catch the one we want. If she gets out, we'll have to wait for them to calm down before we can round 'em up again." He circled the flock, scattering them, then lunged in and caught the hind leg of a ewe. He pulled her up and looked at her. "That ain't the one." He lugged her over to the gate, and Mattie let her out. Chas worked at the flock this way until they'd released another twelve. Finally, he caught the one he was after.

"How can you tell which one you're looking for?" Mattie said.

Chas lifted the animal so she could see the udder. "She's got a bag."

Mattie grimaced at his choice of words.

The ewe struggled to free herself from his grip. "You can let 'em out now." He lugged the animal into the barn. "Can you git the gate for me?" he called over his shoulder.

Mattie raced ahead of him, splattering muck on her jeans up to the knees.

He pushed the ewe into the pen with her lambs, then stood back and watched. The babies ran to her, but she stamped her feet, warning them away. One of them butted her udder with its face, trying to nurse. She butted it away in turn.

Chas hopped into the pen and swatted her across the nose with his glove. "Knock it off!" He gave her another chance, but she refused to let the lamb nurse. "I promise you don't wanna piss me off," he growled. He cornered her and dragged her to the front of the jug, where Mattie noticed for the first time, a medieval-looking apparatus of metal bars and levers.

"What's that?"

"A stanchion," he said, pushing the ewe's head through the opening, then levering it closed.

"You'll hurt her," she gasped.

"She'll be okay. She can stand up and lay down. I'll git her some water."

"You're not going to leave her in that, are you?" Mattie was horrified. But the ewe immediately calmed down.

"If they don't git colostrum they won't make it. It's got antibodies in it. If she won't feed 'em on her own, I'll force her." He checked the stanchion to make sure it wasn't too tight. "See." He pointed at the nursing lambs. "She can't hurt 'em, and they can git as much as they want."

"How long will she have to be in that?"

"Depends on how quick she decides to be a mother. A few days, maybe."

"A few days?" Mattie's mouth gaped.

"Hey, when sheep can drive tractors she'll have career choices. Until then, this is it. Mother or mutton." He rubbed his stomach. "Speaking of mutton, I'm starving. How 'bout you?"

"You're on your own. I'm taking a shower."

"This your first time working livestock?"

She stared at his wide grin. What a stupid question, she thought.

Chas drank black coffee while he fried bacon and eggs in a cast-iron skillet. He hadn't made a real breakfast for himself in so long he couldn't remember the last time. He made extra for Mattie, who was showering on the other side of the wall. His mind wandered into the bathroom with her, and he imagined her naked, shampooing her hair, soap suds rolling over her round breasts. He thought about it a moment longer, then turned his attention back to the eggs. "Over easy," he said aloud as he slid a spatula under the eggs and rolled them over without breaking the yolks.

Mattie emerged from the bathroom in her robe, a towel wrapped around her head. She looked over Chas's shoulder. "You *can* cook. You've been holding out on me."

"Holding out?"

"All this time you could've done your fair share."

He thought of making a crack about cooking being a woman's job, but held his tongue. "You never gave me a chance. Besides, I can't find anything in my own damn kitchen now."

"Mm, I see what you mean. The pots and pans are in the cupboards instead of scattered all over the counter and stacked in the sink, greasy. And the dishes—"

"You made your point."

"Hope so. I wouldn't want to find a nasty skillet in that freshly scrubbed sink later."

"You want breakfast? Or you just here to nag?"

She looked into the skillet again. "Sure, I'll have some. Let's see what kind of cook you are. Maybe I'll work out a schedule for you."

He shook his head. This is what I get for trying to be nice and making you breakfast.

Mattie sat down and waited to be served. She rubbed a

fresh purple bruise on her forearm. "I thought sheep were supposed to be docile animals. I never knew they were so hard to handle."

"It's Blackbellies. They're kinda flighty. Love 'em for their hardiness, but they can be wild as deer." He turned to her. "You could git some dishes."

She smiled, but stayed in her seat.

Chas turned back to the eggs. Was she baiting him? Was she being playful? Maybe she was mocking him. Should he be angry? When he turned back, she'd pulled the towel from her head and was raking her fingers through her wet hair. He went a little weak in the knees. "I need to go back to Salmon City today. Forgot to order your alternator yesterday." Which was a lie. He had ordered it, but thought he might do something stupid if he didn't get away from her in short order.

Searching for Nuri's van, Chas drove up and down the streets of Salmon City. It was a tiny hamlet, almost too small to be called a town. The city fathers had clearly been optimistic in deeming it a city. But he didn't find the familiar vehicle or face he searched for. He started up the steep grade of Highway 14, along the river toward Lewiston. Had decided to talk to the nursing home manager, just in case. As he wound along the narrow highway, he glimpsed a gray van sitting in the driveway of a rundown cabin close to the road. He pulled onto the shoulder and walked the twenty-some feet back to the driveway. The van was Nuri's. He knew it by the large dent in the left rear panel. He hesitated, now that he'd found him, to speak with the man whose house he was suspected of burning down. What would he say? What if the Teleghanis called the police? As he stood in the driveway with his hands shoved in his pockets, a child came into the yard and saw him. Chas knew if he didn't go say something now, it would look suspicious. The boy went back inside and a moment later Nuri appeared on the front step. The cabin looked as though it hadn't been inhabited for some years, and it was clearly too small for a family of nine to live comfortably.

"Mr. Teleghani," he said, "I hope I'm not disturbing you."

"No," Nuri said, but remained on the porch. He neither seemed happy to see Chas, nor afraid of his presence.

"I thought I saw your van in Salmon City yesterday. I've . . . I've been hoping to speak with you."

"I know you did not set fire to my house, Mr. McPherson."

Chas blew his breath out in a puff of steam.

"A man who shares his food is not a hateful man."

Chas didn't argue about the gift, it seemed pointless, and perhaps even dangerous to deny it now. "How's your family?"

"They are alive, *Alhamdulillah.*"

"I butchered a lamb just the other day. Have extra. Can I bring you some?

"No." Nuri's demeanor was commanding, and Chas didn't insist.

"Will you be coming back to Sweetwater?"

Nuri looked over his shoulder at the sagging cabin. "I have lived in Idaho for almost thirty years, Mr. McPherson. In that time, you might think a person would become part of the place where he lives, where he raises his family."

Chas knew that wasn't true. Or, if one did become a part of the community it was on the community's terms. No one is allowed to define their own place in society. It is a collective appraisal subject to the influence and prejudice of others. Chas realized how much alike he and the Teleghanis were—chosen by others to be set aside in one way or another. He imagined the citizens of Sweetwater, with their good intentions, applauding themselves for accepting a foreign family, for their forward and progressive thinking, their grounding in the ideal of an American melting pot. But only so far as the ideal didn't interfere with their own lives, or touch them too deeply, would they maintain that view.

"We have not decided where we will go now," Nuri said. "My wife would like to go back to Persia, so our children can learn about their heritage. But I am an American. And I have American children. We are between places, and neither one is home to us now. I sometimes wonder if my greatest mistake was coming to this country in the first place."

"I hope you'll stay," Chas said. "It'd be a pity for whoever did this to think they won."

Nuri regarded Chas a moment without giving insight into his thoughts. Finally, he said, "If we stay, I will look for some land, perhaps I will buy some sheep from you. I would not mind having a flock of my own."

Chas nodded. "I'll save you my best." Then he turned and started back toward his pickup, feeling oddly enlightened, having realized something new about the nature of things. Hoping Nuri would stay, but understanding his wife's desire to go—sharing her desire to leave this place. He turned at the end of the driveway and called to Nuri, "I suspect if the sheriff knew I was here, it'd look bad for me."

Nuri nodded, leaving Chas with the belief his visit would remain a secret.

CHAS DECIDED NOT TO GO ON TO LEWISTON after all. It might bring bad luck on him to prepare in advance for Mattie's departure. And he didn't want to spoil the odd euphoria that touched him after his visit with Nuri. At home, he checked the ewe in the stanchion, then his lead ewe. "Still waiting, huh?" he said, rubbing his hand down her nose. She was the only one tame enough to touch that way. It was perplexing to him—why she was different from the others.

Inside, his father sat looking out on the melting snow. The gutter, jammed with leaves and moss, overflowed, sending water streaming onto the porch. Chas was thankful his father didn't comprehend the lack of household mainte-nance, and thought for the first time about getting out the ladder and cleaning the gutters. In the spring, he decided.

He kicked his boots off next to the woodstove to dry. "I'm back," he said to Mattie.

"Did you order the alternator for my car?"

He stared at her blankly, having forgotten his lie. "Uh-huh," he finally said. "Be a couple a weeks, though."

Her eyebrows went up. "Two weeks?"

"You're living in the boonies now. And you ain't driving the customary American-made car like the rest of us hicks."

She went back to mashing boiled sweet potatoes with the back of a fork. She'd pulled her hair up tight again, out of her way.

Chas got a glass and filled it with whiskey. "Want one?"

She paused, eyeing the bottle, then nodded. "Okay."

He poured her a glass. "You're pretty hardcore."

"You offered."

He watched her take a sip, then went to the living room. He turned his father's wheelchair to face him and sat down. "Hi, Dad," he began, after a long scrutinizing stare. "She's making sweet potatoes. I'm enjoying the cooking, how 'bout you?" As he looked at his father, he made a firm decision to kill himself before he wound up like that. If he could see it coming. He wondered if his father would've committed suicide if it hadn't been for his faith. Probably he would have–probably he had to struggle not to. He'd once been a powerful man, physically as well as mentally.

The effects of his drink eased the awkwardness. Chas couldn't take his eyes off the shriveled hands that'd once broken horses and cut raw lumber dragged down from the mountains. It seemed a cruel ending. But there was an irony here that didn't escape Chas. He'd always wished he could have his say–wished that his father would just listen to him. And now, he couldn't think of what he wanted to tell the man.

"I went to see Nuri Teleghani today. He's living up Highway 14, outside Salmon City. It's a terrible place. Falling down around 'em. Didn't ask, but wonder if it even has indoor plumbing." He sighed. "The fire must have taken all his violins. Has to start over now."

Chas turned the empty glass over in his hand, letting the last drops roll onto his palm, then rubbed it into his skin like lotion. He turned the lamp on and surveyed his father's vacant face, as if he might find something new there. "I had so much to tell you all these years, but now I can't remember what it was. Funny, ain't it? Now I can only think of questions . . . like whether you ever regretted anything . . . or if you're okay with the way things played out."

He took his glass to the kitchen where Mattie was setting his father's supper on the table. He poured another drink, took the bottle with him and walked out onto the porch. The temperature was plummeting under a black, cloudless sky. Chas stepped out into the yard, the ice-crusted snow caving beneath his feet, and looked up at the starry sky. The big dipper sparkled overhead, and he followed a line to the North Star, remembering his father pointing it out to him when he was just six or seven, teaching him how to navigate in the wilderness by it. That was the father he liked to remember. A vast oracle of practical information who never seemed to come up short, no matter the circumstances. His father knew all the constellations, even the ones that couldn't be seen from North America. He could survive in the wilderness with nothing more than a sharp knife and a warm coat. He had showed Chas how to build a dead fall for trapping raccoons, and how to put up a crude shelter in case he got lost in bad weather. He was a 20th century Daniel Boone, and when Chas was eight, he'd watched the Hollywood version of the frontier man get the details wrong so many times in a single episode that he never took interest in TV again.

He went to the fence and looked across the meadow at his sheep. They watched him passively. He felt tired of them—tired of their daily demands, their constant care. Tired of treating eyes, trimming hooves, administering shots, mending fences. And now he looked ahead with dread to the dozens of lambs on the way. The inevitable struggles just like the one he'd experienced that morning—a mother with no instincts for her job.

He finished his drink while contemplating his wards, but didn't pour another. He didn't know what pressed in on him more—the sheep, his father, or the sheriff. But it was becoming hard to breathe under the weight of it all. What would happen if he started walking and just kept going? How long would it take Mattie to figure out he'd left, and what would she do? It came to him that he didn't know very much about Mattie, despite their spontaneous exchange of grievous sins. What happened after her parents died? Why didn't she want her sister to pay for her trip to Florida? What could make a woman like her come to Sweetwater, live in a rundown farmhouse, cook for an ass like himself, and care for a man like his father? She wasn't stupid; that was plain. But he couldn't see any other reason she would be here at all.

Chas turned his back to the meadow and leaned against a fence post. The house lights cast a yellow glow across the snow, and he watched Mattie spoon-feeding his father. He tried to imagine her gone. What would it be like after his father died? Chas tried to imagine life as it had been before Mattie arrived–warming cans of condensed soup amidst the piles of dirty dishes, falling asleep in his chair after drinking whiskey alone all evening. And rising to a bleak landscape, starved for the sound of another human voice. It made him sick to his stomach to think about. He kicked at the snow with the toe of his boot, chipping the icy surface away until he turned up hard chunks of dirt. He tipped the bottle back and sucked down another swig before turning to the sheep once again.

Mattie left the light on in the kitchen so Chas would find his supper on the stove for him, then climbed the stairs to bed. His pickup was still parked in front of the barn and no light came from that direction. She hoped the whiskey could keep him warm; his coat still hung from a peg in the entryway. She'd thought about going out to see if he was all right, but the place scared her after dark; wild animals lurked in the meadow.

Shortly after midnight Mattie awoke to the old man's familiar persecution. "Why are you doing this?" she whispered into the dark. "If you think I'm going to fall on my knees and beg for forgiveness, you're wrong, old man." She didn't believe in the absolution of sin any more than she believed a man lived in the moon. To her it served no purpose but to lull the soul into a false sense of atonement. There was no forgiving God—if there was a God at all. She pulled on her robe and crept to Chas's door. His bed was empty, the covers in a tangle.

She slipped downstairs quietly, went straight to the old man's room and took him by the shoulders, shaking him roughly. "Wake up, Mr. McPherson."

He opened his eyes.

"I've had it with you." She closed in on his face, her lips nearly brushing his cheek. She held his ears firmly in her hands—a tight grip, an unmistakable warning. "You let me sleep! You hear me?" Her knuckles went white. "If you don't leave me alone, I'll make the rest of your life a living hell. You'll pray for death with every beat of your heart. I promise."

He blinked three times in rapid succession.

She pushed his head back against the pillow and straightened up, then sat next to his bed. In the moonlight, the tip of Mr. McPherson's nose shone like the slim arc of a sickle blade. "I'm not a nice girl, Mr. McPherson. But you already know that, don't you? I'm not one to be pushed. If it comes down between you and me, you know who's gonna win."

She leaned back and stretched her arms, releasing the tension from her body. It felt good. "How about a bedtime story? Once upon a time, a little girl named Mattie went to school wearing a short skirt and no panties. She did it on a dare." Mattie leaned close to the old man again. "I think you'd probably have called her whore, wouldn't you? Just like that little girl Chas got pregnant."

Mr. McPherson closed his eyes.

She yawned. "Well, it's late. If I have to come back down here, you'll regret it."

Sheriff Edelson leafed through the latest tips called in, or given in person to his secretary, about the comings and goings of Chas McPherson before and after the fire. Well-meaning citizens seemed anxious to provide evidence to convict a man they all believed guilty. This latest report had been phoned in by Mrs. Watson, a Sweetwater resident since her birth in 1927, and president of the county Methodist Women's Club. She'd seen the guilt in Chas's face when he refused to acknowledge her in passing on the street.

"Thanks, Mrs. Watson," the sheriff sighed, "but psychic readings don't count in court." He dropped the note into a manila folder filled with similar notes and tossed it on his desk. He leaned back in his chair. Sun streamed between the buildings setting icicles ablaze like diamonds dripping from the eves. He couldn't stop thinking about Chas's philosophy of God and trees. It struck him as almost absurd, its simplicity. But also brilliant in that he couldn't find a hole in it. And it had compelled Edelson to begin looking for clues to God's intent in the world all around him.

Lorraine appeared in the doorway holding a piece of paper. "Another one. That's two since eight o'clock."

He looked at his watch: Eight-forty-five. "Hope it's more useful than the last."

She handed it to him. "Eric Mullen says he saw Chas's truck up in Salmon City."

"So?"

She shrugged.

He opened the folder and showed her the contents. "Look at these. There must be sixty-five or seventy tips in here, and not a goddamn one of 'em is anything more than a hunch. Some of 'em I suspect are outright lies." He dropped the latest on the pile. "I've never seen a town so bent on blaming a person they've known all his life."

"He ain't a very popular man."

"Lorraine, this isn't a popularity contest. I have a mind to make a public statement that Chas McPherson is no longer a suspect just to put an end to all this foolishness."

She shook her head adamantly.

"All I've got on him is a gasoline match, but it also matches the fuel at the only filling station in Sweetwater. If that was evidence enough to convict the man, we'd all be going to prison."

"You know he did it," she said.

"No I don't! And neither do you."

"Sheriff–"

"In fact, the one statement I have that makes any sense at all is Nuri Teleghani's claim that Chas gave his family a lamb on the night of Eid. He showed me the hide. It was one of those blackbelly sheep. Who else raises those animals? I can't find a single person within a–hundred–and–fifty miles."

"You've got Pam's testimony. She said that Chas shouted at her that if we're going to get rid of Christmas, we may as well get rid of the Golden Rule too."

The sheriff fished through the folder and held up the tip from Mrs. Watson. "And this sweet lady, who *could see the guilt in his face* was the one who organized a counter campaign to the petition against the Christmas celebration at school. She stood on the front steps of the school for two weeks telling everyone that evil had come to Sweetwater. If I used Pam's logic, Mrs. Watson would be a far more likely arsonist."

"Yeah, but you know about Chas's dad."

Sheriff Edelson stared at his secretary, mulling her propensity to blindly pin Chas with this crime no matter what the evidence suggested. She'd grown up in Sweetwater; he'd only moved here to run for office. He'd heard stories about Franklin McPherson, even a hundred miles away as a rookie officer in Sandpoint. Stories he largely discounted. He thought about telling Lorraine what Chas had said about the trees. But this philosophy, which from any other source might cause a person to pause a moment and think about, would only spawn suspicion and ridicule for Chas.

"Sheriff, you tell folks Chas McPherson ain't a suspect in the arson case and you can kiss reelection goodbye."

He squinted at her. "That a threat?"

She shook her head and smoothed her skirt. "It's a fact. Can I get you a cup of coffee?"

The morning sun broke through where the shingles of the barn roof had gone missing, lancing the nerves at the back of Chas's eyes like white probes. He sat up and a stinking, manure-caked blanket, used for warming new lambs, slid onto the floor of the loft. Hay stuck like Velcro in his hair and on his shirt. Next to him were an empty whiskey bottle and an upturned glass. He stared at them, taking the scene in with more clarity than that afforded a man in his condition. "I'm a fucking drunk," he muttered. He looked at his watch. It was almost nine. He groaned and got to his feet, leaving the evidence of his indulgence where they lay, and climbed down the ladder to the barn floor. His sheep were hungry. But he limped past them, his knees feeling arthritic in the cold, out of the barn and across the yard. When he stopped and tried to brush the hay from his shirt, his fingers were numb with cold.

Mattie stood at the kitchen counter slicing an apple. He couldn't read her expression. He looked for evidence of crying, hoping his father hadn't tormented her during the night, pushing her closer to leaving.

"If you don't mind," she said coolly, "I'd appreciate it if you'd let me know when you're going to be gone all night."

He nodded, took the last of the coffee and leaned against the counter. "You fare okay last night?"

She turned to him, the sharp little paring knife gripped in her hand. "Better than you, by the looks of things."

He peered down at his shirt, still littered with hay.

She reached over his head, and he flinched. She paused, then continued, pulling a long twig from his hair and handing it to him. "Sleep with the sheep?"

"No," he said, taking the twig from her. "They can't climb the loft ladder. Might have been warmer if I had."

She nodded and sliced the last of the apple, then held the plate out to him. "Hungry?"

"Just cold." He watched her take the plate and sit down. "Guess I'll git in the shower."

She smiled to herself, and he wondered if she had sexual fantasies about him. She was probably just happy to get rid of his smell, which was apparent, now that he was inside away from the animals.

"Have you ever considered getting a cat?"

"Why? I don't have enough animals?"

"Too many. Mostly mice. This place is crawling with them. I had to throw the pancake mix out this morning because they'd chewed a hole in the bag."

"You threw it out?"

She gave him a pointed look. "I'm not eating it after mice have gotten into it."

"Try plastic containers. I'll pick up some rat poison today." He set the empty cup on the counter and started for the bathroom. His entire body ached from the cold. He sat on the edge of the tub and pulled his boots off. He tried to remember last evening but couldn't recall anything after a dim vision of looking out at the river, seeing the reflection of the moon in the ripples, while he thought about having sex with Mattie.

Chas fed his sheep, then started for town to get vaccine and rat poison. He was glad he didn't have to drive to Salmon

City for that, like everything else these days.

At Ruark's he stood at the large refrigerator near the front door, where Dean kept an assortment of vaccines for nearly every animal ailment. Dean looked over Chas's shoulder as he lifted serum bottles, read the labels, and put them back.

"Help ya find something, Chas?"

"Clostridium C & D."

"Here." Dean picked up a small bottle with pink liquid and handed it to Chas.

"Thanks. Rat poison?"

"Aisle eight. Before ya head off to git it, I have to ask if you can pay cash."

Chas spun on his heels. "What for?"

Dean looked sheepishly at his feet and fidgeted with his hands. "Can't risk running a tab with all this arson stuff goin' on. Hope you understand, Chas. Just can't afford it."

Being clubbed on the head might've stung less than the blow Dean delivered. He and Chas had managed a business-like respect, if not a friendship, for twenty years or better. Now this insult? "When have I ever not paid my bill?"

Dean shrugged. Chas did pay his bills—always.

"What about Maynard? You never asked him to pay cash, and he's always late paying his bill. You had to write off half the feed he bought last year."

Dean glanced up, but didn't hold Chas's gaze. "I'm getting some pressure."

"From who?"

"Folks."

"*What goddamn folks?*"

"Bob Hinkler. He's trying to git everyone in town to close your accounts, or drop 'em so low they ain't any good to ya."

"I see." Chas walked back to the counter and set the clostridium down.

Dean fumbled to punch the numbers into the register.

"I always thought you were an upstanding kinda man, Dean."

The storekeeper's left eyelid twitched.

Chas lifted the bottle in his fist, and Dean flinched. "I find it hard to believe you're doing so well you can afford to chase off paying customers."

"Nobody's chasing you off, Chas. Just asking you–"

"Fuck you! You can take your vaccine and go straight to Hell." Chas slammed the bottle down on the counter, splitting the sides. Sticky liquid sprayed the register and both men. Chas went to the front window and picked up a bandana from the display, wiped his hand with it and tossed it on the counter. "Put it on my tab."

Chas sped up Highway 14 toward Lewiston, screeching around curves at breakneck speed. He gripped the steering wheel hard, the tips of his hot fingers beginning to tingle into numbness. His jaw flexed, amplifying the pounding in his temples. He pressed the accelerator to the floor.

"Goddamn Hinkler! Fucking Ruark! Son-of-a-bitch . . . " But the names were too numerous, and he ran out of profanities in short order. It was the organization and forethought of a group, a cohesive, organized group with a leader that struck him.

Chas thought about Bob Hinkler, but he couldn't bring his face to mind, only his snowy cap of hair, thick and bright in his old age. He could only see him as he'd been that night at the revival. His father had called that name too–the last name he called. And he quoted Proverbs: *Bob Hinkler, A scoundrel and villain, who goes about with a corrupt mouth, who winks his eye, signals with his feet, and motions with his fingers, who plots evil with deceit in his heart.*

But Hinkler hadn't fallen into the aisle weeping, or begged God for forgiveness. He made his way to the center of the tent with a strawberry face and a bluish vein raised on his temple. Chas had watched it pulse. Hinkler stood there, staring at Franklin McPherson. Seconds stretched taut between them as everyone waited for this red-faced man to explode like a rocket. Someone muffled a cough in the back rows. The woman across the aisle stopped fanning herself with her program, forgetting about the oppressive heat, eyes fixed on Hinkler.

Finally, Hinkler had shouted, "You're nothing but a witchdoctor, Preacher McPherson!" And stormed out with all of Sweetwater's stunned gazes following him. All eyes turned forward again and waited for the preacher to respond. It was Franklin McPherson's undoing—that last accusation. Everyone knew Bob Hinkler was a respectable, honest man. He'd plotted against no one. And nothing came to light afterward to prove any evidence to back the charge.

Chas zoomed along in a white fury—his anger blinding. In the split second his wheels left the pavement and his truck began to roll, it came to him; perhaps it hadn't been a declaration of what Hinkler had done, but a foretelling of what he would do. His head hit the roof and glass shattered in on him from all sides, tiny shards stinging his hands and face.

CHAS SAT ON THE EMBANKMENT below Highway 14, barely able to process his surroundings. A slow trickle of blood dripped over his left eye from a gash along his hairline. He was in pain, but it was an all-over, general sort of pain that left him unable to assess where it came from—his ribs, his neck, or his head—except for his left wrist, which had turned into a ball of hot, tight flesh.

Below him his pickup sat on its roof, sides crushed in, windows out. It'd rolled twice for sure, he thought, possibly even three times, before coming to rest in the shallow edge water of the Sweetwater River. He could plainly see it was totaled. He didn't remember getting out, or climbing onto the embankment. But he'd thought to bring his keys, which he grasped tightly in his right hand. He glanced at his watch; almost three. He tried to calculate how much time had passed since the wreck, but the morning was a blur. All he remembered was the interchange with Dean and clostridium splattering against the cash register. And for the first time since boyhood, he had to forcibly suppress tears, which horrified him.

He dropped his keys on the ground and picked up a fist-sized stone. It was blue, like Mattie's stones, but bigger. Worn smooth from the river, it felt nice against his skin—heavy and cool. He heaved it down the embankment, hitting the passenger door of his truck. A magnificent pain rocketed through his middle, doubling him over. His stomach lurched, and he thought he would puke. He sat very still, sucking in slow breath after slow breath until the nausea passed. He spit, splattering the stones near his feet with blood.

Finally standing on shaky legs, Chas looked up the highway toward Lewiston, then in the opposite direction toward Salmon City. He'd gone off the road in a notorious stretch of curves, where the highway was flanked by a steep, forested mountain on one side and the boulder-strewn river on the other. He wasn't the first to find himself in the river and he wouldn't be the last. He figured he was closer to Salmon City, but still a good ten miles away. He doubted he could make it on foot—just getting the rest of the way to the road would be trouble enough. But it would be dark soon and no one would find him where he was, so he started to climb, falling to his knees and crawling most of the way up.

With an awkward, uneven gait, he started south, hoping someone would come by and offer a ride. His right ankle was stiff, forcing him to tread lightly on it. And he kept his wrist tucked up along his ribs, held it in place by his other hand. He leaned forward, like an old man who'd forgotten his cane, and made his way with small, laborious steps. Snow had begun to fall again. Light, dry wisps that swirled on the air like pixies. He wondered if he should go back for his coat, but the idea of climbing down the embankment turned the thought away. He reckoned it was wet anyway. As he wandered, he began to shiver.

In the twilight, a pickup sped past, giving Chas a wide berth, but didn't slow. A fine sheen of icy water sprayed over him. He realized, as if coming out of a dream, that he wasn't paying attention, hadn't heard it approaching. He had lost an opportunity—the only one to present itself so far. His muscles were stiffening in the frigid air, his skin nearly numb. He kept moving, one foot ahead of the other, knowing if he stopped, he'd freeze into a knot of ruined muscle and die. This thought was not entirely unattractive to him, and he lingered on it for some time, calculating how long it would take a man of his size to lose consciousness. Then he saw the cabin. He limped across the road and into the driveway.

He tried to lift his foot to mount the first of four steps, but could not get it off the ground. He laughed aloud at the absurdity of walking all the way to safety, only to die at the entrance. Delirious and in shock, he fell forward onto the steps, laughing.

In the living room, Matti was drinking Chas's whiskey from a plastic cup. Mr. McPherson sat near her with his wool blanket across his lap.

"If there's any justice in the world, you'll go to Hell for what you do to people," she said. She didn't survey his face for signs now, but turned her gaze to the newly falling snow as she pulled the silver clip from her hair, letting the dark locks spill down around her shoulders. She raked her fingers through it. "Like it?" she said, tipping her chin up. "Chas loves it–can't keep his eyes off it. Says I should always wear my hair down like this."

Long, narrow lights fluttered overhead, setting off a buzzing in Chas's ears. He was alone, separated from a hacking woman on his left by a thin white curtain dotted with tiny blue triangles. The smell of iodine burned in his nostrils. He ran his hand over his forehead and felt a thick bandage along his hairline, and the smoothness of his skin where his head was shaved in an arc above it. His left arm was encased in a cast equal in weight to an anvil. It was neon blue. He wished he'd been awake enough to protest. Vague yellow memories of Nuri's house, warm and bright, came to him.

Then the dark interior of a car, a wool blanket scratching at his neck, the road jarring his bones.

He sat up, starting a strong, familiar pulsing in his head. His right ankle was wrapped, but without a cast, so he assumed it wasn't broken. He nodded, happy for that, and swung his legs off the side of the bed. He looked at his watch, but it was missing–replaced by the neon cast. He scanned the tiny space for his clothes, finding them stacked on a chair. He eased himself to a stand, balancing on one foot, and began to dress, stopping to take inventory of his wallet, which he found in the front pocket of his jeans along with his watch.

As he buttoned his shirt, a petite, middle–aged nurse appeared from behind the folds. "Oh, you're up."

"Can I use your phone?" he said, limping into the florescent–lit aisle between rows of curtained beds, his boots in his hand.

"Mr. McPherson, the doctor hasn't released you yet. Please stay here while I get him."

"I need to make a phone call. I need a ride."

"There's a gentleman waiting for you in the lobby."

"He's still here?"

She nodded. "Please sit down until I get the doctor. You have a concussion."

Chas was already limping toward a sign pointing the way to the lobby.

"Mr. McPherson, please," she called after him.

Nuri was watching the evening news and immediately got to his feet when he saw Chas. "Are you okay?"

"Yeah, thanks for waiting."

"I did not want to leave you here alone." An awkward silence stretched between them. Finally, "Are they letting you go?"

"Yeah." Chas sat down to put his boots on and eased his right foot in as far as he could. "I hate to ask any more favors . . . but d'ya think you could give me a lift home? I'd call the nurse that's taking care of my father, but her car won't start."

"Of course."

"Thanks," Chas said, loathing this position of having to ask for help, particularly from Nuri.

Nuri didn't speak as he drove the dark highway back to Sweetwater. Chas tried to stay awake, focusing his mind on the licorice smell of spilled root-beer permeating the front seat. He wanted to express his gratitude, but the only words he could think of sounded stupid. It irked him to be at the mercy of another man. The silence between them only served to illuminate the bizarre position they were in: one man suspect, one man ruined. Perhaps both ruined, he thought, then wondered if Nuri had doubts about his innocence. It's one thing to ease a man's fears when he shows up on your doorstep, but to be compelled to help him in his hour of need, is quite another.

"Do you remember what happened?" Nuri said.

Chas looked at him, unsure of what he meant.

"What caused the accident?"

"I was going too fast."

"I saw your truck. It's obliterated."

Chas laughed. It was an odd way of putting it, carefully articulated with an uncommon accent. "Yup. And I only carry liability. My truck is ruined and I'm screwed."

Nuri didn't laugh.

Chas went quiet, certain that Nuri didn't have insurance for his home either.

As they turned into the driveway, Chas sat up to see if Mattie was awake. It was after ten. He wished he'd called from the hospital to let her know he was okay, especially after not coming in the night before. The lights were on, but he couldn't see her. He sat back and surveyed the meadow for the dark bodies of his sheep.

145

Nuri slowed and looked past Chas, through the passenger window. "Lambs yet?"

"A few."

Nuri craned to see them in the darkness. "You have got everything a man could want here."

Chas gave him a sideways glance. He couldn't recall ever being envied for what he had. And this—this was a muddy, shitty sheep ranch. He had more work than a man could finish in a lifetime, and that was just to stay even. Not to mention a decaying father, who haunted the only nurse willing to take care of him. What did he have that *any* man would want?

Nuri didn't turn off the ignition, but waited as Chas climbed out.

Chas thanked him again, and again offered him some lamb, which Nuri declined. Chas stood on the porch and waved another thank you at the retreating taillights before going inside.

Mattie sat on the sofa, her face stern. He believed she was angry and his very soul rebelled at the idea. What right did she have to place demands on him? But immediately she got to her feet.

"Oh, God. What happened?"

"I'm okay," he said, turning to take his boots off. The right boot fell to the floor, but he had trouble standing to take the left boot off.

"Here, sit down," she said, sliding under his shoulder and leading him to the sofa. "What happened?"

"Wreck," he said, easing down. He suddenly wanted to sleep more than anything in the world. Didn't care about his other boot, or recounting the accident for Mattie. "Think you can git me a pillow? And a blanket maybe?"

She'd crouched to pull his boot off, and watched him slide horizontal, his feet still flat on the floor. "Okay," she said and gently lifted his feet onto the sofa.

Chas dozed, but awoke as Mattie pulled his head forward and slid a pillow under his neck. She ran her fingers over his forehead, lingering near his bandaged wound, then conducted a silent assessment with her eyes. "Do you want to change out of that bloody shirt?"

Chas looked up from behind heavy lids, hearing, but not comprehending her words. When he didn't respond, she unfolded the blanket and draped it over him.

Sheriff Edelson stood along the shoulder of Highway 14, his jacket collar buttoned against the icy morning wind, and wondered how Chas had survived the accident. And where he was now and who had helped him. A wrecking truck dragged the vehicle up the embankment, scraping it over jagged boulders, sending sparks dancing downriver on the breeze. Was it really an accident? Attempted suicide, perhaps? That didn't seem likely. Or could someone hate Chas McPherson enough to try to kill him?

He hiked back to his patrol car and turned the heat on. Then he jotted down the mile marker, the condition of the truck, the absence of Chas.

As he started back to Sweetwater he passed the Teleghanis' new place. It was just a few miles from the accident, and that bothered him. What were the odds of an arson suspect wrecking his truck so near the new home of the victims? He pulled to the shoulder and waited for a pickup to pass him, then did a 180 and headed back. He coasted into the Teleghanis' driveway and killed the engine. The van was not there, but a light glowed in the kitchen window, which was covered over with a plastic sheet to keep out the drafts. He surveyed the sagging roof. The crumbling chimney. An undeniable step down from the less than luxurious house that had burned to the ground.

He'd only spoken with Mrs. Teleghani once, when he questioned her about the fire. The intensity of her emotions

147

had rendered her unintelligible, which was compounded by her unfamiliar accent. He stepped up to the door and knocked.

It took a long while for her to answer the door, and she stood back startled by his presence. "What is wrong?" She looked past him, as if to see why he was there.

"Nothing, ma'am. Nothing is wrong." He shifted on his feet, feeling the porch groan beneath him, and wondered if it would fail. "There was an accident up the road. Someone drove into the river."

"I know," she said curtly. "Chas McPherson."

He waited for her to go on. Her words were taut. Not an ounce of forgiveness in them.

"He comes to us for help. Can you imagine?"

"He came here?" He paused to look over his shoulder at the road. It made some sense—being the only home out there for a long stretch.

She huffed. "What more will we suffer from this man? He finds us wherever we are."

Edelson turned back to her. "Where is he now?"

"My husband took him to hospital. He was talking nonsense, laughing like a crazy man."

"Laughing?"

She nodded.

"It's a long drive to the hospital. Did he leave him there?"

"No, Nuri took him home." She shook her head in disgust. "He does not believe Mr. McPherson burned our house down. He believes he is a victim. Like us."

"You don't?"

"I don't know what to believe."

"Your husband told me Chas gave you a lamb. Do you know if that's true?" He wished he'd phrased his question differently. He was asking her to contradict her husband, and he didn't believe she would.

"Hinkler believes it was a trick to throw you off, Sheriff."

"Hinkler?"

"The man who owns the grocery store." She stared at him as if he must be stupid not to know who Hinkler was.

Edelson nodded. "Thanks for your time. I appreciate it."

When Chas awoke, he found Mattie asleep in his chair with her legs draped over the armrest. His father's blanket was wrapped around her shoulders, but her feet were bare. He imagined they were cold, wanted to stoke the fire, but more than that he wanted to get up and touch her hair. He wondered why she'd slept in the chair all night. He touched the bandage on his throbbing forehead, could feel where it'd been peeled back, a corner that wouldn't stick. Had she done that? Then he had a vague, disquieting recollection of her waiting for him on the sofa, like an angry wife. And like an avalanche on a quiet mountain morning, the whole of yesterday crashed back–the interchange with Dean, the revelation about Hinkler, his pickup on its roof, Nuri Teleghani . . . his rescuer–annoyance, anger, frustration.

He sat up gingerly and examined his injuries. Broken arm, sprained ankle, stitched head. His shirt stank like a dead animal. He pulled it off and threw it in a heap on the floor. After hobbling to the bathroom, he brewed some coffee, hopping around on one foot. He thought about his sheep, hungry, waiting, and wondered about his lead ewe. Almost worried about her.

"What are you doing?" Mattie asked, standing in the doorway, her hair touseled, her eyes still full of sleep. "Go lay down. I'll take care of the coffee."

"You gonna take care my sheep, too?"

She frowned, then nodded. "Yeah, I guess I'll have to."

He laughed to himself. "I don't think so."

"I can do it," she said, rubbing the back of her neck. She tipped her chin back as if working the kink out.

"I might let ya help, I guess."

149

She shook her head and disappeared into the living room.

Chas heard her stoking the fire, adding logs, adjusting the flue. She'd become quite masterful at the task. Maybe she *could* feed his sheep. It wasn't out of the realm of possibility. But the vision of her up to her knees in sheep shit depressed him. He hoped she'd never have to feed sheep for living.

Mattie returned and examined his wounds. She ran her hand over his shoulder. "That's some bruise you've got started."

He shivered, as if she'd swept a feather across his skin, and closed his eyes.

"How's your head?" She touched the bandage.

He flinched.

"I'm not gonna hurt you."

He tipped his head back a little as she peeled a corner of the bandage up. She stood so close. She smelled like a mossy brook—an earthy scent that was deeply pleasing. "How many stitches?"

"Eight. Looks like you were lucky you didn't bash your brains out."

"Probably hurt less right now if I had."

"What about your truck?"

"Totaled. Probably get fined for leaving it in the river."

"Who helped you?"

He pushed on the bandage, trying to get it to stick in place. "I walked to the Teleghanis' house. Of all the people in the world, I had to ask *them* for help."

"How'd the wreck happen?"

"You just gonna ask questions, or you gonna get us some coffee?"

She pressed the bandage down again before getting the cups, but it curled up.

"I was pissed off and driving too fast. Ruark closed my account at the farm store."

She glanced over her shoulder. "What are you going to do now?"

"'Bout what?"

"Well . . . my car's dead and yours is totaled."

"Jenny."

"Who?" She brought the coffee to the table.

"Happy New Year," he said, lifting his cup to her. "We're off to a great start."

Chas limped around to the side of the barn that faced away from the house, where a massive sliding door hung on a rusty metal track. He gripped the handle and leaned his weight into it. The track was too long unused; the door didn't budge. He rocked it back and forth, then gave it another shove, pressing his jaw against the splintery wood, heaving it open. Dirt and diesel odors burst through the opening, and he peered inside. Dust particles danced in the still air. He sat down to rest on an empty oil drum lying on its side.

As his eyes adjusted to the dim light, he took inventory of the room that had been his father's workroom. A tall, sturdy workbench stood along the wall, cluttered with tools and spare parts. A carburetor from a 1967 Cougar was suspended in a vise—suspended in time. Chas immediately recognized it; it was from his car. He and his father never did fix it. But the two of them spent hours trying. He finally bought a rebuilt carburetor and sold the Cougar. He missed it a little—its masculine V8 power packed beneath a sleek white, feminine body. It was the only vehicle he had ever owned that wasn't a truck. Sarah had loved it. She squealed with delight when he revved the engine. He got up and twirled the pin on the vise, releasing the dirty carburetor from its prison. He rolled it over in his hand—dry now, dead—and dropped it onto the workbench with a heavy thud that rattled the graveyard of tools.

He wasted no more time looking for memories in the

piles of trash his father had kept, but focused on his purpose. He worked his way to the back, past a dirty red tractor, to the tarp–covered vehicle next to it. He yanked the corner of the dusty green cover, unveiling a lovingly restored '51 Chevy pickup. Canary yellow. Its paint still glowed. He brushed his hand across the chrome grill and followed a rounded fender back to the driver's door.

"Hello, Jenny," he whispered reverently. He opened the door with a squeak, and stepped up on the running board. Mice had nested in the upholstery, scattering stuffing over the floorboards. Their malodorous scent burned his nostrils. He brushed his hand across the seat and found the hole. Wished he had the rat poison he'd promised Mattie.

He slid behind the wheel and examined the dashboard. It was shiny black and simple; gas gauge, speedometer, battery, oil. No radio, no tachometer. Nothing electronic or fancy. He laid his hand on the stick shift. "Four on the floor," he said aloud. Then leaned down and pushed open the vent lever under the dash. A small rectangular vent popped up on the hood. Simplicity at its finest, he thought. Who needs a fan when you've got the open road?

Chas stepped out of the truck and examined the tires, gone flat from sitting. And set about, slowly in his handicapped condition, to bring Jenny alive. Oil, lube, antifreeze. Charged the battery. All the care she required. He was meticulous and methodical, just as his father would have been. As his father had taught him to be.

It was nearly one o'clock when he filled the tires, taking note that two needed replacing. He climbed up into the cab again. The key was in the ignition, just where his father had left it. He turned it to the "on" position, then kicked the seat stuffing away from the starter protruding from the floor like a giant caterpillar. He pressed his right heel against the gas pedal, sending a painful spasm through his calf, but he ignored it and pressed down on the starter with his toes.

Jenny chugged a few times and fell silent. He pulled back on the choke and tried again, his ankle aching. On the third try, she sputtered to life, coughing, then settling into a rhythmic purr. Chas let out a whoop of excitement.

13

SHERIFF EDELSON FOUND CHAS, bruised and bandaged, in his barn, feeding his sheep. "Looks like some work for a man in your condition," he said as he approached.

Chas heaved a third of a bale of hay through the open barn window with one arm. He didn't turn to look at Edelson, but bent and scooped oats into a bucket. "Don't matter what condition I'm in. Still gotta feed 'em."

"I guess that's why I never fancied becoming a farmer."

Chas stopped and faced the sheriff. "Can I help you?"

"Seeing you on your feet walking around is a good start. Found your truck this morning."

Chas grunted.

"What happened?"

"Nothin'."

"Pretty smashed up nothing." Edelson wondered if this man was ever agreeable.

"If you think I was drinkin', I wasn't." Chas went back to scooping oats.

"I never said that." The sheriff pulled his hat off and scratched his head. *Let's try again.* "I have to file a report. It would be helpful if you'd give me the details."

"There aren't any details to give. Ruark closed my

account and I was on my way to Lewiston. I need vaccine. I've got lambs comin'." Chas leaned out the window and poured the oats over the hay. "I mighta been goin' a little fast. I was pretty pissed off."

"Trouble with your bills?" Edelson hoped he wasn't prying too much.

"Shit! I haven't got two pennies to scrape together to start a fire. But somehow . . . somehow, I always manage to pay my bills. And Ruark's been carrying half the town for a year or better, but he closes my account. Says he's worried I might not pay. Thinks you're gonna haul me off to jail."

"Ruark, you say?" Edelson considered the shopkeeper, remembering that he'd been among the first to suggest that Chas had burned the Teleghanis' home. Ruark hadn't claimed to have seen him do it, but when Edelson stopped by his store to pick up dog food, the merchant intimated Chas was the most likely suspect.

"Ruark yesterday, Hinkler before that."

"You're not a very popular man I'm coming to find." He guessed Chas already knew his standing in the community, but he was curious what the man thought of it.

Chas limped past the sheriff and out of the barn. "You got enough for your report?"

Sheriff Edelson followed him out into the light. His eyes went to the walnut trees, then the firs on the ridge. "I guess so." He turned and left, still wondering if Chas cared a whit about what the town folk thought of him, or if he was simply angry because they'd inconvenienced him.

Chas had finished his lunch, but sat at the table drinking a cup of coffee.

"Here, I brought some clean clothes down for you," Mattie said, knowing he always showered after feeding his sheep, before going to town. Not that he could go to town without a car.

Chas frowned at the stack of clothes, his underwear on top, in plain view.

"I thought I'd save you a trip upstairs."

He pulled the shirt out and laid it on top to cover his boxer shorts. "You know how to cut hair?"

"No."

"It can't be that hard."

She looked over her shoulder at him from where she stood at the sink. "No."

"Feel like trying?"

"Feel like walking around looking like a dork?"

"Can't be that hard."

She shrugged. "As long as you don't get mad if it doesn't turn out."

"Can ya cut it like my dad's?"

Her eyebrows went up. He looked so much like his father already. They'd be twins from different generations. "I already told you, I don't know how."

"I'll git the scissors."

"Wash your hair first. It needs to be wet; I know that much."

As Chas showered, Mattie spoon-fed his father in the kitchen. He choked and sputtered on the applesauce, and she added water to it. The fruit was like soup, and she spooned it into the old man slowly, giving it time to roll to the back of his throat. He needed a feeding tube really, but she didn't know how she'd get him back to the doctor again. Secretly she hoped nature would take its course with Mr. McPherson and soon, but then what would happen to her? Where would she go?

When he had finished sputtering and choking, she wheeled him into the living room to look out the window and it was there she saw the truck sitting in the driveway. For a moment she thought she'd imagined it. It was so out of place there in the dirty snow, like a bright yellow dahlia blooming in the dead of winter.

"Wow, where'd he get that?" She turned to Mr. McPherson. His eyes were locked urgently on the yellow truck, his mouth sliding open. "Is that yours?" she asked, surprised by this small, but significant movement of his mouth. He claimed ownership with every ounce of his presence.

Chas came and stood next to his father. "Ain't she still just the prettiest thing, Dad?"

"Where'd that come from?" Mattie asked.

"That's Jenny. Dad's pride and joy. Ain't been outta the barn since . . . I don't know when."

Mattie looked at the old man. "Look at him. He recognizes it."

Chas glanced at his father, but shook his head. "You gonna cut my hair?"

"Just promise you won't be mad if it doesn't turn out. I told you I don't know how to cut hair."

"Can't be that hard."

"Promise me."

"All right, I promise."

When Mattie stood back and looked at Chas, a hot ripple went up her spine like she'd licked a nine-volt battery. He *was* his father.

Chas looked in the mirror and suffered a pang of nausea. She does too know how to cut hair, he thought. The haircut was as good as any he'd gotten at the barber. He went to the hall closet and took out his father's field jacket. It was a pale khaki color with big brown buttons, green corduroy cuffs and collar, and a brown plaid lining. His father had never gone to town without it. It was his "preachin" coat, as he liked to call it, priding himself that as ministers around the world were donning their blue and gray suits, he wore a farmer's garb. Kept him in touch with his flock, or so he imagined. Chas pulled the jacket on and adjusted the sleeves. The two of them were the same size, at least had been until Parkinson's ravaged his father's body.

"I can't tell you how much you look like your father," Mattie said with haunted eyes and a clenched jaw.

"I know," he said grimly. "That was my intent."

Chas parked Jenny outside Hinkler's Market, dead center in front of the door. He rolled the window down, despite the cold, but didn't get out. With a thermos of coffee on the seat next to him, he picked up a book about native American religious practices he'd been thinking about reading for more than a decade. He sat back to enjoy the afternoon convalescing in his father's pickup, basking in the charm of 1880s Sweetwater.

The checkout clerk came to the front window to get a better look, then disappeared again. Chas watched as each car that pulled up sat idle a moment, then pulled away again. It was as if no one was willing to walk past Franklin McPherson—ghost or not—sitting in front of the market. Mrs. Watson tottered down the sidewalk, nearsighted and severely bent in the shoulders. When she drew up alongside the bright yellow pickup she took notice of it, her eyes wide with sudden understanding. Chas laughed out loud when she finally found his face. She stood visibly shaken, her mouth agape, her wrinkled lip trembling with age or fright, or both. She turned on her heels as quickly as her arthritic bones would allow and started back in the direction from which she came. Chas saw to it that Hinkler's Market did no business that day.

It was well past dark when Chas got home. He parked Jenny in front of the barn and limped down the walkway along the jugs to check his lead ewe. Still no lamb. In all his years he'd never been so far wrong guessing a lambing date. "What's keeping you, old girl? You cook it any longer it'll kill ya coming out." He ran the back of his fingers down her face, then gave her an extra scoop of grain. She sniffed it, but didn't eat. Good sign, he thought. She's going into labor. He watched for a time, making sure she was chewing her cud, wasn't showing signs of toxemia, then limped back to the house.

"Man, you look more like your dad than your dad does," Mattie said with a shudder when he came in.

He smiled. "That's what the folks at Hinkler's thought too."

She sipped from a large blue cup, practically sucking on the rim.

"Funny, not a single one of 'em wanted to walk past me. Afraid I might read their sins, I guess." He gave a hoarse laugh at the remembrance.

"What did you do?" She was staring at him, puzzled.

"Nothin'. Just spent the afternoon readin' a book and drinkin' coffee." He grinned. "Sittin' out front of the store in Jenny."

A slow smile broke across her face. "He get any customers?"

Chas shook his head. "Not a one. If I keep this up, I just might put him outta business."

"You are pure evil, Chas McPherson."

"Indeed I am."

"Can I get you a whiskey?"

He thought about it a moment. He had told himself he was going to give it up after waking up in the barn, but as long as she was offering, what the hell? "That'd be all right I guess. Thanks. Have one, too?"

"Maybe one."

As Chas relaxed with his drink, Mattie put supper on the table: scalloped potatoes with ham, green beans on the side.

"When you gonna stop buying all this meat and use the lamb in the freezer?"

"I wondered when you were going to ask that. You know, I never really acquired a taste for lamb."

"Ya ever had a blackbelly? They're mild, tender—not like woollies."

"You talk about those sheep like they're . . . I don't know. Like they're sacred or something."

Chas leaned back and put his ankle up on the chair next to him, tilting his head to the side. "I know some folks subscribe to the whole ant, grasshopper theory of life. Not me."

"What?" She joined him at the table.

"You know, the old tale of the grasshopper that doesn't do a damn thing, mooches off the ant that's busting his ass all summer storing up food for the winter. We're all supposed to be like the ant."

"I've never heard it quite that way before."

"I subscribe to the way of the blackbelly."

"What the hell are you talking about?"

"Blackbellies—they're the path of least resistance. Well, in the sheep ranching world anyhow. Think 'bout it. No shearing, hardy. Good lambers—the one in the stanchion notwithstanding. Independent. And they have a mild, tender flavor—even when they're old. I ain't a grasshopper. But I sure as hell ain't no ant." He swallowed the last of the whiskey in his glass. He could already feel the effects of it, and wondered if his injuries were more serious than he'd first believed. He was fatigued, but noticed that Mattie was considering his words seriously.

Mattie held her gaze on him, pondering. Then she reached up and pulled the barrette from her hair, letting it cascade down over her shoulders. She ran her fingers through it and pulled it away from her face. "I guess that was rude, to let my hair down at the dinner table," she said. "Sorry."

Chas stared at the lustrous locks as they danced across her bosom.

"How's supper?"

He looked down at his plate, then back at her hair and nodded, still unable to find his words. He loved her hair, couldn't see anything else.

She stood and leaned across the table to pour him another drink. Her shirt gaped, giving him a fine view of her round breasts tucked up tight to her chest by a pale pink brassiere. She sat down again and brushed her fingers across his knee. "How's your ankle?"

Chas's hand flew up and snapped hold of her wrist. "You're teasing me," he said with a breathy voice. "Don't tease me." He felt his eyes go hot.

Mattie yelped. He tightened his hand around her wrist. She pulled; he pulled back. "I didn't mean to," she pleaded.

He pulled again, hard, dragging her out of her chair.

She cried out, "No, Chas! Please, stop!"

As if jolted awake, he saw her fear. She wasn't one of those women after all. And he understood how depraved he'd become—a man who had to pay for affection. Affection on his terms, without consideration for the one who would render it. He had become an animal. "I'm sorry," he said, standing abruptly, sending his chair clattering to the floor. "I'm sorry." He turned and started for the stairs.

Mattie massaged her wrist, spoke after him. "Wait," she said. "Don't go."

He paused, his back to her.

"I wasn't exactly teasing you. I was . . . trying to attract you."

"You did that a long time ago." Chas almost blushed. What in God's name had he said?

She didn't seem to mind. "Then stay."

She picked up his chair. He hesitated, staring at it, then sat down. She put her hands gently to his face, and he pulled her down on his lap. He gripped her shoulders, hard at first, then eased off, reminding himself to be gentle. She was a woman, not a whore. A real woman he'd often imagined making love to.

She kissed him tentatively. He watched her red lips as she pulled away, then chased after them with his own. She tasted warm and spicy, and he explored her mouth with his tongue. She pulled back and covered his forehead with dainty kisses. She moved down the bridge of his nose, across his eyelids, and to each of his ears. He swelled beneath her, wanting to open his jeans. Imagined his cock in her hand, in her mouth. He pushed up her shirt and slid his fingers under her bra, releasing her breasts, then dragged her top hastily over her head. She put her hands up, covering herself.

"Let me see," he whispered.

She dropped her hands to her waist, shy and self-conscious. That excited him, and he ran his fingers over her white skin. He sucked her swollen nipple into his mouth, rolling his tongue and flicking it softly. When he released it, blue veins pulsed around it like an aura. She stood and led him up the stairs. Hesitating between bedrooms, Chas guided her to his.

He stripped his clothes off, then hers, slowly taking time to taste her skin and explore her mysterious curves and silky skin. She closed her eyes as he roamed her body with his fingers. She gave him time. He liked that. Finally, she ran her hand up his stiff penis and he moaned almost painfully. She pressed him back against the bed and crawled over him, kissing his stomach and chest, letting her breasts fall against his member. He arched his back, grinding against her breastbone. She sat back on her haunches and slid her mouth over his penis, sucking hard. He closed his eyes, unable to fathom how he deserved this blessing after such a long while. He couldn't hold himself, bursting in her mouth with the urgency of an adolescent boy experiencing his first time.

Mattie lay against Chas's side, their limbs entwined. His cast pressed heavy against her ribs. He was snoring. There was something about his mischievous mind that evening that had made him suddenly irresistible. He'd taken matters into his own hands at last. With quiet, calculated action. He wasn't so much a coward after all.

She thought of his father and knew she had to get up again. The sex had been somewhat of a disappointment, but she imagined it was circumstance. She'd experienced enough of Chas to believe it could be better. Thought him off to a good start, despite her bruised wrist. His warmth felt good now, and she didn't want to let it go just yet. She wondered if she would experience it again. He was so difficult to predict. She imagined it was just as likely he'd be cold to her in the morning.

She gently pulled away, trying not to wake him. He tightened his hold. "I'll be back," she whispered. She stood a moment watching him. He seemed so peaceful, more so than she'd imagined he could be–the tortured sort of man he was. And she took a little credit for his childlike slumber.

Downstairs, she stood outside the old man's bedroom. She could feel him, as if he were standing behind her, with her. His presence was as strong as a starving piranha. He had called her a whore. She could hear him as clearly as if he were speaking. She found an undeniable liberation in accepting the truth. It was as Chas had said, there was no point in getting her gear on–but not because the mountain was too tall. That's where Chas was wrong. Because climbing the mountain was pointless, even if she could reach the top.

She ran her tongue across her lips–the lips she'd parted over Chas's penis–and entered his father's room. The helpless old man stared up at her, awake and knowing. As she went to work, she told him what she'd done in explicit detail. When finished, she sat down next to him on the bed.

"I imagine having your gift is like becoming a vampire," she told him. "You're probably not the sort to read that kind of stuff, but I am. And I think feeding on the sins of others is like joining the dead, understanding beyond any doubt that you're damned, and waiting with shameless anticipation for the next opportunity to suck the very life from someone." Mattie ran the tip of her tongue over the point of her right canine tooth. "My crimes feed you, so I guess I'm damned, too."

Chas awoke with an erection. Mattie's skin was moist where she lay against him, nearly the full length of him, naked. He thought back on the night and suffered a mild embarrassment for not containing himself. He ran his hand over her head, smoothing her hair. She had a sweet, floral scent. He kissed her temple, bringing her closer to awakening. She moaned and turned onto her side, facing him, her breasts against his chest. He rolled her under him in a smooth, quick movement. She opened her eyes, startled. They glistened in the darkness. He smothered her mouth with his as he forced her legs apart with his knee. She reached a hand to guide him into her velvety pocket.

The barn was cold. The temperature had dropped into the teens. Chas's breath puffed out ahead of him as he limped down the hallway, making his rounds, checking his sheep. He thought of Mattie as he went, shooting an occasional glance over his shoulder toward the house, as if he could see her. He had an urgent burn to go back and make love to her again. She'd seduced him. Blatantly! He thought of her in the kitchen, brewing coffee and humming softly, her hair all tangled and her cheeks flushed after their early morning tryst. His crotch rose, a painful bulge of suddenly over-exercised muscle. He had to get a hold on his mind. He couldn't allow her to control him like this. He spit in the walkway, as if to rid himself of her enchantment.

He looked in on his lead ewe. And his heart skipped. She

lay in a round lump of brown hair, a white eye turned toward the ceiling. Her mouth gaped, tongue crusted with straw. The other end, a half–emerged lamb–back legs protruding. Both dead. He sucked back something near to grief, and closed his eyes. *Why the hell didn't I check her again last night?* He turned from the ewe's tortured death, and leaned against the pen, staring at the floor. It was dotted with ice circles from the leaky roof, like so many lily pads on a muddy pond. "Goddamn it," he breathed, quietly. *"Goddamn it!"*

After dragging the carcasses out of the barn and digging a hole in the frozen earth with his tractor, Chas returned to the house. He kicked his boots off outside and quietly closed the door behind him. He hoped to sneak a thermos of coffee out without Mattie hearing him, then head for town. She was in his father's room, talking again, the way she had when she first arrived. He paused and listened as she explained, in rich detail, the clothing styles of sixteenth-century Italian nobility. Chas wrinkled his brow, wondering where the hell she had learned that. Imagined his father bored out of his mind–had he been able to understand her. He slipped into the kitchen and filled his thermos, then paused again on his way out. She was talking of vampires now. He shook his head, baffled. There was so much about her he couldn't comprehend.

14

SHERIFF EDELSON LEANED ON HIS ELBOWS, his hands pressed against his temples. Pale winter sunlight streamed through the dirty office window. The phone had rung constantly for two days. Chas McPherson, or Franklin–the reports were split down the middle–was sitting in front of Hinkler's, terrorizing shoppers with his presence. The phone rang again, it was the inside line Lorraine used after screening his calls. "Yeah?"

"Sheriff, Bob Hinkler's on the phone. He's real hot."

"Put him through," he said with a sigh.

"Sheriff? This is Hinkler."

"Let me guess, Chas McPherson is sitting in front of your store again."

"You think this is some kind of joke?"

"No . . . no, I don't. But it's not against the law either. He's parked on a public street."

"He's chasing off my customers!"

"What exactly is he doing?"

"Not a damn thing! Drinking coffee and reading a book."

"It's perfectly legal, Mr. Hinkler. I can't do anything about it."

"Some goddamn sheriff you are! See if you get reelected!" Hinkler slammed the phone down.

The sheriff sat back, twisting a pencil in his fingers until it snapped in two. Fine slivers of yellow paint littered his uniform. "Assuming I run," he said aloud. "Bunch of lunatics." He stood and got his jacket.

His secretary met him at the door. "You leavin', Sheriff?"

"Thought I'd go down and see if I can reason with him."

"Hinkler?"

"McPherson."

She snorted, then turned to go.

He thought a moment and called her back. "Tell me again why everyone hates this guy so much."

She looked at her watch, as if there wasn't enough time in the world to explain it. She cocked her hip to one side, and said, "It ain't really Chas. It's his father. Well . . . maybe it's both of 'em."

He listened.

"See, Preacher McPherson has this . . . power. He can see people's sins."

"C'mon, you expect me to believe that? Like he's some kind of wizard or something? He can't see people's sins."

"Oh, yes he can!" Her eyebrows arched in a challenge. "He told everybody my mother was having an affair. My dad left because of it. Us kids never saw him again."

He stared at her in disbelief.

"It's true. Ask anyone."

"*Was* your mom having an affair?"

She jutted her chin out. "Yeah. But that ain't the point."

"Could it be Mr. McPherson came on this information in the usual manner? He saw, or heard?"

She blew out her breath, her patience gone. "Sheriff, he had a meeting in the park–a 'come to Jesus' meeting. And he called people up one at a time, announcing their sins to *every-body*. There's no way he could know all those things about all those people. The only one that didn't confess to his sins was Hinkler. He never admitted that he cheated anybody, not in all these years. But everybody knows he did, or preacher McPherson wouldn't have said he did."

Sheriff Edelson stood back a little, regarding her carefully. "What did McPherson say Hinkler did?"

She waved her hand in the air. "I can't remember it all, just that Hinkler was lying and cheating people."

He frowned.

"Yeah, go ahead and try to reason with him," she said, walking away. "Take my advice, though, and say your prayers before you go. Ask God for forgiveness, for whatever you done."

"Even if the old man could know people's sins, this is Chas, not his father."

She turned and faced him again. "You seen him lately?"

He shook his head.

She nodded once, as if she'd made her point, and disappeared down the hall.

Sheriff Edelson shook his head. *Lunatics. They're all a bunch of lunatics.*

Edelson pulled up behind the shiny, yellow pickup, and called in the expired license plate to confirm the truck wasn't stolen. He got out and approached the driver's door.

Chas rolled the window down. "Mornin', Sheriff."

"Mr. McPherson." Edelson looked the vehicle up and down. "New truck?"

"Belongs to my dad. I'd git out, but I've got a sprained ankle, you know." He held his arm up. "Broken wrist too."

"Any particular reason for sitting in front of Hinkler's Market?" The sheriff pointed at the store with the brim of his hat. Bob Hinkler stood in the window with his arms across his chest.

"Ain't it a nice spot to recuperate? I like Sweetwater. It's a pretty little town." Chas poured himself a cup of coffee. "Can't do much work right now. Got a nurse living in my house.

Thought I'd come down here and enjoy the scenery. Read a little." He looked up at the Sheriff. "That's okay, ain't it?"

"Not against the law."

"Didn't think so."

"Getting some complaints, though."

"'Bout what?"

"Some folks think you're Franklin."

Chas gave the sheriff a wide grin. "I do resemble him, don't I?"

"Wouldn't know." *Lunatic.* "Guess your dad has a reputation with the locals."

"Yeah. Guess he does." Chas squinted at him. "Ain't against the law for a man to look like his dad is it? I git mixed up 'bout what's legal and what's not these days. Ever since finding out that refusing to sign petitions and parking in front of the school can git a man in trouble."

Sheriff Edelson suppressed a smile. "Anything ever happen between your father and Bob Hinkler? I mean, I heard a rumor this morning your dad accused him of cheating people."

Chas shrugged. "He accused a lotta people of a lotta things. He was the preacher after all."

"You wouldn't be sitting out here to scare people away, would you?" Edelson watched Chas carefully, but knew the answer.

"No . . . no, I'm just enjoying the view. It's a pretty little town, like I said."

"Might I persuade you to park somewhere else? Give Hinkler some peace of mind you're not deliberately scaring away his customers?"

Chas shook his head. "I don't think so, Sheriff. See, I have a sprained ankle. I thought it would be best to sit in front of the store . . . in case I need something, you know." Chas gazed up at him, innocently.

"Your plates are expired."

169

"Hmm. It's a long way to Salmon City for a man in my condition."

"You've got ten days. Then I'm gonna write you up."

"Thanks, Sheriff. I'll git it taken care of."

Edelson didn't look at Hinkler as he walked back to his patrol car. Hinkler was a powerful man in Sweetwater, and Edelson knew his threat was real. He wouldn't get reelected if he didn't take care of Chas McPherson. But he didn't take kindly to threats, either. Would've written another man up for expired plates.

Chas recognized the rich aroma of roasted lamb when he got home. It greeted him like an old friend. Mattie worked in the kitchen, her domain in his house, her hair down, flowing and sleek. He paused in the doorway, looking at the dark fall shimmering down her back. His senses were alive, his stomach and lower regions aching for fulfillment. He wondered if her spell would be so potent without all that lovely hair. Wondered if she'd be so flavorful steeped in the aroma of another dish. He shook his head and went to the sink to wash up.

She smiled at him with the sweetness of new spring grass.

He turned away.

"Hungry?"

"Uh-huh." He went to the table.

She followed and draped her arms around his neck. "Where'd you take off to this afternoon?"

He closed his eyes. "Hinkler's."

"Tell him to wait his turn." She nuzzled his neck.

Chas groaned and struggled to keep his mind about him. She'd caught him in a web, and he couldn't shake himself free. The harder he struggled, the more tightly bound he became. "Mattie," he rasped. "You gonna feed me?"

"Mmm," she breathed in his ear. "I'll feed you."

"I mean supper," he struggled. Her lips were against his cheek. Warm. Wet.

She released him and sighed. "Okay." She opened the oven door. "I hope I did this right. I've never made lamb before."

"It smells like ya did all right."

After supper, while Mattie washed dishes, Chas went to the barn to check on his sheep. He'd let the ewes with new lambs out into the meadow that morning, and brought in the next few due. He walked along the jugs, assessing each animal, the image of his lead ewe heavy on his mind, filling him with an unwelcome sense of guilt. If he hadn't fallen into Mattie's trap, the ewe would still be alive. He'd have found her in time; he was certain of it. He would have assisted. He would have saved her, if not her lamb. Just as well, he told himself, acutely aware of his shortcoming. A good rancher doesn't get attached to his animals, just like a good dealer doesn't smoke his own crack. It clouds your mind, messes up your priorities.

His father had taught him that. "You git attached to your animals and the next thing you know you're squandering all your profit to keep a sick one alive. You gotta be able to make the hard decisions, Chas. Gotta be able to put a bullet in her head before she costs you more than she's worth." He bent close to Chas's face when he said the words, to make sure his son understood. It was the summer his mother left, and he'd found some small comfort in rubbing the ears of a friendly ewe–a ewe not unlike the one he'd lost that morning.

His father was right, goddamn it! Chas had an intense welling of anger as he remembered his father's words. He stumbled down the aisle, fingertips hot with rage, moving blindly through the barn. He found his way to his father's workroom. In the gray-black dusk, the carburetor from his

'67 Cougar just a hunk of metal among shiny tools. He picked it up and rolled it in his hands. His heavy cast made it awkward, stunting his movement. Stifling him. He threw the carburetor at the tractor, hitting it squarely in the grill. *Gotta be able to put a bullet in her head . . .*

A tortured laugh raked the stillness. Chas turned back to the workbench and fumbled for another object. His fingers found purchase on a heavy crescent wrench, which he heaved over his head at the tractor, too. It missed, clanging against a hubcap hanging on the wall. The hubcap fell with a clatter. He turned for another. A screwdriver. It lanced the tractor's radiator. A terrible pleasure descended on Chas, and he tore the room apart, destroying all he touched. Tools took flight, aimed or not, at all that his father had held dear. The room was in ruin when Chas fell against the dusty, rotting floor, spent.

Had he been a man capable of tears, they would have come. But he lay quiet, his eyes open, looking at the underside of the workbench, passively inventorying the ball bearings and tools it had swallowed up through time. A vantage point wholly new. A mysterious treasure trove of oddities. His eyes came to rest on the smooth, white swell of something round. A skull. He focused. Came alert again. No, it was a baseball. He closed his eyes. When would he stop looking for his mother's bones in the lonely places of his father's ranch?

Mattie massaged the old man's legs, quietly annoyed by Chas's lack of interest in her now. He couldn't keep his hands off her the night before, making love three times before morning light flooded his east-facing bedroom. Pleasing a man in the bedroom was never a talent she'd questioned. Not long after the death of her parents she had discovered food and shelter could always be gotten by soothing the primal desire common in all men. But now things weren't the same. She sagged in new places. She'd noticed the new wrinkles between her breasts. And it struck her as almost hilarious that she'd be rejected by a man like Chas. A troll-like recluse with an appetite for misery. Still, it left her hollow, the idea he wouldn't want her again. She questioned the wisdom of her seduction.

"Your son is so odd," she said to the old man. "You must have done some serious damage to him. How else could he have ended up like this?" She covered Mr. McPherson with a blanket and moved to the chair. "I'm tired of reading this book." She tapped her fingers on his Bible. "It doesn't make any sense to me. We need some good fiction. I'll see what I can find." She observed her patient carefully. The more blatant she'd become in detailing her crimes to him, the more his haunting her seemed to fade. After mulling that over, she got up and turned out the light. "You rest, Mr. McPherson."

In the kitchen, she got Chas's whiskey down, filled her plastic cup and put the bottle away. He'd think it was water.

She'd drunk two good-sized glasses of whiskey and water before Chas returned. He was covered with a fine, silty dust. And he smelled like diesel fuel. "Have you been crawling around under the barn?"

He stood in the middle of the room, looking at her. As if she'd interrupted some important thought. His forehead heavily creased.

"Chas?" His eyes were intent on her, making her apprehensive. Did he suspect she'd been stealing his liquor? "Can I get you a drink?"

He advanced on her so rapidly she had no time to think. He embraced her with the force of a grizzly bear; squeezing her so tight she couldn't get her breath. He seemed about to cry. He pulled her against him and dug his fingers into her hair, his breath huffing against her ear. He mashed his lips to her forehead, as if she were a child who'd wandered off, giving him a scare. His lovemaking was intense—ravenous and vulnerable.

173

Chas listened to Mattie's breathing, calm and quiet in the dark. He pulled her closer, wanting to pull her inside him and keep her there. It puzzled him that she wanted him at all.

It was a sunny day, the third day Chas sat in front of Hinkler's Market. Warm. If he hadn't known better, he might've believed it was spring. Jenny's yellow paint glinted brilliantly under the blue sky. Chas rolled the windows down, letting in a breeze to keep the heat from lulling him to sleep. Mattie had packed two ham sandwiches and a sliced apple—he liked the way she cut his fruit into neat wedges—and she'd filled his thermos with coffee. She'd been quiet and introspective that morning, and he questioned himself for leaving her alone. Half believed he'd find her gone when he got back. But she still didn't have a car.

As Chas bit into a tart apple, Hinkler came to the driver's window. "The sheriff tell you to move your ass from in front of my store?"

Chas hadn't seen him walking up. "No."

"*I'm* telling you then. Get this piece of shit outta here!"

Chas chewed the apple slowly, watching Hinkler. He took his time swallowing before he spoke. "The sheriff told me I could sit here if I wanted. It's a public street. You don't own the street."

"No, but I own the store you're sitting in front of. And I know what you're doing out here. You can't play dumb with me, McPherson. Convalescing, my ass!"

"It's true. See." He held up his broken arm.

"You'll have two of those, you don't get the hell outta here."

"You threatening me, Hinkler?" Chas assessed the old man. He was at least sixty. It was audacious of him to believe he could whip the younger man, even with a broken arm.

Hinkler went red in the face. "I can sight you like a sitting duck from my cash register."

Chas leaned his head out the window to see if Hinkler had a gun with him. "Guess that'd be right stupid. Might put me in my grave, but you'd spend the rest of your life in prison." He frowned. "Prison ain't no place for an old man can't defend himself."

"Seems to me the satisfaction might be worth the hardship."

"Mm," Chas shook his head. "You think that now. But the minute they snapped those cuffs on ya, you'd change your mind. Somebody's just waitin' for a little darlin' like you. Hell of a price to pay for killin' me."

"I'm warning you, McPherson. There's more than one way of getting rid of you."

Chas nodded. "That's a fact. You stop badmouthing me 'round town and harassing my . . . nurse. That'd be one way."

Hinkler scoffed.

"I never did anything to you, Hinkler. And I didn't burn that house down, either." Hinkler stepped back, and Chas caught a flicker of acknowledgement in his eye so fleeting he questioned it. But it was there. "You know who did it, don't you?"

"Yeah, I know who did it, and I'm looking right at the son-of-a-bitch."

Chas spit out the window, landing a slippery wad next to Hinkler's foot. "I think *I'm* lookin' at him."

"I'm warning you, Chas." Hinkler pointed a crooked finger in through the window.

Chas's epiphany on Highway 14 that Hinkler was lying and conspiring against him was confirmed by the menacing deformed digit. His stomach jellied, the way it always did when his father's words scorched true. He turned the key and pressed his foot against the starter. Jenny roared alive. He looked back at Old Man Hinkler one more time. He had no words for him. But he nodded. A knowing nod. A nod designed to come back to chill him in the darkest moments of the night.

15

AFTER SHOWING MATTIE THE PECULIARITIES OF JENNY, Chas
watched the yellow pickup bounce down the driveway and
out of sight. She had asked him to buy some books. But his
confidence was thin when it came to selecting good reading
material, especially for a woman. He'd thought to go with
her, but was so vexed by his encounter with Bob Hinkler the
previous day he wasn't in the mood to go anywhere. So he
reluctantly agreed to send her off with the only vehicle they
had. She'd have to drive to Salmon City. It had the only
bookstore this side of Lewiston.

"Don't worry, she'll be careful with Jenny," he said to his
father. Chas looked at the old man. Mattie had assured him
all his father's needs were taken care of before she left, and
that she'd be back before he needed anything else. He turned
the wheelchair to face him and sat down. His father seemed
older today. His cheeks were more drawn, his eyes sunk
deeper in his head. His wrists curled under, his fingers contracted like talons. Mattie had warned him the massage
wouldn't prevent this. It would only slow it. Seeing this next
stage of deterioration in his once powerful father made
Chas's stomach knot.

"I think Hinkler burnt down the Moslem family's house,

177

Dad." Chas raked his fingers over his head, pulling the curly locks straight and letting them bounce into place again. "I can't describe it, but I saw it in his face." He studied his father's eyes. "God, I wish you could talk. You'd know who did this. You could tell me."

Chas stood again. He knew his father didn't understand, despite what he'd been told. Early on, the doctor assured him Parkinson's patients generally kept their mental faculties to the end, as if that were some consolation. A horrifying concept. Could not imagine his father now, fully aware of all that happened to him but unable to make his thoughts known. It would be the cruelest sort of ending.

"I'm sorry, Dad. I know you don't know. You've taken off to other parts by now. Ain't that right?" He tipped his head back and spoke to the ceiling. "You're probably having a good laugh with God right now, watching me, making sure I fulfill my obligations. This is a test, ain't it? To make sure I honor you to the end, even though you've already left town."

Chas sat down, resigned. "Just when I needed ya the most."

Sheriff Edelson watched from the lobby of the old bank building as Chas McPherson's yellow Chevy rolled past on its way out of town. He recognized the nurse behind the wheel. She was a curiosity. He had meant to run a background check on her after questioning her at Chas's place.

He took a sealed envelope from the counter. *Idaho State Crime Lab* was emblazoned across the upper left corner. He resisted the urge to open it on the spot, instead, turned to Lorraine and said, "Hold my calls." Then he strode down the back hall to his office. He shut the door behind him, increasingly guarded about the information he shared with his secretary. She didn't seem to understand that her position with his office required nonbiased reasoning. She seemed unable

178

to keep her opinions to herself, particularly where Chas McPherson was concerned.

He laid the report out flat on his desk and scanned the information, looking for new data to convict Chas–sheep fiber–anything. He started at the top and carefully read each line. Nothing unusual or incriminating caught his eye. Then, *White cat hair.* His eyebrows went up, and he jotted it down on a yellow post-it note. The next line, *traces of Bacterin-Toxoid.* In parenthesis it said, *Clostriduim Chauvoei-Septicum-Novyi-Sordel-lii-Perfringens.*

"What the hell is that?" he said aloud. He turned the page over and read the lab technician's summary. Bacterin–Toxoid: A vaccine commonly used for sheep and cattle in the prevention of blackleg, malignant edema, black disease, and enterotoxemia.

Maybe McPherson's guilty after all, he thought. The information wasn't exactly a smoking gun, though. Chas wasn't the only rancher in Sweetwater–far from it. But it was something. The sheriff leaned back in his chair and contemplated the lamb skin in Nuri's shed. He wondered again if Chas was so clever he had given the Teleghanis a lamb before burning down their house, like some sort of last supper. It was the common theory among Sweetwater residents, but one Edelson was having difficulty accepting. Was Chas's claim that God favored variety also a ploy? He realized the thought saddened him.

Chas worked the handle of his pitchfork one–handed. The jugs were a foot deep in wet, mucky straw that had begun to turn black with rot. The smell sickened him. He'd never been able to stomach shitty straw left too long. Cleaning the jugs was the one chore he performed faithfully through the years. His broken wrist angered him now. It would take all day to rake the rancid bedding out with one arm. Sweat beaded on his forehead as he worked. He didn't want his barn reeking of rot. Diesel fuel, maybe. Hell, even blood. But not this. It heightened his frustration over Bob Hinkler. Chas knew the man was guilty of burning down the Teleghanis' place or knowing who did, but he hadn't the slightest idea how to prove it. He'd picked up the phone to call the sheriff twice, but put it back as he played the conversation out in his head. It sounded stupid—a gut instinct is all it was. He'd never convince Sheriff Edelson of anything without proof.

Worms wiggled naked and exposed as he cleared layers of stringy, black slime. He'd always marveled at how they got through a concrete floor to find a nest in his animal stalls. He paused and stared at them, then fumbled for an empty Ball Mason jar. He collected a dozen, dropping them into the dusty, web-infested jar, watching them writhe.

He leaned the pitchfork against the jug and limped down the hallway and up two steps to a dry, hazy tack room. Bridles hung along one wall, the leather curled to a brittle gray from years of neglect in the dry climate. A trio of saddles, thick with dust, sat astride lifeless horses of pine. He dragged his index finger across one, cutting a line in the thick dust, and remembered his parents galloping through the meadow—racing. Laughing. His mother always won. His father denied it. She teased him relentlessly about losing to a woman. She had a gray roan that Chas loved. What was its name? Bindy—Rabindranath.

At the back of the room a tangle of fishing poles lay horizontally across a row of small windows. He wondered if Mattie liked fishing. Of course not; she's a city girl. Still, the thought lingered. What if she would go fishing with him?

The idea of fishing suddenly seemed silly. What was he thinking? A waste of time was all it was. But as a younger man he seldom missed a weekend. It helped to clear his mind. And he needed to clear his mind now. In a few short weeks his life had careened out of control. Before he knew it, it wasn't just his father and him anymore, but a woman too. And he was keenly aware that his need for her went beyond what she provided for his father. She inspired ambitions he'd forgotten. But he also knew dreams were nothing more than tricks of the mind, fantasies that happiness could truly be attained. And this woman was nothing more than an intoxicating drink that would leave him empty and sick in the end. He'd lain in bed just that morning drunk on her juices, watching her pull on her blouse, and wondering what it would be like to marry her.

He opened the door and tossed the worms out on the ground.

Chas carried a handful of spiny teasels with him when he returned to the house. He'd wandered up and down the river for most of the afternoon, tossing rocks into the pewter ripples, listening to the dull plunk they made, and surveying the grassy knob on the back parcel where he'd always imagined building a cabin of his own. Plotting out where he'd put the kitchen so he could look out on the river while he drank his morning coffee in the winter. Or where he'd build the deck for evenings listening to the elk whistle. He paused at the door and studied the dead plants in the growing dusk. What if she thinks they're ugly? They looked kind of ugly to him now, in the fading light. She hadn't seen them silhouetted against the pink sky like tiny, space-age towers. She hadn't heard them rustling in the breeze. But he thought a woman who liked plain old pinecones might enjoy teasels too. His mother had made barnyard animals out of them with toothpicks legs and bright felt ears. The pigs were the best—just the right shape for them. He took a nervous breath and opened the door.

Mattie sat on the couch, reading one of her newly acquired books. He wished he'd left the teasels outside. But it was too late now. "Brought ya some flowers," he said. He closed his eyes; they weren't flowers. "You don't have to do anything with 'em . . . I mean . . . if you don't like 'em."

She got to her feet. "They're lovely. What are they?"

He studied her face for signs of deceit. He didn't want to be patronized. Would hate her for that. "What d'ya mean, what are they? They're teasels."

"Teasels?"

"Ain't you ever seen teasels before?"

"No." She collected the rough stalks from him and took them into the bright kitchen light.

He sat at the table and watched as she arranged the dead plants in a tall, glass jar, then filled the bottom with stones. She moved the pinecones to the living room, and placed the teasels in the middle of the table, stood back, and admired her creation.

"Isn't that beautiful?"

He looked at it. It seemed to him like the kind of art a cavewoman might make. He nodded, and guessed he did okay.

Sheriff Edelson leaned against the counter and studied a crosscut illustration of the innards of a horse as he waited to speak to the veterinarian. Next to the horse was a graphic depiction of the stages of a flea's life. More than he cared to know about what lived on his dog—or worse, his wife's cat, which liked to burrow under their bed covers with them.

"Sheriff," Dr. Beck said, drying his hands as he came down the hall behind the reception desk. "What can I do for you?"

"Gathering some information about this," he said, sliding a piece of paper across the counter with Bacterin-Toxoid printed out carefully.

The vet squinted at it. "Common vaccine for livestock," he said, handing it back.

"Would I buy that here if I needed it?"

The vet shook his head. "No. You can get it at any feed store. Ruark carries it."

"I don't need a prescription for this?"

"I wish. I'd be a rich man."

"Thanks, I'll talk to Ruark then."

"Are you thinking of raising some livestock, Sheriff?"

He paused, his hand on the doorknob. "No, just following a lead, that's all."

"Does it have anything to do with that house someone torched a couple of weeks ago."

"Might."

"McPherson's got sheep. He'd use that kind of vaccine."

"He's not the only man with sheep in the area. Or cattle."

"You ask me, he's guilty."

"What makes you say that?"

The vet shrugged. "A hunch."

"You're an educated man, Dr. Beck."

The vet nodded.

"You ever hear of anyone being prosecuted on a hunch?"

"It's not my job to prove it. I can have all the hunches I want."

"Guess so." The sheriff jerked the door open, sending it shuddering on its hinges. When he got to his car, he sat in the parking lot for a few minutes, going over the interchange and wondering if Chas had a single friend in all of Sweetwater.

Chas sat in front of the farm store, reading a newspaper he'd picked up in Salmon City while renewing the registration on his father's pickup and replacing the dry rotted tires. It was a tough choice between Hinkler's and Ruark's. He preferred to torment Hinkler, but something held him back. If the man had burned a house down, Chas reckoned, he shouldn't underestimate him.

He peeked over the top of the paper into the farm store. A few customers had been there when he pulled up, but were gone now and no one else stopped. Dean Ruark paced in the window, glancing frequently at the pickup. Chas knew he didn't have the balls to confront him. Not like Hinkler.

The sheriff pulled up beside him. Chas popped the glove box open and took out the new registration. "Renewed it this morning, Sheriff," he said, holding up the proof.

The sheriff examined the paper, then handed it back. "Get tired of Hinkler's?"

"Not really. Just needed a change of scenery."

He put his hands against Chas's door and leaned in a little. "Well, as long as you're here, mind answering a couple more questions?"

"When have I ever refused to answer your questions, Sheriff?"

Sheriff Edelson pulled a piece of paper from his pocket. "You vaccinate your sheep with bac-teerin tox-oid?"

Chas frowned. "I use eight-way. It might be Bacterin-Toxoid, but I'd have to look at the bottle." He eyed the sheriff. "You gittin' into the sheep business?"

"Hardly."

Chas nodded at Dean, still at the window. "You should ask him. He sells the stuff. Lotta people in Sweetwater who vaccinate with Bacterin-Toxoid. You're lookin' for a needle in a haystack."

The sheriff appeared to think about that, but made no move to leave, or ask more questions.

"Say, Sheriff, you consider anyone like . . . maybe Hinkler?" Chas squinted up at the tall man, trying to read his eyes.

"Consider him for what?"

Chas was quiet a second. *What do you think?* "I ain't the only one who coulda burnt that place down, you know."

"What motive?"

"I haven't got any idea . . . except maybe to set me up."

The sheriff looked up the street at Hinkler's Market, six or seven buildings away on the opposite side of the street. "Hinkler is a well-respected man. That's a pretty big charge you're leveling."

Chas looked down at his broken wrist, the cast now a dirty blue-black to match the bruises beneath. "So what you're sayin' is that it's okay to level a charge like that at me, but not Hinkler because he's an influential man? Did he support your campaign, Sheriff?" He looked up in time to witness a flash of anger in the sheriff's blue eyes.

Sheriff Edelson's jaw flexed. "Do you have a cat?"

Chas sneered. "I hate cats."

The sheriff kept a fierce eye on Chas.

"Ask my nurse. Mice got into the pancake mix."

"Speaking of that nurse—"

"This ain't about my nurse! She doesn't have anything to do with this."

The sheriff took a step back. "As long as she's not an arsonist."

"Not likely."

"You got anything more on Hinkler than a hunch? I'm getting pretty damn tired of hearing about people's hunches," the sheriff said.

Chas thought about it. Psychic premonition is what he had, just like his father. And that wasn't any better than a hunch. "No," he finally said. "And I guess I have more to gain than anyone in pointing fingers at people based on hunches. All the same . . . I got a sense Hinkler has something to do with the burning. He confronted me the other day while I was convalescing. Threatened to shoot me. Said he could sight me from his cash register."

"It's against the law to threaten people," the sheriff said, eyebrows raised. "Why didn't you report it?"

Chas just stared a moment, then went on. "At the risk of sounding like a complete nutball, there was something in his eyes that gave him away. He did it. I know he did."

"Yeah, you sound like a nutball, all right. But God knows you're not alone."

"Glad to hear I've got company." Chas rolled his eyes. He knew the hunches Sheriff Edelson referred to were about him. The story was all over town. Everyone believed he did it. "You have any more questions for me?"

The sheriff lifted his hat and smoothed his hair back, then pulled it down low on his forehead. "No. I'm going to see Mr. Ruark about that vaccine now."

"Nice day, Sheriff."

Edelson ignored him and walked to the store. He was greeted by Dean, ranting and pointing at Chas like a maniac. Chas watched from his pickup, wondering what Bacterin-Toxoid had to do with the Teleghanis' house burning down, and believing he'd found a finger hole in the sheriff's tight façade. A glimpse of doubt.

Mattie rolled the old man onto his side and pulled his nightshirt down over his hips. "You know, Mr. McPherson, I was accused of elder abuse once. Can you believe that? He was about your age. He wouldn't get into the bathtub. The jerk spit on me. Seventy-eight years old and pissed off at me because his kids stuck him in a nursing home." She sat down so she could see his face. Watched for a reaction, but saw none. "It wasn't that bad. He was only bruised."

The old man closed his eyes.

Mattie shook him. "Hey, I'm talking to you."

He opened his eyes again and stared blankly ahead.

"Anyway, the painkillers might've been nice if they'd let me stay on to take care of him."

16

CHAS LOOKED ON AS A PALE LAMB STRUGGLED to stand next to its nervous mother. It was the color of new-cut pine. He reached for it and lifted it to the light, peering at the uniform tan of its underbelly. No markings over the eyes. No black on the neck or ears. Just tan. He returned it to its mother—a first timer—and noted the number on her ear tag: eighty-eight.

Inside, he looked up the parentage of number eighty-eight and made notes about it in his records.

Mattie set a plate of scrambled eggs in front of him and looked over his shoulder at the notebook. "New lamb?"

"Yeah. But it's not marked right. It's all tan, no black any-where on it."

She joined him at the table with a cup of coffee. She sel-dom ate breakfast, herself, a fact that didn't go unnoticed by Chas every morning when she served him.

"Guess I'll castrate it."

She grimaced. "What happened to the one with the twins? She still in the McPherson torture chamber?"

He smiled. "No. They're out with the others now." He dug into the eggs. "Too bad it wasn't the other way around."

"What?"

"The stupid one had nice lambs. The good one had a cull."

"What's a cull?"

"Anything you don't wanna keep. Sick, lame, tan."

"It's not the lamb's fault it's not marked right . . . or the mother's."

He shrugged.

Her eyes roamed Chas's face. "Maybe you're not marked right." Her eyebrows arched. "I mean, it *is* all in the eye of the beholder."

"Yup." He nodded and eyed her back. "Maybe we should check to make sure *you're* marked right."

"And if I'm not?"

"Might have to eat ya."

"Yeah, well if *you're* not, we might have to castrate *you*."

"Hey, now—" He reached for her.

She shrieked and jumped out of her chair.

"C'mon, let's check," he said, chasing her upstairs.

Sheriff Edelson parked several hundred yards from Hinkler's Market and watched as the merchant opened his store for the day. He'd taken to running the place himself, since Chas McPherson began sitting out front. Once Hinkler was out of sight the sheriff turned his attention to a list Dean Ruark had given him. Everyone who'd purchased Bacterin-Toxoid in the last two years. There were a dozen names, Chas McPherson at the top in deliberately bold letters. He ran his finger down the paper: Robert Van DeHey, Kip Martin, Car Stevens, Albert Minot . . . the list went on. Most of these people he'd encountered at least once in the two years he'd served as sheriff. But some he only knew through their teenage children who boarded at the Grand Hotel during the school year, where he broke up underage parties and fist fights. Old Idaho families from the back country with kids too old for home-schooling, sent off to the city to finish or quit. Kids accustomed to one trip out in the spring, another in the fall, suddenly thrust into the world on their own. An almost legendary existence, and a rite of passage, spoken of by locals with a reverent awe. But these parents were hardly likely to come to town in the dead of winter to burn someone's house down.

Hinkler swept the slushy snow from the front walk with a large push broom. The sheriff watched. What would a grocer be doing with livestock vaccine? Chas's theory seemed as unlikely as the others. And Bob Hinkler was a meticulous man. Finely manicured and clean-shaven, he kept a standing, bi-weekly appointment at Gene Lang's barber shop. Edelson doubted Hinkler would own a cat either, any animal for that matter. He'd investigated Hinkler's dealings all the same. McPherson was right about one thing: leveling a charge against someone shouldn't have anything to do with how influential he was. He regretted having given the rancher the opposite impression.

He pondered what motive Hinkler would have for burning down the Teleghanis' house. He'd been quiet about the petition to change the Christmas celebration at the school to a non-religious event, though he hadn't signed it. But he could hardly have hated the family. Mrs. Teleghani had an account at his store, and he often bought fresh vegetables from her for resale. Chas was wrong about Hinkler, Edelson concluded. And that was too bad. The sheriff had taken a liking to the suggestion.

He ticked off the names of the ranchers in the back country with a new, sharp pencil. He'd interview them last if it was necessary. He drew a line through Chas's name because it galled him that Dean Ruark had put him prominently at the top.

Mr. McPherson's lips were blue, his hollow cheeks translucent white. His bedroom was fifty-seven degrees. And his blankets bunched around his knees.

Mattie rifled through the medicine cabinet, unaware the fire had gone out. "God, doesn't this guy ever get sick?" She read the labels on the sparse smattering of over-the-counter medicines: aspirin, antacids, hydrocortisone cream. Nothing. She thought back on Chas's accident–concussion, broken wrist–where was the Vicodin? Why didn't he have anything for pain? She'd already had two large glasses of whiskey and water, but what she really craved was narcotic. She stepped up on a stool and peered into the high cupboard over the vanity. Jackpot! Prescription cough syrup. She uncapped it, sniffed once, and sucked it down before stepping off the stool. It was old and there wasn't much left in the bottle. Sugar granules crusted the opening. She licked them away and held the bottle upside down, waiting for the last drops to roll onto her tongue. Knowing she'd be wishing for more in short order.

She went to the kitchen and chased the cough syrup down with a shot of straight whiskey. Stood looking at the bottle, and wondering if Chas would notice. Doubted it, with the amount he drank. But still–maybe she should add some water. She decided against it, this time, and put the bottle away. Then rekindled the fire and went to get Mr. McPherson up for lunch.

Snow was falling in great, heavy clumps, coating everything in pristine white when Chas returned. Cedar branches lay low over the backs of his sheep, seeking the tree's shelter. He opened the gate to a lean-to-style structure that his father had added to the back of the barn decades before, giving the sheep access to some small shelter. He despised cleaning it, so generally kept them out. But conditions today warranted giving in.

In the house Mattie greeted him with a drink. He saw she already had one of her own, half drunk. He didn't care for their whiskey routine–not that it was anything new for him, but he worried about her. Too much booze. He pushed his glass away. "Think I'll make some coffee," he said, and poured the whiskey in the sink.

Mattie opened her mouth in silent objection as the brown liquid disappeared down the drain.

"Want some?"

She shook her head and went back to stirring a large pot of chili. Her hair was down and messy. She looked like she'd been sleeping.

Chas fumbled with the paper coffee filters, trying to peel them apart with his thick fingers. "What's next for you?"

"Huh?"

He paused to look at her, then focused on the filters again. "I mean after this. Where will you go?"

"I don't know."

He measured out four heaping tablespoons of coffee.

"That's too much. It'll be too strong."

"I got by on my coffee before you came along."

"Fine." She shrugged. "I'm not drinking it."

"You already said that."

"Are you getting rid of me?"

"What?"

"You asked where I'm going next. Does that mean I'm finished here?"

He stared at her. Couldn't follow her logic. Were all women like this? Or just this one? "I didn't say that." He filled the coffee maker with water and turned it on. Paused to watch the first brown drops splatter into the pot. "Alaska is nice. I'm thinkin' about Alaska. And I hear they need nurses up there."

She faced him, giving him her attention.

"Maybe when the time comes, you know . . . " He nodded toward his father's bedroom. "We could make a new start . . . the two of us."

* * *

Sheriff Edelson rolled over in bed, the blankets hobbling him, and thrashed to get free. The cat slid off the end with the sound of its claws dragging along the bedspread. The clock read one-forty-two. Insomnia again. It was becoming a habit now to wake after a couple of hours of sleep only to stare at the ceiling most of the night, thinking about Chas McPherson. And walnut trees, fir trees, and apple trees.

He got up and pulled his boxers on. The cat skittered under the bed and hunched down watching him.

"Kip?"

"Shhhh, go back to sleep." He leaned and kissed his wife's cheek, then tiptoed out into the dining room, where he sat under the dim chandelier and paged through her Bible, a book so foreign to him when he'd started this a week back he didn't know it was split into two parts. Sifting for a needle in a haystack, some evidence to prove or disprove Chas's theology. Going on faith the needle was there in the first place. Just like police work.

Chas lay in bed, Mattie snug against his side, and watched for the first inkling of dawn. She slept so soundly now, that he fancied it was the safety he provided. She hadn't got up and cried on the step since she had moved to his bed.

He realized it had been snowing most of the night. He crept downstairs in the dark, wanting to see how deep it was. But it was night still and all was black, so he got his boots on and walked out on the porch. The world was as still and silent as a photograph. And he breathed in the sharp, cold air, feeling a wonderful sense of being alive.

"You've made it too easy, McPherson."

Chas started.

"I thought I'd have to sneak inside and kill you in your sleep." Hinkler held a hunting rifle pointed at Chas. His face was a pale moon illumined by snow. "I was thinkin' to wake you up first. Make sure you knew it was me. But I was worried I'd have to kill the nurse first. The nurse'll be second. Your old man'll be last. I want him to savor the moment."

Chas felt the blood drain from his fingers; his breath flew away. "Why?"

"Why what? Why kill you?"

"Yeah," he rasped.

Hinkler laughed. "You still tryin' to convince people that you didn't burn that house down?"

"You know I didn't. We both know . . . "

"Know what? That it was me?" Hinkler took finer aim. He smiled. "I loved her; why would I burn her house down?"

Chas blinked.

"And then you scared her away."

Chas could feel the bullet hole burning between his eyes. At ten feet there was no chance of a miss. He wondered if his mother was watching. Was she waiting for him on the other side? Or was it just a boyish fantasy, all these years believing she couldn't have really left. Must have died. Wouldn't have left him.

Hinkler pulled back on the trigger. The hammer fell. The dull click was dampened by the snow-insulated world around them.

The two men locked eyes, neither one quite sure the gun didn't fire. Chas lunged, grabbed a stick of firewood and advanced like a demon from Hell. A swift, overhead crack and Hinkler was down, his skull split, even through his Stetson, and his blood ran brilliant red in the snow.

Chas stood stunned and wheezing, his lungs burning from the cold.

They'd crucify him now.

Mattie's stomach lurched when she saw Hinkler's body laid out in the snow. She ran inside to retch. Chas followed, but she slammed the bathroom door in his face.

"Mattie?" His muffled voice came through the door.

She vomited. And vomited again, dredging up the green bile from the pit of her stomach. Sticky and bitter. Then came heaves—dry, painful.

Twenty minutes passed, and when she emerged Chas still waited in the hall. "Mattie?"

She winced and turned away.

"He tried to shoot me, Mattie. He came to kill all of us. He said so himself."

Her fingers trembled, and she refused to look at him. Her thoughts went off like bottle rockets—too many directions to focus on any one. Should she run? Would they blame her, too?

"Mattie, please."

She suppressed persistent nausea. The dead man's pale skin tinged with black, snow melted away in an arc around his crushed skull—nothing she'd ever witnessed as a nurse. Nothing she would ever forget, no matter how long she lived.

"I'll call the sheriff. I'll explain what happened."

"No!" she snapped. "Are you out of your mind?"

"It was self-defense."

"You think anyone's gonna believe that?"

Chas walked a steady line to the front window, pausing to look out at Hinkler's body, now dusted with snow. The coming light making the scene more real. "What else can we do?"

We? Mattie stared at him in disbelief. "You have to hide it."

"*What?*"

"They'll put you away for this. You'll never see the light of day again. Murder is a capital offense in Idaho."

"Murder? I didn't murder him. It was self-defense."

"You have to get rid of the body, Chas. You have no choice. If they find out he's dead in your yard, you'll never convince them of anything. You have no choice." She stood close, her countenance urgent. "Chas . . . you have no choice."

A heavy slab of snow slid from a low branch of the cedar tree, snapping it skyward and causing an avalanche from the upper branches. Chas's flock darted across the meadow. Midway, the animal in the lead leaped high in the air, as if hurtling a wire. Each one followed in turn, leaping over the unseen object.

"Why'd they do that?" the sheriff asked with fascination.

"'Cuz they're stupid. Whatever one does, they all do. They don't have to see to believe," Chas remarked with intensely waning interest in the antics of his sheep.

The sheriff took pause. "Sounds like some people I know."

"Sheep *were* God's pick to symbolize mankind." Chas kept a wary eye on the sheriff, wishing him away with every ounce of himself.

Edelson made no move to go. Began scanning the trees again, up, down, around. Over the snow. Across the yard.

"Wanna cup of coffee?"

The sheriff turned abruptly and stared. " . . . okay."

"Come on inside then." Chas led him up the steps, keeping his gaze down, away from the mound of snow he'd plowed out of the driveway and into the yard only moments before the sheriff arrived. Cutting it close. His heart pounded in his throat so loudly he was certain the sheriff would hear it if he listened hard enough.

"Hear about Mrs. Teleghani?" the sheriff said as he pulled his hat off in the entryway. Mattie was standing stone-still.

"You met Sheriff Edelson before?" Chas asked her.

"We've met," the sheriff said, nodding politely.

She disappeared into the kitchen, but shot a dismayed glance at Chas when they followed her.

"We have any coffee made?" Chas's words were thin and sharply punctuated, like barbed wire cranked down too tight.

"Yeah, I'll get you some."

"Looks like she left for good," the sheriff continued.

Chas and Mattie exchanged a confused glance.

"Mrs. Teleghani. She left. Her husband hasn't seen her for two days."

Mattie set two cups of coffee on the table and went to Mr. McPherson's bedroom without a word.

Chas's eyes were stuck on the teasels. They looked somehow sharper now than before. He imagined brushing too close to them would puncture his skin, releasing this terrible secret on a rush of air. How good that would feel. To unleash this suffocating pressure expanding in his chest.

"She took all her things."

Chas's mind was numb, focused on Hinkler, now five or six feet beneath the meadow on the far side of his barn, snow steadily covering the evidence of a newly dug grave. A grave not nearly deep enough, but as deep as he could scrape from the frozen earth with his backhoe. His greatest fear was the blood. Red snow on white. A trail he had tried to cover up. What had he done? Something he'd never imagined in his wildest dreams.

"You seem a little tense. Everything okay?"

Chas looked up, caught the sheriff's eye briefly and shrugged. "Got into a little spat this morning. That's all. Women have a way a gettin' in your head and wrappin' your brain around the silliest things."

The sheriff twisted in his seat to see where Mattie had gone. "Didn't realize you two were . . . "

"Yeah," Chas whispered.

Edelson smiled into his cup, a fleeting gesture. "So you're sure you haven't seen Hinkler?"

"Yup."

"Strange . . . why would his truck be parked in the brush across the road from your place and no sign of the man anywhere?"

"Maybe he just went fishin'. It ain't the weirdest thing for a man to take a day off and enjoy the outdoors."

Edelson glanced out at the haze of thick snow still obliterating the landscape. "Hinkler? He didn't open his store this morning. Don't you think that's odd? Legend has it he's never missed a day in forty years. Besides, who'd go fishing in weather like this?"

"The man lived in Sweetwater; he was used to the snow."

The sheriff squinted at Chas. A hard, line-invoking gaze. "Lived? Was?"

"You know what I mean."

Sheriff Edelson set his cup down and gave it a mild shove, watched it slide on the pine table. Then stood. He positioned his hat firmly on his head. Low over the eyebrows. He cinched his waistband, running his fingers along his belt, over his pistol. At the door, he turned. "I don't think this conversation is over."

"We can have it again, but it'll be the same."

As the sheriff's patrol turned out of the driveway, Chas burned to follow and tell him the truth. Why had he listened to Mattie? How would he possibly explain burying the man if he didn't have anything to hide?

Mattie appeared in the doorway with a rancorous glare. "What the hell were you thinking, inviting him in for a cup of coffee?"

"I couldn't very well tell him to leave. And he was just standing in the driveway waiting for the first clue about what we did to jump out at him."

"We? *We* didn't do anything. Don't drag me into this."

"It was your idea to hide the body. I wanted to call the sheriff and tell him the truth."

"I was just trying to save your neck." She brushed past him into the kitchen. He followed. She opened the whiskey and poured a glass.

"What are you doing? We need to keep our heads about us."

"I'm having a drink. I'm sorry if that bothers you, but it's not every day the man you're sleeping with brains someone with a stick of firewood." Her fingers trembled noticeably.

He pulled the glass away. "You drink too much."

"Oh, you're one to talk." She got another glass.

"Mattie, please. This isn't the time for it."

"It is the time for it. If ever there was a time for it, *this* is it!" She left the glass on the counter and took a swig straight from the bottle.

"Look at you."

"How dare you start in on me like this? You're lucky I'm here at all. If I hadn't come along, you'd never have found a nurse."

Chas's stomach ached like she was dragging his intestines out through his bellybutton. "Why'd you take the job if it's so bad?"

She laughed cynically and tipped the bottle back for another guzzle. Her lips glistened, and Chas could smell the spice of liquor. "I thought being out here in the middle of nowhere would help me kick my habit."

"What are you talking about?"

"Drugs. I . . . have a drug problem. I took this job because I needed to get away. I needed to be where I couldn't get drugs, where I would have to get over it. What better place than here?" Her agitation had evaporated. She just sounded sad now. "But I guess that's the skewed logic of an addict. Like I could just sequester myself out here in the middle of nowhere. With a patient who doesn't take the kind of drugs I fancy. I didn't count on living with an alcoholic."

17

CHAS TRUDGED THROUGH THE SNOW to the barn. It was already ankle-deep where he'd plowed, but it was easing up. The flakes were smaller and drifting down in a lazy, half hearted manner. It was the first time in his life he honestly felt happy about snow. The landscape was blinding white. Everything white. Trees, buildings, fences, cars–white. It was like a great blank abyss. As if nothing had ever happened there in all of history. Only the silence of white.

He fumbled through his toolbox for a wrench, then pulled a Mitsubishi alternator from a plastic bag on his workbench. Before going back outside, he stopped to gaze on the tan lamb in the jug with its mother. Earlier, he'd gotten the banding pliers out and loaded a thick, green band. Stretched it out and let it snap back, but didn't go any further. Didn't castrate the animal. He had set the pliers down again, deciding to wait another day. For what?

Sheriff Edelson sloshed along the unplowed county road near the McPherson ranch. Too many four-by-fours had already traveled it that day, obscuring any evidence of Hinkler's footprints, if there had been any in the first place. He felt inept, as if his skill as a law enforcer, his wellspring of confidence, had atrophied like an unused muscle. During his two years in Sweetwater the most important arrest he'd made was stopping Benjamin Harper from beating the brains out of his cousin after a manipulative little trailer-trash mother of six, probably another cousin, started flirting with him. But now he had a real crime—the worst kind of crime, an arson. And he was making no headway investigating, was even alienating the community in the process. Now a missing grocer—so he assumed. Maybe Chas was right, maybe Hinkler simply went fishing. He hadn't been gone more than a day, and he had no family to file a missing persons report. But the sheriff knew Hinkler would never leave his store unopened to go fishing, especially in this weather. Never. His gut told him there was more to it. And that McPherson knew something.

He wondered if he was losing his objectivity. The Teleghani case was affecting him deep in his personal life. Perhaps his judgment was blurred now. He seemed always to come away from encounters with Chas McPherson with some unsolicited revelation about God's divine hand. He found himself looking for reasons to question McPherson, not because he thought the man had some clue about the arson, but because the sheriff simply wanted to understand him, to see the world as he saw it. Edelson had found himself irresistibly drawn in by McPherson's liberating perspective. And he could not reconcile the community's strikingly different view of the man he was coming to admire. Was he wrong about McPherson? Was he losing perspective?

The sheriff left Hinkler's vehicle in its place along the road, thinking not to disturb it yet. He radioed Lorraine. "Call in search and rescue. If he's out in this weather, we need to find him."

"Will do, Sheriff."

He headed back to town. He'd meet the crew and give

them what information he had, then join them in the hunt. But he lacked the urgency this case should have spawned. Felt disconcertingly resolved that Hinkler was already dead.

A volunteer search and rescue crew convened at Dean Ruark's, where they bought bright slickers to keep dry. Snow fell off and on all day. Thick, wet snow, that gets into your bones and freezes you from the inside out.

Ruark rang up the merchandise with a wide grin, as if fortune had suddenly smiled upon him. He seemed even less urgent than the sheriff that his fellow businessman and proclaimed friend was out there somewhere, probably dead.

"Can I use your bathroom?" the sheriff asked Dean.

"Sure. Down the back hallway on the left. It ain't for public use, so don't expect too much."

Sheriff Edelson made his way through the aisles of cow and calf supplements, prods, and electrical fencing equipment, into the rear of the store where he found the dim hallway. The right wall was littered with flyers for free kittens, professionally trained stock dogs, used tractors, haybines, you name it.

He found the john and yanked the lightbulb chain over the sink, startling a cat that hissed and disappeared into the dark warehouse at the back of the building. He followed it, the blur of white vivid in his mind. The cat slunk behind a twelve foot monolith of alfalfa hay. Edelson surveyed the warehouse. Shelf upon shelf, row upon row, of neatly inventoried boxes on one side, banks of hay, ten tons to a bay, on the other. Straw, grass, alfalfa—sweet, honey—like aroma. How had he missed it? One man's name not on his list, one man who'd bought more Bacterin-Toxoid in a year than most buy in a lifetime.

Mattie's head hummed like a wire in the wind. She sat in

Chas's chair, Mr. McPherson next to her, and nursed the last swallows of her fifth drink. Outside, Chas worked under the hood of her car, his shoulders dusted with snow.

"I really wanted to make it, Mr. McPherson. It's the honest-to-God truth. I came here to make you comfortable, and to get back on my feet myself. I really only wanted to be a better person."

The old man watched Chas, his eyes moving with him from one side of the vehicle to the other.

Mattie tipped her head back against the chair and gazed at the living room ceiling, the acoustical tiles added in the sixties sooty black from the smoke of the woodstove. A testament to the hopelessness of trying to change anything. For all her cleaning, still the place was a cave. Tears began to well.

Chas came in on a gust of frigid air. He pulled his coat off and shook the snow out in the entryway. He looked at Mattie, held his gaze for a moment. "Your car is fixed."

She wiped her cheeks, but tears still came. "I'm sorry . . ."

"You're drunk. Tell me what you're sorry for when you can look me in the face sober."

Mattie cried quietly, a dull, but persistent ache in her middle. Chas somehow held the key to her highs and lows now. His regard for her had become a barometer of her self-worth. A man over whom she once believed she held the moral advantage was now so plainly out of her league.

Chas took the glass from Mattie's hand. It'd been empty for some time, gripped to her middle like a teddy bear. Her head drooped to one side, her breathing rough. He might have carried her upstairs if it weren't for his broken arm. But wouldn't have known which bed to take her to if he had, so he left her there to sleep off her drunk.

He wheeled his father to his room and lifted him onto the bed, then stood over him, wondering what he needed to do. He worked silently, methodically, and with a gentle touch. Undressing the old man with deliberate effort, hiding his shock when he saw how thin and frail his father had become. He turned him on his side, facing away, while he wiped the feces from his skin. Hoping beyond hope his father lay unaware, but knowing in the deepest part of him that he could no longer pretend things were different from what they were. His mother would not light on his shoulder and whisper the one thing he longed most to hear. Or that Nuri's wife hadn't betrayed and devastated her family. He thought of her children and the sense of abandonment he shared with them, bringing the sting of tears to his nose. If only his sheep weren't gently treading over a man entombed, and a search party weren't risking their lives to try and find him. If only he had not believed a woman could restore his forgotten soul.

He rolled his father onto his back and bathed him with warm soapy water, wiping his skin dry only to splatter it with his tears.

When the old man was tucked in his bed, the blankets pulled up around him, Chas sat and took a long contemplative pause.

"Dad, I killed a man." His voice cracked beneath the words. He endured a new volley of tears, but did not try to stop them. Bent forward and let them fall to the floor, gripping his temples, rocking.

Finally, "It was Hinkler. He came to kill us—you, me, Mattie. I don't know why Mattie, I guess because he couldn't leave a witness. You were right about him."

Chas sat quiet for a time.

"I'm sorry, Dad. I don't know how to fix it. I don't know how we got to this place, and I don't know how to fix it. I should've told the sheriff what happened . . . the truth. But he wouldn't have believed me. So I listened to Mattie; I did what she told me."

Her words echoed in his head, *you have no choice.*

"I guess I had a choice. You always have a choice, don't you? Prison would be better than this awful torment." Chas watched his father's face, hoping for understanding, forgiveness. "I'm sorry about Mom. I always blamed you for her leaving. But that was *her* choice. I only wonder if she wishes she'd made a different one.

"Hinkler was having an affair with Mrs. Teleghani—Nuri's wife. I'm probably telling you what you already knew. But it was a surprise to me. That's why he came to kill me; he thought I burned her house down." Chas studied his father more closely. "I thought he did it."

The old man's chest rose and fell, reminding Chas of his father's stubborn inability to give up, to quit—even when everything was done. The idea of pulling a pillow across his face and gently holding him until his body fell slack occurred to Chas. He lingered on the idea. Would his father curse or bless him for it? And what of God? Only a day ago he'd snapped the neck of a new lamb born with a cleft palate. A brutally compassionate gesture his father had taught him to carry out with swift decisiveness. It would've been a grievous sin to allow the creature to suffer. His eyes rested on his father's leathery skin as he tried to fathom the difference between his father's suffering and the lamb's.

After another thoughtful moment Chas stood and turned out the light. "Forgive me, Dad," he whispered. "Please . . . forgive me."

Mattie dreamed the old man was sitting on the ammunition box next to her. He reached a frail hand and clasped her fingers between his gnarled joints, like an ancient raptor gripping its prey.

She tried to pull away from him, but she was fixed there. Her arms and legs would not respond.

"I never knew your sins, my dear. I never knew them."

She looked into his stony face. He did not smile, but he gazed on her with compassionate eyes. Eyes she could not recognize.

"You're not such a bad girl, Mattia Elaine Sly." Then he got up and walked away.

She couldn't move, couldn't follow.

"Chas, wake up," Mattie whispered.

He heard his name called out as if in a dream. Sleep had finally come, heavy and thick, like a great wave smothering him in a sea of dread.

"Chas, please wake up."

She was peering into his face, her hair spilling on the pillow around him. An angel. A devil. Then the reality of Hinkler's frozen body drifted closer to the surface of his conscience. A torment to dwarf all torment.

"Chas?"

He sat up.

"He's gone."

He came alert. "Hinkler?"

"Your father."

Chas called the coroner, then went directly to the barn. The snow had ceased, and the day was pristine white beneath a radiant sky. A fresh morning, with the unmistakable promise of a coming thaw. He resented nature for it. How dare the day dawn on his father's death with such bold ambition?

As he worked his way down the jugs, he was greeted by a brave little ewe lamb in the last one. She came to the gate and sniffed him, just as she'd done the day before. He turned to fill the water bucket, but turned back again. She waited there, expectantly. For what? Lambs don't understand oats or alfalfa. Not at day three, anyway.

"What's this?" he said, slipping his hand between the

slats to touch her, expecting her to run away. She sniffed his fingers. He smoothed her velvety nose, then pulled away, perplexed, even disturbed.

Mattie was putting her things in her car when he crossed the yard. He stood his distance, watching.

"I'll wait for the coroner," she said.

"I never said you had to leave."

"Don't you think it would be best?"

"I guess the choice is yours."

She nodded and went back inside.

Chas scanned the snow, the porch, the driveway for evidence of Hinkler, but found none. The sound of the search party getting underway again echoed from across the road. The sheriff would be out. Maybe with helicopters. He hoped he'd plowed enough snow out into the meadow to hide the grave.

Sheriff Edelson stood at Ruark's refrigerator filled with vaccines and medications, reading the labels and thinking that whoever called farmers uneducated never had to sort out the finer points of bovine and ovine health. He straightened up and waited for the last customer to leave.

Ruark stood behind the counter, smiling like the sheriff had never seen him smile before. "Sheriff, what can I get you?"

Edelson approached the counter. He was still waiting on the search warrant, and was careful not to tip Ruark off to his suspicion. "Business must be good. Had to wait a long time."

Ruark smiled again, brighter. "Never knew a search party could go through so much stuff. Like they didn't bring anything of their own. Bought it all from me."

"Guess you're having a better day than Hinkler."

Ruark shrugged. "He'll turn up. I don't think he's lost."

"Where do you think he is then?"

"Who knows? He probably parked his truck there as a

hint. He's pretty mad that you haven't hauled McPherson in yet."

"You really think Chas McPherson burned that house down?"

Ruark's face went serious. "Who else could it be?"

"What do you think his motive was?"

"He's old Idaho. His grandfather was born down on the Salmon." Ruark nodded as if that answered the question.

"So?"

"Guess he didn't like them Moslems moving in and . . . you know."

Edelson squinted at Ruark. "No, I don't know. Why don't you explain it in plain English for me?"

"C'mon, Sheriff." Ruark tossed his head. "Lotta people don't like foreigners movin' in here and raisin' kids like they're part of the community. I mean think about it. Who are those kids gonna grow up and marry but the sons and daughters of white folk."

Edelson's eyebrow went up and he caught himself staring at Ruark. "Yeah, guess you're right," he said, trying to sound agreeable. "Well, I gotta get up the road and check on this crew. You gonna be around later?"

Ruark looked puzzled.

"Got a late crew coming down from Spokane. They'll be in after closing time. Just want to make sure they can get what they need."

Ruark smiled again. "Oh, yeah, I ain't goin' anywhere. Best business I've done in years."

18

THE CORONER TOOK HIS TIME COMING, and Mattie had begun to drink long before he arrived. She stammered out the details of Franklin McPherson's condition, his recent propensity for choking, and the natural conclusion of his life. The coroner, a graying man with a deeply etched face, undoubtedly the toll of his profession, seemed to accept her explanations without question, while displaying a clear disdain for her as he listened.

He turned to Chas. "Cause of death is consistent with Parkinson's. But I hope his nurse wasn't this drunk when he died. He might've had a better chance at holding on."

Chas flushed with embarrassment. "I took care of him last night. And I didn't have anything to drink."

The coroner nodded and proceeded with his work, moving the old man's ashen body to a stretcher and covering him from head to toe before loading him in the van. "What funeral chapel will you be using?"

Chas went blank. "He . . . he was the preacher. I don't think he'd want a service."

When the coroner was gone, Chas closed his father's bedroom door, knowing he'd never open it again. He experienced an odd mix of longing for the man he could now remember without the marring effects of illness, the man he had admired and feared, and a guilty sense of relief. It was over. Finally, the hour for which he'd waited had come. And he couldn't believe how ashamed he was to have looked forward to it so.

He turned to Mattie, who was gathering her coat and purse. "You're not leaving now. You've had too much to drink."

"I don't need anyone telling me what to do."

"You'll kill yourself. And if you don't, you'll kill someone else."

"Oh, and now you're worried about killing people?"

Chas's ears instantly burned hot. "Goddamn, but you *piss me off*!"

She paused, one arm in her coat, standing there looking at him.

"You can't just come in here and rip my heart out and then walk away," he shouted, his ears disbelieving what his mouth was saying. "You said you came here to kick the habit. Well do it, damn it! Do it!"

"I can't!"

"You can if you want to."

"No I can't. You don't understand," she cried. "You don't know."

"Then tell me."

She sat back on the sofa, appearing stunned by his anger. He sat beside her. "Tell me."

"I wouldn't even know where to start. Just let me go, Chas. It's better for both of us."

"No."

"Chas, please."

"Just tell me, Mattie. Don't I deserve that much? Don't I deserve an explanation?"

"Fine," she said, sitting up with marked determination. "But remember you asked."

He waited.

"I don't know when it started. When I was still a kid, I guess, after my parents died. But it didn't really become a problem until I was a nurse. When I could get pain meds. One day I just couldn't stop. I had to have them. So I . . . I started stealing from my patients."

Chas sighed.

She looked into his face. Waited for him to look at her before she went on. "I never did that here. I took this job because people with Parkinson's don't take those kinds of meds. I really meant it when I decided to quit this time." She glanced around his living room, then out the window. "I thought I'd be too far away to get my hands on any prescription drugs out here. It was supposed to be a forced withdrawal."

"Why not just go to rehab?"

She shook her head as if he didn't understand.

"Isn't this a fairly common problem? I just read an article about it a week ago."

"I didn't want anyone to know. I thought it would ruin my career. Chas, you have to understand, this job can be so hard. You don't know how it is."

"So I hired a nurse who is addicted to pain killers to take care of my elderly father." Chas's face was grim and he wouldn't look at her. "And I watch her stealing my whiskey for weeks. Then I have sex with her," he said, mostly to himself. "What kind of fool am I?"

Mattie stared at her fingers.

He turned to her abruptly. "Did you care for me at all?"

Tears came again. "Of course. You have no idea." She snorted back an absurd sort of laugh. "The other reason I took this job is because I thought you were an ass and I'd never have to worry about getting involved."

He didn't see what was funny. In fact he found her confession profoundly painful.

"I was wrong," she whispered.

"Are you saying this because you're afraid of me? Everyone is afraid of me."

"I'm not afraid of you."

He bit the skin on his lip as he tried to read her mind, to see for himself what kind of person she was. To know if there was any reason he should trust her at all. "Then why are you leaving?"

Sheriff Edelson hiked along the roadway behind Hinkler's Bronco. It was time to tow it in to the station, get it off the road, go through it for less obvious clues. The keys were in it, but he thought it best to do everything by the book. The man had simply vanished. He couldn't overlook anything. He had concluded it was no coincidence that Hinkler's truck was found across from the McPherson ranch. The two hated each other. Was the merchant coming to exact revenge for Chas's recent protests? Was he that foolish? In the sheriff's estimation, McPherson was a man to be reckoned with.

He remembered his last conversation with Hinkler. The grocer had threatened him again and ranted on that Edelson would never serve as sheriff in Idaho County again if he couldn't even arrest an arsonist sitting right under his nose.

"Give me proof it was him and I'll go cuff him right now," he'd replied.

"You're the fucking sheriff."

"Then let me do my job."

"Well, if you don't we'll get someone who will."

He wasn't a vindictive man, the sheriff. But he also wasn't disappointed that Chas was still on his feet and it was Hinkler they were searching for. As he passed the McPherson driveway he saw the coroner's van pull onto the road. He flagged him down.

"Sir," the coroner greeted. They didn't know each other.
"May I inquire?"

"Franklin McPherson. Natural causes."

Edelson stepped back and surveyed the van. "Thanks. That's all I need."

"What's going on here?" The coroner nodded at the trucks and horse trailers parked along the shoulder of the road.

"A man came up missing the other day. Found his truck parked nearby."

"Guess I'll be making another trip then."

The sheriff scowled. Didn't appreciate the dark perspective. "Don't know the man is dead yet."

"Call me when you find him."

The sheriff slapped the side of the van as a signal for the coroner to be on his way. It moved on and Edelson tried to think of a reason to walk up the McPherson driveway—to come up with just one unanswered question that he hadn't already asked. But the only questions that came to mind didn't have anything to do with Hinkler, or the arson, but about the apple trees, walnut trees, and the nature of God.

He turned and headed for his car. He needed to check on that warrant to search Ruark's warehouse.

"You still haul stock?" Chas gripped the phone to his ear. "Two trips. A big one to the sale ring. A small one up the road a piece." He jotted notes. "I do, but I wrecked my truck. The rack doesn't fit on the other one." He listened. "Tomorrow morning? That'll work fine. Thanks.

"Oh," he said quickly, before the man hung up, "I have a classic pickup for sale too if you know anyone interested." He craned to see Jenny out the front window. "Fifty-one Chevy half-ton. Yellow. She's as pretty as they come." He nodded and smiled. "Make me an offer."

Edelson found Ruark behind his till the following morning, still smiling.

"Mornin', Sheriff."

"Good morning." The sheriff paused at the counter, glancing around for other customers, but the store was empty. The last of the search and rescue crew had headed down the Sweetwater to take their turn at hunting for the missing grocer. A state trooper followed on Edelson's heels, but Ruark didn't seem alarmed with all the commotion.

"Any news about Bob Hinkler?"

"No. It's the damnedest thing, Edelson said."

"He'll turn up."

Sheriff Edelson surveyed Ruark with his usual scrutinizing squint, then produced a search warrant. "We need to take a look at your warehouse, Dean."

Ruark's face went gray. "What for?"

"Just working my way down the list of people with access to Bacterin–Toxoid, that's all."

"Surely you don't think . . . "

"Can't leave any stone unturned. I wouldn't be doing my job if I didn't look at all the possibilities." The sheriff nodded to the officer, who snapped a pair of rubber gloves in place and started through the store.

"Wait." Dean called after them. "Can't we discuss this like gentlemen? There's no need to go ransacking my warehouse."

"We're not going to ransack anything. We're just checking."

Ruark appeared so distressed Edelson fancied he could hear the man's heart hammering away like a combustion engine suddenly gone dry. "I thought McPherson was your man."

"So far we haven't found anything to support that. And the victim is adamant about his innocence."

"If you're talkin' about that lamb he gave to Teleghani, everybody knows he did that to throw you off. You're fallin' for it. He's fooled you, Sheriff."

"You seem a bit nervous. Anything you want to tell us before we search your place?"

Dean stood red-faced and silent.

The sheriff followed the officer into the warehouse.

19

CHAS COUNTED OUT ONE-HUNDRED-AND-SIXTY DOLLARS in twenties and handed them to a lanky cowboy in dirty Levis. "That's highway robbery, Hal."

"Gotta feed my family."

A large stock trailer rattled down the driveway filled with sheep. Chas turned away without emotion.

"This the truck?"

"Yeah. It was my dad's."

"Heard about it, all the way over in Riggins. She's a fine one."

"Make me a reasonable offer and she's all yours." Chas rubbed his hand over the fender, wiping away winter grit.

"Eighteen."

"I said reasonable."

"Shit. How much work am I gonna have to put into her to keep her runnin'?"

Chas popped the hood and showed him the engine. "Practically none."

Hal peered inside, twisting his mouth. He turned and spit in the snow. "Twenty-five then."

"Got yourself a deal."

"What about these other sheep? Where they goin'?" Hal

strode to his pickup and looked at the flock they'd loaded up with Chas's stock rack. Two ewes, one with a ewe lamb and one with a ram lamb–a tan lamb. He reached in and rubbed the ewe's ears. "You're a sweetie." The others darted to the far side of the truck.

Chas gave him a hand–drawn map. "They're goin' to this place up Highway 14. He doesn't know they're comin', but don't let him refuse."

"What if he don't got a place to keep 'em?"

"Leave him the rack. He'll get somethin' up when he realizes they're his."

Hal nodded and folded the map into his shirt pocket.

"Listen, I need ya to tell him something for me."

Hal stared off in the direction of the search party. "What d'ya suppose happened to that storekeeper? Bet he run acrost a bear. Probly shit him out already."

"Hal, pay attention. This is important."

Hal turned and made eye contact.

"Tell the man that the tan one is special. Not to eat it. Tell him to use it as his herd sire. Got that?"

Hal grinned. "You're a strange one, McPherson. Yeah, I got it."

"It's important."

"If you say so. I'll be back for the truck." He climbed into the cab and pulled away, waving a hand out the window as he started down the driveway.

Chas watched the little faces of the sheep get smaller; they kept looking back at him like children separating from a parent, eyes bright and curious. He waited for the truck to pull onto the main road, out of sight, then turned and scanned the meadow. Empty. The gate stood open. He'd never seen the gate stand open. He walked through the barn and unlatched the jugs. He swung the big door wide, then went to the lean-to in the back and pulled the gates open, like arms outstretched in an inviting gesture.

Sheriff Edelson called the crime lab and asked the technician to expedite analysis of the samples he'd sent with the state trooper. Ruark was his arsonist, he knew it. A match on the fabric or cat hair was all he needed now. He glanced at his watch: two-thirty. He gathered his hat and jacket and headed out to check on the search crew.

He parked at the mouth of Chas's driveway, leaving enough room for a vehicle to pass. The search party was coming in, empty-handed again. Tense-lipped. The coordinator approached his window.

"No luck?"

"No," the man replied. "Snow's too deep. Whatever tracks he left are long covered. If he fell, he's froze to death by now."

"What are you saying?"

"I think it's time to wrap this up."

"Are you sure he can't be alive out there?"

The man looked up the canyon. "Anything's possible, Sheriff. But not probable."

"Okay. Thank the boys for their hard work. I imagine it's a disappointment."

"Yeah, it is."

Edelson pulled into Chas's driveway to turn around, but paused to look at the little white homestead nestled against the base of the mountain. From a distance it was quaint. Inviting even. He should tell Chas the news about Ruark. It was the least he owed him.

He coasted down the driveway. The place seemed deserted. The cars were gone, the sheep too. He craned to see inside, wondering if Chas had pulled out after his father died. The man wasn't even laid to rest yet. But then who would go to Franklin McPherson's funeral?

Chas stepped out on the porch, surprising the sheriff. Edelson got out and nodded his greeting.

Chas leaned a shoulder against the porch support and

waited with a nonchalance that unnerved the sheriff.

"Afternoon, Chas."

"Sheriff."

"What happened to your vehicles?"

Chas glanced around as if the missing vehicles were news to him. "Sold the truck. Mattie left."

The sheriff scowled.

"No reason for her to stay, I guess . . . now that my father has passed." Chas stared off to the west, a distant, unreadable thought passing through his mind for an unusually long time. Then, "More questions?"

"No. Just some news." But even as he prepared himself, he decided not to tell Chas what he'd turned up on the nurse—too late. Didn't see any point in it now—now that Franklin was gone. She had lost her license for elder abuse, and her name was not Holden, but Sly. *Sly,* he pondered the irony a moment and briefly wondered if she had anything to do with the preacher's death. What purpose would it serve to tell Chas now? Edelson understood little about Chas McPherson, but he knew this woman had fulfilled a deep need. Another victim left in her wake, Chas was. Besides, the sheriff had done his part in notifying the state medical board about her recent employment with the McPhersons.

Chas sat on the top step, bringing him eye level with the sheriff.

"Think we've finally got our arsonist."

A weak smile cracked Chas's face, but slipped away as quickly.

"It was Dean Ruark."

"He admit it?"

"No. And I haven't arrested him yet. Waiting for results from the crime lab. Today, though."

Chas frowned at his feet. "Why'd he do it?"

"I suppose he was afraid his daughter would wanna marry one of those kids someday." A silence fell between them, and Edelson thought of Hinkler again. "The search party is pulling out."

Chas's eyes were fixed out to the west, where the searchers were loading up their horses. "Too soon. Maybe he's still alive."

"I don't think so."

Chas finally looked at the sheriff. "Why not?"

"A hunch." Edelson climbed the steps and sat down with Chas. "I think you could tell me for sure."

Chas made a slow and deliberate motion of nodding. "Sheriff–"

"Kip . . . my name. It's Kip."

". . . Kip." He spoke it with crisp enunciation. "Everything I ever did in my life, right up to not begging that woman to stay, was purely out of self-preservation." He paused, glanced at the sheriff, then back to the western skyline. "I woke up alone this morning. And for the first time, didn't think I could go on. If I don't start living my life, there ain't gonna be any of it left to live." He pointed to his meadow. "See that?"

"Your sheep are gone."

"Yup. And soon I will be, too. Whatever happened to Hinkler wasn't anything I invited or planned. Like I said, it was self-preservation." Chas drew a circle in the snow on the step with his index finger, dotted the center, as if setting up a target, then scuffed it out with his boot sole. "If you keep at it, I suppose you'll find what you're looking for. But I ain't gonna be here when you do. I guess if you're planning to stop me, you better kill me now and get it over with," he said, gesturing to the sheriff's gun. "All I've got left is what I can salvage of my future. I'm not giving that up willingly. If you're gonna take it, you'll have to take it all."

The sheriff reflected. Thought about his oath to uphold the law. Understood that Chas had given as much a confession as he'd ever hope to hear. And according to the moral compass that drove him–made him a cop in the first place–

Chas deserved prosecution. He looked out on the meadow now void of God's rich symbolism, and somehow the world no longer showed itself in the stark hues of black and white. "My take is that Hinkler fell in the river." He scratched his chin, twisted his mouth. "Probably half-way to the Pacific Ocean by now. I doubt we'll ever find him."

Mattie sat at a remote rest stop equipped with a one-hole outhouse and a rusty spigot, tracing her finger across a map. Her gas gauge was nearly reading empty, she was hungry, and her head ached. If she could just get to a pay phone she could call her sister.

Perfect Kathy. Broken Mattie. It would be as it always had been.

The old man was with her again, there in the car. A forgiving smile. A redeeming touch. Her dream relived, over and over in her every waking moment. A compassion so undeserved and confusing, she didn't know whether to take her own life to escape the guilt of treating the man so cruelly, or to accept his forgiveness. Had she imagined his persecution? Was it simply the effects of drug withdrawal? The different Franklin McPherson she encountered in the last visitation, seemed so real. It brought undeserved hope.

Chas made his way up Highway 14, listening for cars, turning with his thumb out as they passed. He turned again, for his ninth or tenth car; he'd never really started counting. A bright red and white Ford F-250 roared toward him. He looked at the driver. The driver looked at him. Ruark. He screamed past without slowing. Hell-bent for parts unknown.

Chas hiked along the roadway a few more miles, wishing he'd asked the sheriff–Kip–odd for him to share his name like that . . . to tell Nuri his place was now empty. A barn full of hay. Spring pastures for his flock. As he thought about it he tuned his ear to the throaty drone of an engine. He turned and readied his thumb, waiting. Seconds passed, then an eighteen-wheeler rounded the last curve, blowing its air brake. Chas jutted his thumb up, standing still at the shoulder of the highway. The semi slowed and squeaked to a halt. He pulled himself up to the cab and waited for the driver to lean over and unlock it.

"Where ya headed?" He was an older man. Chas guessed sixty-five. His bald head was smooth and tan and his face wrinkled like a prune.

Chas hesitated, hadn't actually decided where he was headed. "BC," he finally said.

"Goin' as far as Spokane."

Chas climbed in and pulled the door shut. "Thanks. I appreciate the lift."

"Long hike to BC," the driver said, lurching the rig forward. Powering through the low gears, building speed.

"Wrecked my truck. Just a few miles back."

"Didn't see it."

"It was about a week ago."

The driver glanced over, appeared to be assessing Chas's character. "What's in BC? A woman?" He smiled.

Chas pictured Mattie with her hair down, her cherry lips, her small breasts. Where was she? Did she think of him? "No. I'm gonna try and git on with a fishin' outfit in Vancouver. Maybe see Alaska this spring."

"Ain't you a bit old for that kind a work?"

Chas nodded. "Yeah, but I guess ya gotta start somewhere."

They rode along in silence, Chas scanning the roadway, half-hoping to see Mattie's blue sedan coming back his way. His disappointment solidified with each passing car, settling into his bones in a familiar sort of ache.

"You say you're just startin' out?" The driver didn't look his way, but deftly maneuvered the rig through the narrow canyon, careful not to cross the center line. Smooth.

"Been raisin' sheep the last forty years."

"Ah." The driver nodded. "No wonder ya wanna be a fisherman."

Chas looked over, waiting for him to elaborate. Not that his opinion was all that unusual.

"I'm a cattle man, myself. Gelbviehs. Ya ever heard of those?"

"Nope."

"German. Big suckers. Put on good muscle, fast. But mean? Son-of-a-bitch!"

"That why you're truckin' for a livin'?"

The driver's face went serious. "No. My wife passed away a couple years ago. I just couldn't take the loneliness. Had to get outta the house."

"Sorry to hear that." Chas looked over his shoulder into the sleeper. "This is less lonely?"

"Got you to talk to, don't I?"

Chas nodded and squinted out at an oncoming car. A red Mustang. He sat back in his seat and watched the Douglas firs fly past his window in a blur of deep blue.

"What's the real reason you're headed for the coast?"

The question startled Chas. "Already told ya."

"Bullshit. People don't just start over like that. Not after forty years of ranchin', and with nothin' more than a duffel bag."

Chas scowled. "Maybe I need to git away from the sheriff."

"I knew it." The driver looked in his side mirror, kept his eyes fixed there, until Chas thought he was going to pull over and demand he get out. But a car sped past, cutting the curve too close, raising the hair on his arms as he watched for oncoming traffic.

"What did you do?"

Chas had hoped the trucker would back off with his

questions if he thought Chas was running from the law. "You can pull over and let me out here."

"Aw, c'mon. Ain't no need for that." The driver reached down and turned his headlights on.

Chas was possessed with a sudden desire to go home. He looked out at the coming dusk and wondered just where he was going. This idea of finally living a new life life, of going out there and doing something–anything, as long as it was his idea–carried considerably less appeal as he hurtled toward his future at sixty-five miles an hour, next to a nosy stranger. It irked him to be questioned about his doings– questions that would inevitably follow him wherever he went. The privacy of his ranch, its seclusion and familiarity, now seemed a treasure beyond any other. But it was not just that; it was Mattie too. How would she find him if he wasn't there?

"You don't have to tell me," the man said.

Chas just looked at him. It was sad in a way, this old man picking up hitch–hikers and grilling them for their life histo- ries. "I was kidding. I'm not running from the sheriff. I think he's my friend. Told me his first name just this morning."

The driver seemed disappointed.

"My old man passed away. I was only staying for him." As he said it, the idea set in with him that it wasn't his father's ranch he left behind. The place was as much a part of him- self as it had ever been a part of his father. And maybe you couldn't separate a man and his father so easily after all. The admirable things he had forgotten about his father, his strength and unwavering confidence, or the quick and bril- liant solutions he produced when the road ahead seemed impassible, were bubbling up in Chas's memory now. Chas recalled those small, extraordinary moments when his father was his hero, and he wished he had lived up to the man's example.

"I'm sorry to hear it," the trucker said.

Chas shifted in his seat, a dull pain replacing the bubbles. Why did the sheriff tell him his first name? He recounted their exchange, not for the first time. That Edelson had let him off the hook for Hinkler's disappearance had dominated his thoughts all day. It was almost like the sheriff was apologizing for suspecting him of arson. Like he was trying to make it up to him, now that he had Ruark. Ruark–Chas recalled the man's startled face, speeding along highway 14. Not coming back.

The driver fiddled with the radio. "Country okay?"

Chas nodded.

"Never can tell with your generation. I've met rodeo bull riders who listened to Mozart. But they mostly just like rock."

Chas wasn't listening. He was thinking about the sheriff. No arsonist in custody. A missing grocer–presumed dead. Not even a suspect to put Sweetwater's mind at ease that he was doing his job. Making any sort of progress.

20

MATTIE SENSED THAT CHAS WAS GONE before she'd come halfway up his driveway. The meadow was wiped clean of that tie binding him to this place, the gates open. She stood next to her car a moment and took in the sheep's disappearance. Once again she had underestimated him.

She climbed the steps and peered through the window at the darkened interior. Then she pushed the door open and stood in the entryway, feeling no perceptible difference in temperature from the outside.

She spoke his name, as if he might step out of the kitchen. Only silence. She had imagined Chas's face all day, his smile when he saw her. She cursed her stupidity. When would she get anything right?

She cried a long while, her tears puddling, until she had nothing left. Now what? Even the swayback barn, once a symbol of Chas's perseverance, seemed to mock her. She had come back because she had believed Chas could save her. She'd returned ready to let him guide her, make her well. But of course a man like Chas would not wait for her. He would get on with his life—accept the truth about them, two drunks off the deep end, not a help to each other. And she understood at last that the running, the hiding that had articulated her life, had to stop. Now. Only she could change herself, no one else could do it for her—not even Chas. She had only one choice if she were to salvage any part of her life. Rehab—her only escape, really. She had in mind to be a better person—a more forgiving person.

Chas waved his thanks to a battered green Volkswagen Beetle; the kid inside rolled his window down and flashed him the peace sign as he pulled out. He'd been generous in insisting on driving Chas all the way home rather than dropping him in the middle of town. Chas watched the kid go, wishing he'd had the guts to do that when he was younger—to take off and see the country. No plan and less money. Just a map and the idea that things would work out. Chas had given him twenty bucks. The kid grinned and thanked him.

He saw Mattie's car by the house when they pulled up, a light glowing in his front window. His heart thudded to a momentary halt. He started up the steps, but she opened the door before he reached it, and just stood before him like she'd never left.

He'd never seen anything so perfect in all his life. Her hair a mess, her cheeks red and streaked with tears. He cupped her chapped face in his hands, and kissed her gently on her lips, her nose, her cheek.

She said, "I was afraid I'd never see you again."

Mattie drove Chas to the sheriff's office at first light. She hadn't tried to talk him out of turning himself in, but still ached at the prospect of being separated—maybe for a long time. They expected her at the Snake River Drug and Alcohol Center in Lewiston this morning. Chas had stood by her side and held her hand when she made the call last night. He promised to pay for the treatment—if she followed through and returned to him clean and sober. No small gesture for a man of his means, she knew. But right now she wanted to stay with him, be his moral support. She didn't believe the sheriff would see Chas's part in Hinkler's death as charitably as Chas expected. It seemed unlikely that anyone would believe Chas had killed the grocer in self-defense.

Chas held her hand as they approached the counter.

A harsh-looking woman scowled at them from behind the desk. She recognized Chas and said, "Did you hear? It was Ruark that burned that place down. I knew it was him the whole time."

Chas nodded, but seemed annoyed. "Is the sheriff in?"

"I'll check." The woman eyed Mattie.

Mattie wondered why she wouldn't know if her boss was in.

Chas kissed Mattie's forehead. "You better go."

"Chas, it can wait—"

"You promised. This is important. Please, Mattie, I'll be okay."

She studied his face, his perfect teeth that she hadn't noticed when they first met, his deep and intense eyes that had once frightened her, his blond curls. His unyielding resolve only enhanced his beauty. She nodded.

Sheriff Edelson was getting his coat on, preparing to drive up to Coeur d'Alene and pick up Ruark. He'd gone straight to his brother's house where local authorities arrested him. Edelson had suspected the man was stupid and he was right.

When Lorraine poked her head into his office and told him Chas McPherson was in the lobby, he thought she was joking. She had that sort of humor.

"Really, Sheriff. Him and that nurse."

Edelson followed her out to see for himself. Chas stood alone, waiting.

"Mr. McPherson, what can I do for you?"

"Chas. You can call me Chas."

Lorraine's eyes bounced between the two men, an angry frown forming on her face. She glanced around as if to find the nurse doing something she shouldn't. But Mattie was gone.

"Came to turn myself in . . . for killin' Hinkler."

Lorraine gasped.

Edelson caught himself shaking his head at Chas. Found himself willing Chas to be quiet, even though he'd believed all along Chas would not run. He'd bet his profession on it. Questioned himself again and again since their conversation at Chas's ranch, but knew in his gut the man wouldn't truly run.

"It was self-defense. He came to my house early in the morning three days ago. I was on the porch, couldn't sleep. He had a gun. You'll find it with the body."

"Wait," Edelson said. "Maybe you should have an attorney present before you say anything more." He glanced at Lorraine. Her mouth was gaping, her eyes fastened on McPherson.

"I'm just saying the truth," Chas went on. "Hinkler told me he was there to kill me. He had the order all figured out in his head. Me, then Mattie, then my father. Said he was looking forward to killing my father." Chas closed his eyes a moment. When he opened them, he continued with the same calm he'd possessed before. "I'm a lucky man to be standing here. He pulled the trigger. Wasn't more than ten feet away."

Lorraine's jaw appeared to drop to her knees.

"The gun jammed. I just reacted; I didn't think about it. I hit him with a stick of firewood. He . . . went down and stayed down."

Edelson had long formulated his conversation with the DA—clear-cut self-defense. A man on the fringes, suspect, no alternative but to cover it up.

"He's in the meadow below my barn. I wanted to tell ya, Sheriff. I meant to tell ya. But . . . " Chas looked straight at Lorraine. "Who would've believed me?"

"Why would Bob Hinkler want to kill you?" Lorraine said.

"I'll do the questioning, Lorraine," Edelson snapped.

"Your dad I can see. Those two hated each other, but why you?"

"Lorraine, shut up!"

Edelson stood in the snowy meadow and watched as a forensic team scraped wet dirt from Hinkler's body. He looked out at the road–the body had been right there all along and somehow he'd known the truth, had put it all together in some intangible sense. He knew Chas spoke the truth, and he hoped Chas would not see prison time. Though he doubted the residents of Sweetwater could forgive this deed, no matter the circumstances, he was undeniably on the rancher's side.

Edelson had come to admire McPherson, but knew in his heart that he would not normally have taken the time to understand him. Funny how duty to the job had caused him to find a friend. A friend who had killed a man.

Chas sat alone on the bunk, looking up at the narrow window. Too small for a man his size, even if he could get the bars off. He didn't regret his decision, but he sensed it would be a bleak and lonely one. He thought of Mattie on her way to Lewiston and wished he could be there to hold her hand and help her through the rough times ahead.

Word was out that he'd killed Hinkler. Lorraine had worked on the news for almost six hours, and it hadn't taken half that time for his arrest to sweep through Sweetwater. But he was equally certain that she'd cleared him of arson charges in the deal. He wondered if they'd exhumed the body yet. Edelson had assured him they could prove it was self–defense. He hoped the sheriff was right.

It was just past two o'clock and he'd eaten a tasty ham and cheese sandwich from the bakery next door. He had never guessed prisoners were treated so well in Sweetwater.

"Someone's here to see you," Lorraine said, appearing at the bars.

Chas got to his feet and walked to the front of the cell.

Nuri Teleghani stood before him with his hat in one hand and a folded piece of paper in the other. "I have information that I believe will help you," he said in his heavy accent.

Chas leaned against the bars and looked at his feet.

Nuri held the paper out to him. "It is from Hinkler. He was . . . " Nuri's words choked off.

Chas waited silently, remembering Hinkler's confession.

"He was seeing my wife," Nuri finally managed. "I found this letter in her things. I am sure she meant to take it with her. You will see from the letter why she left. He was a dangerous man."

Chas worked the skin on his lower lip, knowing the shame Nuri must be experiencing to share such details of his wife's adultery.

"He promised to kill you for burning her house down." Nuri worked to keep his composure, finally standing firm and quiet, saying nothing more.

Chas stared at the letter. "Thank you," he said after a time. "Are you sure you want–"

Nuri held his hand up in a motion for Chas to stop. He looked around for a chair, pulled it up to the cell and sat down. "It seems I find myself repeatedly in your debt, Mr. McPherson."

Chas shook his head. "I'd say we're even."

An odd silence fell between them, but Nuri didn't make a move to leave, and Chas was glad of it.

"My barn is still full of hay. I wouldn't mind if ya moved your sheep down there and took advantage of the place. I'm not usin' it right now, anyway."

Nuri nodded, but said nothing.

"You're welcome to the house too. I've been thinking to build a little cabin on the back parcel, down by the river. The homestead was always a bit too close to the road for my liking." He looked up at the man now wiping tears from his eyes. "It needs some work. But there's room enough for your kids. Maybe they'd like to git a horse or two."

"Sometimes God provides for us in mysterious ways," Nuri finally said.

Chas nodded, thinking of Mattie, his little mixed-up lover. The broken but beautiful woman that he wanted so desperately to make happy. His gift from God.

"I received an order the other day for fifty-two violins. Fifty-two! I have never made more than ten in one year. And now a school down in Arizona wants fifty-two by fall." Nuri shook his head, half-smiling and half-wondering.

Chas grinned. "There's a nice workshop around the side of the barn. It's a mess, but you could make a lotta violins in there."

They were quiet a moment. Then Nuri looked at Chas with seriousness. "Your sheep are gone. How will you live?"

Chas looked at his boots a long while, then shrugged. "God provides in mysterious ways . . . maybe you'll teach me to make violins."

About the Author

HEATHER SHARFEDDIN was born in Forsythe, Montana. She is the author of three books, including the acclaimed *Blackbelly*, which was chosen by the Pacific Northwest Booksellers Association as one of the "Best of the Northwest" and was proclaimed by New Hampshire's *Portsmouth Herald* as one of the top novels of 2005. She lives near Portland, Oregon. Bantam Books will publish a paperback edition of her novel *Mineral Spirits*.